Marita Conlon-McKenna is one of Ireland's favourite authors and her books are enjoyed by readers around the world. Her previous novels include *The Matchmaker* and the number one bestsellers *The Magdalen* and *Mother of the Bride*. She is the winner of the prestigious International Reading Association award and is a regular contributor on radio and TV. She lives in Dublin with her husband James and the family.

www.transworldireland.ie

D0522541

Also by Marita Conlon-McKenna

THE MAGDALEN
PROMISED LAND
MIRACLE WOMAN
THE STONE HOUSE
THE HAT SHOP ON THE CORNER
THE MATCHMAKER
MOTHER OF THE BRIDE

A Taste for Love

Marita Conlon-McKenna

TRANSWORLD IRELAND

TRANSWORLD IRELAND
An imprint of The Random House Group Limited
20 Vauxhall Bridge Road, London SW1V 2SA
www.transworldbooks.co.uk

A TASTE FOR LOVE
A TRANSWORLD IRELAND BOOK: 9781848270404

First published in 2011
by Transworld Ireland
a division of Transworld Publishers
Transworld Ireland paperback edition published 2012

Addresses for Random House Group Ltd companies outside the UK
can be found at: www.randomhouse.co.uk
The Random House Group Ltd Reg. No. 954009

The Random House Group Limited supports the Forest Stewardship
Council (FSC), the leading international forest certification organization.
All our titles that are printed on Greenpeace approved FSC®-certified paper.
FSC is the only forest certification scheme supported by the leading
environmental organizations, including Greenpeace. Our paper-procurement
policy can be found at www.randomhouse.co.uk/environment.

Typeset in 11.5/15.5pt Sabon by Falcon Oast Graphic Art Ltd.
Printed and bound by CPI Group (UK) Ltd, Croydon, CR0 4YY

2 4 6 8 10 9 7 5 3 1

For my best friend, Ann Frances Doorly,
who loved life and lived it to the full!

Chapter One

Alice Kinsella checked the oven. The rich aroma of spices and apricots from the slowly cooking lamb tagine was filling the kitchen. The table was set, the white wine was chilling in the fridge and the red wine was on the counter. Everything looked perfect, and she hurried upstairs as she had only half an hour to get ready and change into something a bit more stylish before her guests arrived.

It was a Saturday night in November, and it seemed strange hosting a dinner party on her own, but she just had to get used to it. She was fed up of Saturday after Saturday sitting in watching DVDs and game shows on TV, and just longed for a bit of decent adult company, everyone sitting around her table with nice food and a few decent bottles of wine. She had always enjoyed having friends around at the weekend or eating out at one of Dublin's many restaurants, and it was one of the things she missed most now that Liam was gone.

It was almost a year and a half since their marriage break-up, and she was still trying to get used to the loneliness of it, and adjust to life without Liam. At first friends and family had been great – remembering to include her, and asking her to lots of things and nights out – but she had noticed over the past few months that the number of dinner and party invitations had dwindled. It was bad enough losing her husband, her marriage, and her financial security, but losing people she had considered friends was probably the thing that hurt the most.

As she pulled her pale-grey shift dress on over her black tights, and slipped into black suede shoes, she tried to push all negative thoughts of her ex-husband from her mind and concentrate on the night ahead. She was going to enjoy herself and have a bit of fun, with or without Liam!

'Hey, Mum, is there anything you want me to do?' offered her twenty-two-year-old daughter, Jenny, who was home for a few days from Galway, where she was at university.

'Will you check I put fresh towels in the downstairs bathroom, please?'

Alice glanced at her make-up, understated yet

enough to make an impact. Her eyes looked different with a hint of eyeliner, the smoky grey and beige shadow that Jenny had suggested she try, and the new mascara she had treated herself to. Her light brown hair, longer and recently lightly highlighted, feathered around her face. She added a warm peach-coloured lipstick and topped it off with a little gloss before dabbing on some of her favourite perfume.

She was looking a lot better than she had done this time last year, when it had felt like her world had fallen apart, and she had been literally on the floor with anger and rage at the injustice and unfairness of it all. Liam moving out of their Monkstown home and in with Elaine Power, the thirty-eight-year-old marriage-wrecker he now called his new partner. He and Elaine had scarcely known each other, and yet her husband of nearly thirty years had walked away from his marriage to Alice with barely a backward glance. Their eldest son, Conor, still wasn't speaking to him, and Sean, their twenty-year-old, tried to avoid his father. Poor Jenny, their only daughter, did her best to remain neutral.

'I've put one of those fancy American towels downstairs.' Jenny smiled as she came back into the room and sat down on the bed. 'Wow! Mum, you look great! That dress is so good on you! You've lost weight.'

'Do you think so?' Alice ran her hands over her firmer hips and flatter tummy. 'Would you notice?'

Alice had to admit that the only good thing to come out of the most stressful time in her life was that she had, for the first time in years, without going on the Atkins or Weight Watchers diets, dropped ten kilos in weight. She felt the better for it. She was taking far more exercise, and was eating less as she was no longer cooking the kind of meals that Liam enjoyed. A fridge full of red meat and pork and sausages had been replaced by one containing healthy chicken and fish and vegetables!

'Everyone will notice,' teased her daughter.

It was so good to have Jenny in the house, even if it was only for a few days. She would be heading off on the train back to college on Wednesday evening, and Alice would really miss her.

Sean was a good kid, but he was rarely around, and seemed always to be busy in college doing something or other. Alice suspected he was still in denial about their situation, and was trying to avoid it and home as much as possible.

Alice jumped as the doorbell went.

'Will I let them in?' offered Jenny.

'Thanks, love. I'll be down in a minute. I think it's probably Joy.'

Alice looked at her neck, deciding to remove the

classic pearls that Liam had given her ten years ago and put them away in their box. Instead she took out the silver John Rocha piece that Conor and his girlfriend Lisa had given her last Christmas, and put it on.

'Better,' she said. 'Much better.'

Joy greeted her with a huge hug. Her old school friend was always the first at everything and had already made herself at home in the kitchen. She was clutching a glass of red wine while interrogating her god-daughter Jenny about her love life in Galway.

'Mum, make her stop,' begged Jenny, mortified.

'You're living away from home with no mamma or dadda around,' teased Joy. 'I can only imagine what Alice and I would have got up to in our day. There's bound to be some lovely Galway man around.'

'Well, if there is . . . and I'm not saying there is . . . you and Mum are the last two I'd tell!'

Alice noticed Joy was wearing her regulation black – this time a skirt with a bolero-type wrap-over top – and had made huge efforts with her unruly blonde hair. She was wearing it pinned up neatly.

Ten minutes later Sally and Hugh Ryan had appeared, Hugh carrying three bottles of expensive French wine into the kitchen and putting them on the kitchen island. 'Some very good wine to go with some

11

very good food, judging by the aroma tempting my taste buds.'

'Thanks, Hugh!'

They were her dearest friends, and he and Sally had rallied around when Liam had gone off with 'the witch' Elaine, leaving Alice virtually penniless. Sally had been a rock over the past year, even listening to her midnight tirades about Liam and 'his hussy'. While Hugh, practical as ever, had managed to get her a temporary job in the accountancy firm where he was one of the partners.

In the twenty-five years that Hugh had been coming to their house he had never arrived without bringing a highly recommended wine that added to the occasion. He was a real wine buff, and Liam and he used to spend ages talking about various vintages. She was glad that tonight, despite Liam's absence, he had kept up the tradition.

'And I've got some photos of little Ava, our ten-day-old granddaughter, to show you,' added Sally proudly.

Alice was so pleased for them, having their first grandchild. It was such a milestone.

'Champagne to celebrate?' She laughed as she took the Bollinger from the fridge, Hugh gallantly doing the honours and opening the bottle for her.

'To little Ava,' they toasted, as Nina Brennan and her husband David joined them, too.

'I'll stick with the red wine,' insisted Joy. 'Champagne just goes straight to my head.'

Alice could certainly vouch for that.

They moved to the sitting room, the fire blazing in the grate, as Alice's neighbours, the Cassidys, appeared. Molly Cassidy had been a great friend to Alice over the years, and even though she and her husband Jack were a good bit older than Alice they were wonderful company. Jack, retired from his career in the Garda, still seemed to know everything that was going on in the country.

The last to arrive were Alice's brother Tim, his wife Patsy, and their daughter Erin – who was six months younger than Jenny. An only child, Erin had spent a vast amount of her childhood in the Kinsellas' house, and she and Jenny were great friends as well as being cousins.

Jenny went to get more champagne glasses as everyone relaxed and chatted easily.

'This is such a treat,' declared Molly. 'Jack is always delighted when Alice invites us over, as she's the best cook we know.'

'Good to have a decent meal compared to that awful stuff we ate on holiday,' Jack said.

'Where were you?' asked Joy.

'We got back from Egypt on Tuesday,' explained Molly. 'We went on a cruise on the Nile, visited Cairo and the museum, and of course the Pyramids. We stayed in some wonderful places.'

'Cost us an arm and a leg, but it still didn't stop us getting tummy trouble.' Jack groaned. 'Followed all the precautions, but it made no difference . . .'

'Well, at least you're back on your home turf now,' consoled Joy.

Alice slipped back into the kitchen. Everything was going perfectly. She checked the lamb: it tasted rich and warm, perfect for a chilly night. She would serve it with couscous and a creamy mash that she knew Jack and her brother Tim were very partial to. The green beans were perfect, and there was the obligatory salad as she knew Erin and Jenny were big into greens. She popped her starter of goats' cheese into the top oven to warm. Once everyone was seated she would cover it with some crumbs and herbs and give it a quick toasting before serving it on a bed of rocket, accompanied by the cooked beetroot that went so perfectly with it. Lighting a few candles, she called everyone to the table.

Sitting around chatting as everyone ate and laughed and told stories, Alice relaxed.

David and Tim were on second helpings of the lamb, and Jack had gotten through a mound of

14

creamy mash. The wine was flowing, and Hugh was great at making sure that new bottles were opened as needed. They were all such good friends, and she didn't know how she would have survived the past eighteen months without them. They had bent over backwards to support her and encourage her to stand on her own two feet again; each person at the table in their own way had listened and advised and encouraged her.

'Alice, how do you do it: cook such delicious food and still manage to lose weight?' Sally sighed. With her curvy figure she was constantly trying diets and gyms and weight-loss clubs.

'Heartbreak, Sally, but you well know I wouldn't recommend it.'

'I put on almost two stone after Malcolm and I split,' admitted Joy. 'I was so sad, and I guess I was comfort eating. It was only when I realized that poor Beth was worried about me that I managed to pull myself together, and decided that there had to be a life after Malcolm. It was what both Beth and I deserved. I realized that the only person who could make me happy with my life was me!'

'And you've been enjoying yourself ever since,' teased Jenny.

'Of course!' said Joy, raising her glass. 'That's what it's all about!'

Alice smiled. Joy had refused to let her sit home and mope after the break-up, and had dragged her to dinners and lunches, walks, theatre and gallery openings, weekends in Barcelona and Prague – as well as a few trips to Joy's holiday cottage down in Wexford. Alice would be lost without her best friend, and they always seemed to have fun together.

The talk at the table turned to politics, and Jack and Tim nearly came to blows about the state of the economy and what should be done to solve it, while Hugh the accountant tried to calm things.

At her end of the table Molly told them she and Jack were planning to visit China the next year, to see Beijing and Hong Kong and walk the Great Wall.

'You two are such intrepid travellers, you put us all to shame!' remarked Nina Brennan enviously.

'Well, as Jack says, it beats sitting around waiting for the two of us to get old!'

Jenny helped Alice serve the warm apple and almond tart with vanilla ice cream and whipped cream, and made coffee for everyone. Alice was relieved that everything had gone so well.

'Alice, that lamb had such a flavour! How do you do it?' asked Sally.

'The secret is in marinating it in lots of spices overnight, and then slow cooking it,' Alice explained.

'And you must give me the recipe for this,' begged her sister-in-law Patsy as she finished the last crumb of the light almond tart.

'I'll email it to you,' Alice offered.

'I'm always trying out Alice's recipes, but somehow when I make them at home they never seem quite as good,' Patsy joked.

'That's because she's a natural cook.' Jack beamed. 'Molly has got green fingers; she can get anything to grow. And Alice is the equivalent with food.'

'Cooking makes me happy,' admitted Alice. 'I guess that's why I like having you lovely people over and doing it for you.'

'And we love coming here and enjoying your fine food,' replied Hugh, toasting her.

By midnight Jack and Molly had said their goodbyes and Jenny and Erin had disappeared to the comfort of the leather couches in the family room.

Alice produced Liam's vintage port and a bottle of Baileys, and they all relaxed.

'Sorry, Alice, but we have to head off, too,' apologized Hugh, sipping his glass of creamy liquor. 'We're driving down to Waterford in the morning to see Sally's parents. Her dad is celebrating his eightieth birthday and there is a big family lunch. We'll have to be on the road by ten o'clock tomorrow.'

'Next time it's our turn,' promised Sally as their taxi arrived and they said their goodbyes in the hall.

'The Ryans are a lovely couple,' said Tim.

'I'd be lost without them,' admitted Alice. 'Hugh has been so kind, giving me all types of advice on tax and finance, and even getting me some work in his office.'

'How's it going there?' enquired Joy. 'What's it like working for Hugh?'

'Great. Hugh's lovely, and everyone has been very kind. But to be honest, it's not exactly my type of work. It's all big spreadsheets and debits and credits. Half the time I'm not sure what I'm doing! But at least it's a job for the time being.'

'A job is a job!' declared Nina. 'They are like gold dust at the moment. Poor Lucy has been trying to find work for ages with no success.'

'It's tough out there,' Tim added.

'Will you stay at Hugh's firm?' pressed Joy.

'I'm not sure.' Alice hesitated. She had joined the accountancy firm on a six-month temporary contract, filling in for someone on maternity leave, and she really wasn't sure if her contract was going to be renewed, or even if she wanted to stay. 'I'll have to see.'

As she got up to make a fresh pot of coffee she

realized that there was no point worrying needlessly about what the future would bring. If there was one thing she had noticed lately, it was that one had very little control over fate.

An hour later everyone except Joy had gone home, Joy accepting Alice's offer to stay overnight in the spare room rather than spend a fortune on a taxi.

'Where's that bottle of wine Hugh opened before he left?' asked Joy, topping up their glasses as she told Alice about the man she had been out to dinner with three times.

'Three dates! Why didn't you bring him along tonight?' Alice said, cuddling her terrier, Lexy.

'Are you gone mad? I barely know Fergus, and I'm not going to inflict him on anyone until I'm sure that he's not another of those lunatics I tend to attract.'

Alice tried not to laugh as she thought of some of Joy's previous male friends, who had certainly been a bit different.

'The next dinner, bring him along!' she urged.

'That's if he survives till then,' said Joy.

Alice had to give it to her best friend: when Joy's husband, Malcolm, had cheated on her and left her, and moved to London with his new lady love – who was expecting his baby – Joy had managed to raise their twelve-year-old daughter with very little support from Malcolm and eventually pick herself up and get on. She had made a new life for herself centred round her daughter Beth, her friends and family, and her work as a teacher.

Alice knew that it was a lesson that she needed to learn, too.

Chapter Two

Lucy Brennan stared at the standard polite rejection letter. She had sent twenty-two copies of her CV out to a number of shops and businesses over the past ten days, and only two had bothered to reply. This was the third, saying there were no current vacancies, but that they would keep her details on file. It was so depressing! Lucy rammed the letter into a bundle in the drawer of her desk. She had been unemployed officially now for twelve months, and judging by this letter it certainly didn't look like anything was going to change.

She was broke, single and back living with her parents! Her life was a Tragedy with a capital T! This time last year she'd had a great job, a great boyfriend, and been sharing a house in Ranelagh with Anna and Megan, two old school friends. They'd called it 'the party house' as it was always full of friends. So many great nights had started and ended back in the small red-bricked terraced house on Warwick Road. Then, fast as you could say global recession, economic downturn, banks, builders and bloody NAMA, everything had collapsed around them. Everyone was suddenly broke and looking for work, or trying to hang on to their jobs. Each time she turned on the news or read a newspaper things were getting worse. It was so depressing. She was twenty-five, and this was meant to be her heyday – not the nightmare it had become.

First, she had lost her job. Phoenix Records, the small record store off Clarendon Street where she worked, had closed down. She had pitied Jeremy and Charlie, the owners, as they'd watched sales dwindle week after week, everyone downloading their music to their iPods and iPhones, so that trying to sell CDs had become almost impossible.

She'd felt bad for the guys in the young bands that Jeremy had promoted, putting their posters up in the window and giving their tracks a push by playing their music in the shop and advertising their gigs. Jeremy had had to give them back stacks of unsold CDs and tell them not to give up hope . . . things had to change . . . great music would always have a place in a civilized society. First Jeremy had cut her wages, then her hours, until eventually, heartbroken, he had explained that he could no longer afford the rent and he and Charlie were just going to close up and hand back the key to their landlord. Phoenix Records, for the moment, would have to shut.

'But I promise you, Lucy, if, like our name, we rise from the ashes of this economic mess, you will be the first person we hire back.'

'Thanks,' she had said, hugging him, knowing how much money he and Charlie had lost over the past two years in the failing business. Music was their life, and she knew the two of them were almost broke. She couldn't imagine her life without the small store with the big heart that could sell out a concert or a gig, and had even broken two or three of the big Irish bands and singers over the years. What would she do without the shop and the music and their customers? It had hardly seemed like work, coming in to a place she loved so much. She had immediately tried to get another job, Jeremy giving her an amazing reference, but no one had wanted a girl with no proper qualifications who only knew about bands and the music scene and how it all worked.

At least, as she had told herself at the time, she had still had Josh Casey, her boyfriend of fourteen months. They were mad about each other and joked about having more time to spend together now that she was footloose and fancy-free. At first it had seemed great, but month after month it had eaten away at them. Josh, fully qualified, had become focused on his own job in the big firm of solicitors on the Quays. He had had to work later in the evenings, and had seemed to have less and less time to see her and be with her. He had become bored by the new bands and their gigs in Whelans and Tripod and Slatterys. Bored by her friends, bored with staying in watching DVDs, bored by her lack of funds to go anywhere different, do anything different!

'Josh, I can't afford to go to Paris to watch Ireland play a stupid rugby match! And I've no intention of going to a restaurant that is going to charge me half my week's dole for a meal and a few glasses of wine!'

'I'll pay for you,' he had offered. 'I'm earning.'

'Josh, I don't want your money! I can pay my own way,' she had insisted stubbornly.

Being broke and trying to live on a tiny budget was no fun, and it hadn't really been a surprise when he'd told her a few months later, 'Lucy, maybe we need to take a break from each other . . . not be so intense, and just cool it for a while?'

'Sure . . . maybe you're right, Josh!' she had said, trying not to cry or let him see how much he was hurting her. They'd gone from having fun and being crazy about each other to making each other unhappy. This way she hoped that they could still at least be friends.

'You and Josh will get back together, just wait and see,' Megan had reassured her. 'Anyone can see you two are made for each other.'

'Yeah, Josh will be back in your life again,' Anna had insisted. 'He's far too great a guy to be an ex.'

The girls had consoled her with fun girly nights and lots of wine, pasta and talk, until, after about three weeks, she had realized that Josh had stopped texting and phoning her and was no longer part of her life. Two months later she'd heard he was going out with a girl from his office.

Then Megan had lost her job in one of the big banks. Two unemployed girls unable to pay the rent in their Ranelagh home was not going to work out, and they had all talked about downsizing to a small two-bedroom apartment. Then, out of the blue one day, Megan had announced she was taking off for Canada. She had cousins in Vancouver, and they were hoping to help her get a job there as a credit analyst.

'There's nothing to lose, Lucy. Why don't you come with me?' she had said.

Lucy did consider it, but knew that finding a job might be very hard in Canada. Megan had qualifications and a hefty redundancy package from the bank to tide her over, whereas she would have to borrow the money from her parents.

'I promise to let you know the minute I find a job for you. Then you just book a flight and come over,' Megan had urged. 'You've nothing to keep you here.'

In August the three girls sadly said goodbye to 'the party house', Anna deciding to move in with her boyfriend Ted.

'He's been asking me for ages, so I guess now is a good time to try out living together . . . hopefully we won't kill each other!'

Lucy liked Ted. She was happy for him and Anna, even if it meant that she was temporarily homeless and had to move back home with her mum and dad.

'Your room is still there for you,' welcomed her mum. 'It's good to have you home, Lucy.'

It was good to be home, but she felt embarrassed at twenty-five years of age to be dependent again on her parents. She knew they were puzzled and didn't understand what was happening to her. Her brothers Niall and Kevin both had good jobs: one working in a big insurance company and the other in an up-coming green energy company which he had joined after qualifying as an engineer. Emma, her older sister, was not only married and had a little boy called Harry, but had a great job in Google's Dublin head office. She knew her folks wondered where they had gone wrong with her. Why was she such a disaster compared to her brothers and sister?

She had taken the studs from her ears and nose, lightened her hair colour and even purged her wardrobe of denims and Doc Martens, but it had been to no avail . . . there were just no jobs. Her dad would sit down with a pad and pen with her, and draft and redraft her CV when he came home from his work at the bank.

'Lucy, you must have some idea of what you would really like to do! The sort of career that would satisfy you, the kind of work you want.'

'I loved Phoenix Records,' she said. 'It was a great buzz working there.'

'Given the current climate, no one is going to be opening another record store in Dublin – or anywhere else for that matter,' said her dad, irritated.

'I know.'

'So you need to focus on something else, Lucy, and try to get experience working in a different environment.'

It was easier said than done. Her reams of unanswered CVs were a testament to that fact.

She had done a bit of babysitting and childminding for her brother Kevin and his wife Cassie and their baby Sophie, and also for her sister Emma. She loved minding her little niece and nephew. Sometimes, through one of Jeremy's contacts, she got a bit of work on the promotion side for big gigs coming into the city's large music venues. It was hand to mouth stuff, and she didn't know how much longer she could keep it up as week after week friends headed for London, New Zealand, Australia and Canada.

'Something will turn up,' her mother said soothingly, again and again.

Lucy knew she was a useless case. She'd loved school, and been happy there, but her exam results had been pretty awful. She wasn't academic, and had struggled to get through the Leaving Cert, unlike her brothers and sister. She had scraped into one of Dublin's smaller colleges, realizing after her first term studying marketing and business and French that she had absolutely no idea what she was doing, but enjoyed the social life. She had flunked her first-year exams, and halfway through repeats in her second year came to the conclusion that there was absolutely no point in it, and just dropped out.

She had tried lots of other things: computers, interior design, tourism, massage, web design . . . and hated every single one of them. She had racked up a fortune in fees over the years, and still had no idea of what her calling in life was.

Sure, she'd like to get married and have kids, but

that didn't really count as a career aim. Her sister Emma had Harry, the most huggable three-and-a-half-year-old on the planet, but she still had to work. She and her husband had a massive mortgage on their small house up in Sandyford.

'Lucy, think yourself lucky you are not caught up paying a mortgage like us.' Emma grimaced. She had given up her Volkswagon Beetle, her fancy clothes, her fake-tan sessions, nail bar and spa treats with her girlfriends, and romantic breaks with Gary in order to keep paying the bills. At least Harry was able to attend the crèche attached to her office, and would start school next year.

'Any news?' asked Lucy's mum hopefully, coming into her room with a pile of washing she had brought in from the line.

'Just another letter with a great big no!' Lucy sighed, feeling sorry for herself. 'Mum, I can't see how I am ever going to get a job unless I emigrate.'

'I'm sorry, pet. It's not your fault. It's the stupid politicians and bankers that run this country that have brought us to this. Who would believe married men and women with families and mortgages are losing their jobs, and talented people like yourself not even getting called to an interview? Honestly, Lucy, it makes my blood boil. In my day jobs were ten a penny. If you didn't like a job or your boss you just quit! Upped and left, and usually found something better. There were jobs and opportunities galore. How did we come to this, I ask you?'

Lucy was so fed up of it. She didn't want to talk about her problems and set her mum off on another of her regular diatribes against politicians and political parties. Ever since her mum had gone back part-time to study arts in college she had loved talking about politics – which was one of her subjects!

'I might sign on for another course,' Lucy said hesitantly.

Nina Brennan looked sceptical.

'What kind of course?'

'I saw one on learning the techniques for making stained glass windows. It's starting next month. Or I could learn how to do mosaic tiling!'

'Lucy, why would you want to go making stained glass windows?' asked her mother gently. 'Or do mosaic tiling?

'It's something to do!' Lucy sighed. 'Something a bit different!'

Nina Brennan harrumphed in disbelief.

Lucy stared stubbornly at the 1980s pink floral print wallpaper in her bedroom.

Something had to change. Something really had to change!

Chapter Three

Staring at the figures on the screen, Alice tried to control her mounting panic as numbers began to slide and disappear before her eyes. What had she done? Had she touched something on the computer keypad by accident? Had she hit delete? This job was going disastrously! She looked over at the desk where Kelly Riordan was inputting numbers as quickly as humanly possible, her attention riveted on her own screen.

'Kelly!' she whispered. 'Kelly!'

She couldn't hide the urgency in her voice, and the twenty-four-year-old, looking up, sensed her quandary and immediately came over.

'What have you done, Alice?' she whispered fiercely, surveying the damage on the Excel account before her and leaning forward and hitting an icon. UNDO.

Alice watched incredulously as the figures magically seemed to reappear and the column of numbers began to look some way right.

'Thanks.' Alice was so grateful to the skinny blonde for all her help over the past few weeks. Kelly seemed to be constantly bailing her out of trouble, dealing with her mistakes, and covering up her utter ineptitude at doing accounts. How had she landed herself in this situation, working in Ronan, Ryan & Lewis's at something she hadn't a clue about? Hugh had been more than kind offering her this job, but in her heart she knew that she was in way over her head! At her age she couldn't compete with Kelly and John and Aoife, and all the other young people here who had college degrees, and were studying accountancy, and seemed to be able to just work away at the computers easily. Her simple ECDL computer course, taken last year, had barely prepared her for the kind of work she was expected to do. She was a dinosaur out of step with the modern office world of laptops and digital downloads and iPods. She must have been mad to accept Hugh's charitable offer of work in the accountancy firm.

'Everything OK, Alice?' Hugh looked concerned as he stopped near her desk.

'Mmmm.' She smiled. 'Fine, thanks, Hugh. I'm just trying to sort a few things out here.'

'Good.' He looked relieved, and she watched him walk back towards the door to his bright office overlooking Fitzwilliam Square. He really was a good man, and he and Sally had been so supportive since Liam had left her.

It had been hard, so hard to get back up on her feet after Liam's affair with Elaine and his demand that Alice and himself separate. It had felt like someone had taken a saw and severed her arm and left her raw and bleeding and shocked. She had driven by Elaine's apartment twice and contemplated murder – or something more mundane like throwing a brick through the second-floor wrap-around glass windows of her modern city-centre apartment overlooking the river. Only the thought of the disgrace she would bring on her family had prevented her from doing such an idiotic thing!

So, while Liam and Elaine lived happily in their glass tower, she struggled to keep her head above water financially, pay her bills, run their home of nearly twenty years and make the best of working in Ronan, Ryan & Lewis.

She glanced at the clock. Only two hours and she would be free to take the DART back home to Monkstown. She'd bring the dog for a walk, heat up the remainder of the lovely shepherd's pie she had made last night, put her feet up and watch the TV.

'Alice! Alice, have you got the copy of the Dunderry report?'

Alice jolted out of her reverie to see the large stocky figure of Alex Ronan standing in front of her.

'It's somewhere here,' she said evasively, trying to work out which pile she had put it in and remember if she had done the changes he had requested.

'Where? I'm in a hurry, their finance guy is phoning me in a few minutes about something, and I want to check the figures.'

'I'll find it, Alex, don't worry.'

Alice frantically scanned the in-tray on her desk and the slide-out drawers, looking for the report Alex had given her to update, trying to ignore his exasperation and impatience as he watched her get more flustered and panicked. Having the senior partner standing over her was making her feel useless, like some school kid on work experience.

Coming closer, Alex impatiently began to go through her work.

'I can find it myself,' she said indignantly, as he pulled open the drawer and banged it back before rifling through the polished black leather tray on her desk.

'There it is,' he said, grabbing it.

'That's the Graham—' she began.

'And Dunderry report I want. The companies merged eighteen months ago, and we acted for Dunderry.'

Her face blazed red. She felt stupid.

He peered at the printout figures.

'You've inverted two of the columns,' he said grimly. 'Transport and rent . . . there is a difference, you know.'

She apologized profusely, knowing that Kelly and Aoife and the rest of the office were watching what was going on.

'I'm sorry, Alex.'

'So am I,' he said, marching towards his office door.

Kelly gave her a little reassuring smile, and Alice, trying not to cave in to her overwhelming feelings of inadequacy and embarrassment, buried herself in another deadly dull report.

Since Liam had left she had tried out a few ways of earning money, but this was without doubt the worst. She had worked as a sales assistant in Elegance, the small gift shop in Foxrock, during the busy Christmas period, done bits of babysitting for friends of friends, had even set up a little business selling homemade cupcakes to local cafés and at the weekly farmers' market in Dun Laoghaire until the cupcake market had got totally oversaturated and she had begun making less and less profit. She had done the catering for two funerals and a twenty-fifth wedding anniversary party, but couldn't hope to compete with the more established caterers who were struggling for business.

Alice wasn't proud. She was willing to try most things, but it was becoming more and more obvious that she just wasn't cut out for office work! She'd have to talk to Hugh. Explain how she felt. Money or no money she didn't know how much more of working in Ronan, Ryan & Lewis she could stick. She glanced up at the clock. Only one hour and forty minutes to go . . .

Chapter Four

Rob Flanagan looked out across Dublin Bay. From the bay window of the sitting room of the large Georgian house on Clifton Terrace where he lived he could see the magnificent spread of water that ran between Dun Laoghaire Harbour and Howth Head. There was a strong breeze blowing, and he watched as the sails of the yachts caught the wind and gathered pace, skimming lightly as they raced each other. In the distance the large Seacat ferry, bringing passengers and cars from Holyhead in Wales to Dublin, slowed as it approached Dun Laoghaire Harbour. He sighed to himself, watching the constant flow of traffic below and the groups of people walking along the seafront. Mothers and fathers with strollers, elderly couples, joggers in tracksuits, young lovers hand in hand. Nowadays he seemed to spend hours up here, people watching, wondering what was going on in the lives of others instead of trying to get on with his own. It was still too painful . . . too raw; and today, like some days, he didn't see how his life could ever return to a semblance of normality and happiness again. When Kate had died, it had felt as if part of his life had ended too.

The large sitting room was full of family photos in polished silver frames. A family photographic history displayed for all to see. Their wedding, their silver wedding anniversary. Proud young parents with new baby sons; birthday parties for their two boys; first communions; graduations; holidays in Donegal and Spain and Florida; and one of those expensive family portraits with them all wearing pale blue and trying to pretend that they weren't posing, Kate laughing at the fun of it all as they stared at the camera. That happiness caught for ever. He touched her face through the glass. She's beautiful, he thought . . . was beautiful. He searched his memory, trying to recall the last time he'd told her . . . actually said to his wife that she looked beautiful. To his shame he couldn't remember. He must have said it last year when they were going to his sister Brigid's son's wedding in Wicklow. He surely had admired Kate's outfit, at the very least. All the things he could have said to her, should have said to her . . . to let her know just how

38

much she meant to him, and he had never bothered . . . never taken the time to talk to her, to talk to his wife. Now the time had gone, all run out, and it was too late. Too much had been left unsaid.

Downstairs in the kitchen he made himself a mug of coffee and toasted a slice of bread. He was almost out of the rich roast blend he liked, and there was hardly any milk left, either.

Pull yourself together! he told himself. Go out and do something! Grabbing his car keys he decided to head for his local supermarket. He needed to stock up on a few things.

Rob stood in the aisle of Supervalu utterly bewildered, his trolley in front of him. Shopping should be simple, the purchase of essential nutrients and cleaning products easily accomplished; but standing here, trying to avoid colliding with his fellow shoppers, he had to admit he felt totally out of his depth.

Kate had shopped here weekly, year in, year out, without complaint or fuss. He'd never given the slightest consideration to her purchases, and their connection to the daily meals and good food she pro-duced and the seamless smooth running of their home. He might have helped her the odd time to lift the boxes and bags from the car and pack them away in their kitchen, but choosing what they should eat had always been his wife's prerogative.

Kate used to consult him if they were having a dinner party or a crowd for supper, about the menu or wines, but otherwise the pleasure of sitting down to the table to a good hot meal was something he had just taken for granted. He studied the rows of tins of tuna, trying to recall which brand they had used. Usually Kate had opened the tin and put the fish in a salad, or made a toasty tuna melt.

Ahead of him there was tuna in brine, tuna in sunflower oil, tuna in water, tuna in mayonnaise, tuna in a tomato sauce, tuna with pasta, tuna with curry, tuna chunks, tuna flakes. Tuna was a minefield . . . He had no idea which one to buy, so he grabbed four different tins and threw them in the trolley. He stood for a second, overcome, trying to control himself, missing Kate. He would never get used to this aloneness, this absence. It had been nearly five months since she had died. Everyone kept saying it would get easier but it hadn't. If anything her death was affecting him more acutely with each day that passed.

How did a woman of fifty-nine just die? No illness, no health risks, no strange medical history. Leave home to buy a dress for a friend's daughter's wedding and end up collapsing and being rushed by ambulance to hospital. An aneurysm, the post-mortem had said . . . a balloon that grew and grew in her brain and just suddenly burst as Kate paid for the expensive silk two-piece. No pain, no consciousness, the medics had reassured him. Alive one minute, warm and breathing. Lifeless and still, by the time he had got to St James's Hospital. He didn't want to think about it. Like Groundhog Day it replayed and replayed in his head, continually on a loop. He kept wondering if he had gone into town with Kate, or if she had stayed home, or gone with a friend, would the outcome have been any different?

He took up a can of organic ratatouille, studying the ingredients as if his life depended on it before slowly lowering it into the trolley. He consulted the list he had made: coffee, milk, bread, butter, marmalade, soup, cereal, sausages, cheese, apples, toilet paper, washing powder, shower gel and shampoo. There had to be more he needed. What about a nice bit of brie or the West Cork cheese that the girl on the delicatessen counter offered him to sample on a cracker with a small blob of quince? Different . . . he liked it.

'Where are the crackers?' he asked. The pretty dark-haired girl pointed him to the far aisle. Recognizing his favourite brand, Rob grabbed them and also a packet of fancy biscuits with cracked black pepper flavouring. Up at the busy meat counter at the back of the shop he picked out two large pork chops and a piece of steak before going to the cold section and stocking up on some frozen pizza and five microwaveable dinners. He added some potato wedges and potato gratin, easily reheated judging by the instructions. As he pushed the trolley towards the checkout he chose a tub of ice cream, six doughnuts and some Cadbury's chocolate. He deliberated at the drinks section, opting for a bottle of a decent looking Burgundy and adding a twelve-pack of Heineken cans.

A harried mother whose toddler was sitting in the trolley in front of him piled enough groceries to feed an army on to the moving belt. Meanwhile, the toddler, angel face smudged with chocolate, turned her attention to nibbling the tip of the crusty baguette in her mother's trolley.

'She's so pretty.' The blonde student operating the checkout smiled.

The mother was pretty, too, in a messy unkempt kind of way. Tracksuit bottoms and a zip-up fleece-lined fitted pink jacket. She smiled at Rob as she pretended to chastise her tow-headed daughter. Instead, she gave her a kiss as she bent over to pay and punched her credit card number into the keypad.

Kate had always wanted a daughter, well, for them

42

to have a third child. He'd been happy with their two boys, Gavin and Luke, two great sons! They were good kids, never caused them trouble: bright and strong and happy, independent and grown-up now, Gavin working in Seattle, and Luke doing his master's at Oxford. A third child might have un-balanced things . . . another son? A daughter who looked like Kate? Pretty and dark with those blue eyes and her mother's dimples! They had argued about it. Two is enough, he had insisted, persuading Kate to put motherhood aside and agree with him.

He flinched when he saw the cost of his groceries, aware of the irritated expression of the middle-aged woman behind him in the queue. Flustered, he finished packing his bags and tried to manoeuvre the trolley towards the busy exit.

At home, he contemplated his purchases, cutting him-self a wedge of cheese and opening the peppered biscuits for lunch. He hated Saturdays. He'd read the paper, have two mugs of coffee and some chocolate, and then go out for a walk. It was overcast, but if he was lucky he might escape the threatened showers. He'd take a rain jacket and head over towards Killiney. Walk for a few hours and then come home and cook those chops.

His brother Johnny had left a message on his

phone to say himself and his wife Maeve were going to Finnegans in Dalkey for a few drinks later if he wanted to join them. Johnny and Maeve had given him stalwart support since Kate had died, but he couldn't keep living in their pockets. He'd had so many dinners in their house it was embarrassing, and generous-spirited Maeve always sent him home with something for the freezer. He texted Johnny saying that he'd see how he felt later.

Kate and he had loved Saturdays: dinners and drinks, meeting up with friends or having people in; lying in bed the next morning with the Sunday newspapers doing a post-mortem on the restaurant they had visited, or how the meal had gone, and chatting about stupid things, planning for the future. They'd been going to have a trip to California in May, spending a few days staying with Gavin and that American girlfriend of his, Joanne, and then hiring a car and driving down the Pacific Highway, Monterey, Carmel, San Francisco, San Diego. There were so many other things they had planned to do: Australia, New Zealand, South Africa, South America! Why hadn't they done some of it? Why had they put it off for another few years? Why had he made her wait?

Kate had looked disappointed when he had told her that perhaps it would be better to wait until he was retired in three or four years' time to do the big trips.

'Sydney Harbour and the Barrier Reef will still be there, Kate! Table Mountain is not going anywhere.'

'Well, retirement or not, we are going to see Gavin soon,' she had insisted, booking the tickets herself over the internet. 'I want to see my son.'

He thought about Gavin and Luke now, about phoning them from the hospital to tell them to come home immediately, lying and saying that their mother was ill and needed them. How could he let them go through the torment of knowing that they would never see her again until he had them back on their home ground, here in Dublin?

The boys had stayed home for two weeks while the funeral took place. Rob was glad of their support and love, and realized what wonderful young men he and Kate had raised. He wished Kate had got the chance to meet Joanne Miller, the tall blonde American with the long legs, sparkling teeth, a big, kind heart and intelligent mind that their eldest son had fallen in love with. She had flown over to Ireland for four days, holding Gavin's hand, making endless pots of coffee and sitting up late listening to stories about a woman she had never met, before having to return to work back in Seattle when the funeral was over.

The boys had adored their mother, and Rob had firmly rejected any talk about either of them coming back home to stay with him. Kate would have wanted them to continue with their careers and studies.

'There's no question of coming back here for the moment,' he'd insisted. 'There is far more opportunity for both of you overseas. Your mother and I knew that. She'd turn in her grave if either of you threw up the chances you've been given and came back just to keep me company. I've Johnny and Maeve and the rest of the family, plus all my buddies. They've been great, not to mention your mother's friends, who've been flapping around the house like a load of hens. Anyway, I'm well able to manage on my own,' he'd assured them.

He'd driven them to the airport, the wrench as they said goodbye in Dublin's new busy air terminal harder than he could have imagined. He'd sat in the car park for an hour afterwards, too upset to drive back home.

All the groceries packed away and his lunch finished, Rob pulled on his jacket and some walking shoes and called Bingo, their ten-year-old Labrador. The dog looked up from his red basket in the corner of the kitchen. Even he missed Kate.

'Here, boy, time for a walk,' Rob said, heading for

the Volvo Estate parked in the driveway. Bingo lumbered along behind him and jumped into the rear seat. 'It's just you and me, Bingo,' Rob said, as he slipped the car into reverse and took off for the rest of the afternoon.

Chapter Five

Kerrie O'Neill tried to disguise the nervousness she felt in the pit of her stomach at going to stay with her fiancé Matt's parents for the weekend. Ever since they had got engaged Matt had been on at her to come up to Moyle House, his family home, for a relaxed break, while she felt utter trepidation about having to spend so much time under the nose of his mother and father.

She'd only met the Hennessys briefly a few times, but from the minute she'd met them she had realized that Matt and his family lived a life of privilege and wealth, one that was totally different from her more humble background. She looked at the perfect diamond ring on her finger. Matt loved her! It shouldn't make a difference where she came from, or what her parents' social status was, but she knew deep in her heart that it did.

As they turned off the busy Athlone Road and headed towards Moyle House she didn't really know what to expect. Matt had gone to private boarding school when he was twelve and talked far more about that than he ever did about home. His sister and brother had all left home as soon as they were able, and only seemed to return home sporadically. She guessed the Hennessys weren't as close as her family.

After they'd passed a few shops and a local pub and driven out the road a bit she spotted the name 'Moyle House' engraved on the tall granite pillars of a gateway. Matt turned up a long rhododendron-lined drive, passing under a canopy of tall chestnut and beech trees.

'We're here,' he said quietly, as they pulled up in front of a very large but rather ugly grey Georgian house with sash windows overlooking a well-kept lawn and a fish pond.

Kerrie took a breath. The house was huge, a lot bigger than she had expected. It was like a stately home, or something you'd see in a period drama on TV. Imagine what it must have been like for Matt growing up in such a place! She took stock for a second, expecting Maureen Hennessy to appear, relieved when there was no sign of her.

'Come on, let's go in and I'll get you a cup of coffee,' offered Matt, as he opened the front door and a large black dog bounded out to meet them.

'Down, Jet!' he said firmly.

The house had patterned tiles in the hall and a wide curving stairway. Light flooded in from the tall landing window, illuminating a grandfather clock and a large coat-stand.

'Mum!' Matt called, peering into the drawing room and the dining room before heading down a few steps towards the breakfast room and kitchen. 'Looks like we have the place to ourselves.' He smiled as he filled the kettle and put it on to boil. 'I'll see if there are any biscuits or cake around.'

It was only eighteen months since Kerrie had first met Matt and they had fallen madly for each other! It had been a whirlwind romance, and they had moved in together the previous year. Matt had totally surprised her with his romantic proposal in July. They'd gone to Stockholm for her boss Sven Johnnson's fiftieth birthday celebrations, and stayed on afterwards, renting a blue-painted summer house on one of the islands for a week. They were out sailing when Matt had asked her to marry him.

'Matt, of course I'll marry you!' she'd cried, overwhelmed, as Matt had kissed her and produced a chilled bottle of champagne and a picnic to celebrate their engagement. She had wanted to stay on that little sailboat out on the water for ever! She still couldn't believe that she was engaged and going to marry Matt, the guy of her dreams.

When they'd got home Matt had organized dinner in Shanahan's Restaurant on St Stephen's Green to celebrate, and for both sets of parents to meet. It was awkward as the Hennessys were wealthy and used to money and position and country living, while Kerrie's mam and dad had struggled to raise them all on her dad's sorting office salary. Matt's mother Maureen had quizzed her nosily about her background and family. Kerrie had become a master at fudging exactly where she came from! Matt didn't need to know the full extent of the differences, and Kerrie had done her best to ensure that.

She had been far too busy trying to keep an eye on how many pints her dad was downing and giving her mam a blow-by-blow account of the romantic proposal to pay too much attention to the shenanigans of Dermot and Maureen Hennessy. Matt's parents were the very opposite of hers. His dad was used to getting his way, while Maureen Hennessy was one of the biggest snobs you could ever meet. Dermot Hennessy had begun by demanding some expensive French wine that tasted awful to celebrate the upcoming nuptials of his eldest son, while Maureen had complained that her fillet steak was a bit too rare, even though that was what she had ordered.

By the end of the night Kerrie's nerves had been frayed. Her dad was drunk and so was Matt's! Her mam had kept whispering to her that Matt was a pet, but she wasn't sure about his hoity-toity parents! Kerrie thanked Heaven she hadn't seated them together, as Maureen had spent the evening being absolutely frosty towards her parents and treating them like they were beneath her in social standing. She had gone on and on about some stupid local hunt ball, too.

'I'd shoot anyone I saw on a horse who went after a poor fox,' Kerrie's mother had declared firmly, her cheeks blazing with temper. 'It's just pure cruel . . . barbaric.'

Dermot Hennessy had looked disgruntled, and Matt tried to appease his father as he paid the bill.

Kerrie and Matt had planned to bring their parents for a post-dinner drink but instead watched with relief as both couples got into taxis and went their separate ways, declaring they were feeling tired and wanted to get home. Matt's parents were staying the night in his married sister Georgina's house in Rathgar.

Exhausted, she and Matt had headed to O'Donoghue's for a well-deserved nightcap.

'Poor Georgina!' declared Matt.

It had been a disaster of a night, and had made Kerrie realize the difficulties they faced organizing a wedding!

Matt's life had been so cosseted: growing up on the Hennessys' rambling old country estate in Meath, surrounded by all the good things in life. Following college he had had a brilliant career mapped out for him in corporate finance at PWC, one of the country's top accountancy firms.

Kerrie's upbringing was totally different. She'd grown up on an estate, too, but hers was no country one! Kerrie O'Neill had grown up in Tallaght, on one of Dublin city's largest sprawling working-class estates. One of six kids, her childhood had been a happy one, but her mam and dad had constantly struggled financially as they did their best to raise and educate them. Like her brothers and sisters, Kerrie had fought for everything she had.

At twelve years old, thrown into the busy local community school, she had buckled down and worked harder than the other hundred and fifty kids in her year, determined to secure a vital place at college which would harness her superior maths and analytical skills.

In UCD she had found it hard to find her feet, and

with no schoolmates to hang around with, she felt out of her depth socially and found her first year lonely. She had contemplated dropping out, but refused to let where she came from disadvantage her. In the second year she had done the J1 to the USA with a big crowd from her class. She'd had the best summer of her life in Montauk, where she was just one of a gang of Irish students working summer jobs. Waitressing in a fancy beach club in the Hamptons with some of the other girls in her year, and hanging out with them swimming and drinking and sailing, Kerrie had finally learned to fit in with everyone.

When she returned home Kerrie had realized that she still had much to learn, and using the same diligence that got her through Riverfield Community School she had changed herself, chameleon-like, to adapt to the new world she was now becoming part of. Her parents were proud of her academic success, but puzzled by her transformation. Kerrie was bright and intelligent, but that was no guarantee of success where she came from! So, armed with an honours degree and a Master's in finance Kerrie had begun to build her career. She now held a senior position in Barrington Holdings, one of the city's main asset-management companies.

* * *

She had met Matt on a skiing trip to Meribel with some of the girls she had kept in touch with from college, and immediately found herself attracted to the tall guy with the easy laugh and fun sense of humour who was already a senior manager in a big accountancy firm down on the river. Their lives and backgrounds were so utterly different, but when they were together on their own that did not seem to matter. They had fallen madly in love, and ten months later had moved in together into an ultra-modern 1400-square-foot apartment overlooking Grand Canal Dock.

Little Kerrie O'Neill had transformed herself from a skinny, mouthy kid with ambitions to a well-educated, qualified, polished professional with an amazing boyfriend and a perfect life stretching ahead of her! She couldn't risk losing it. Losing Matt.

So she had drawn a veil over her background and where she came from, letting Matt assume that she was just another of those nice middle-class girls from a good home and good family and good school that he normally hung out with.

She had deliberately kept her family at a distance, deflecting Matt's interest in visiting her home by saying her parents would much prefer to come and have dinner in their new apartment, and ensuring that when Matt did get to meet them it was always on her terms: like treating them to tickets to see Paul McCartney playing at the Royal Dublin Society.

'I never thought I'd live to see this day,' her dad had said, blinking away his tears when Paul McCartney sang 'Blackbird'.

'I never knew your dad was such a music fan,' Matt had laughed when they got home.

'He was in a band! I told you . . . that's how he met my mam. I think she was a kind of groupie and used to turn up wherever they played. Dad played the guitar and the fiddle and sang a bit.'

'Does he still play?'

'Yeah! At the drop of a hat he'll give you a bit of Elvis, the Beatles, the Stones, Led Zeppelin, Bowie or Bob Dylan,' she had said proudly.

'My folks are big into classical music and opera,' Matt had confided. 'They like the Wexford Opera Festival. They're not really into other kinds of music.'

Was it any wonder that she was doing her very best to keep both sets of families apart? The thought of the two families getting together for their wedding was a major stress, which was why Kerrie was determined that it should be a small, simple affair. She had suggested going off on their own to somewhere exclusive like the Seychelles or the Maldives and having a beach wedding, but Matt would hear none of it!

'Hey, if you don't want to have a big family wedding in some castle or hotel at home that's OK, Kerrie, but the least we can do if we go away is have our parents and a few of our family and close friends present!' he reasoned. 'We can well afford it! After all, our wedding day is going to be the most important day of our lives. We want them to be there and part of it.'

Kerrie had trawled the internet and spent hours researching and planning for their wedding, eventually persuading Matt to opt for the South of France. They both loved the area and were busy trying to organize a small wedding next September in the harbour town of Villefranche. They'd have the ceremony in the pretty church overlooking the sea and then a meal for the wedding party in one of the expensive restaurants beside the water. It would be classy and exclusive and stylish, with hopefully as few members of each family present as possible, if she had her way. They were paying for the wedding themselves, and she wasn't going to let what parents or family and friends thought dictate what they should or shouldn't do.

Kerrie took the opportunity to look around the large kitchen as Matt disappeared into what she presumed was some kind of larder or pantry. There was a huge Aga, a massive kitchen table, and ten chairs – including two rather decrepit-looking armchairs positioned at the window, which were covered in newspapers and dog hair.

The kitchen units looked hand-painted and expensive, and when she pulled out a drawer it slid out smoothly revealing an expensive array of dinner and side plates. The kitchen also had a massive American fridge and some pretty fancy electrics.

'I found some Madeira cake,' said Matt. 'And a few scones.'

They were enjoying the scones when Maureen Hennessy appeared in the back door.

'I was up at the golf club . . . I didn't think you would get here for another hour at least,' she said, hugging Matt and flicking her eyes over Kerrie.

'The traffic was lighter than I expected,' Matt explained.

'Well, it's lovely to have you home, Matt. We don't see half enough of you.' Maureen helped herself to a mug of coffee. 'And of course, Kerrie, dear, you're very welcome at Moyle House.'

'Where's Dad?'

'He had some meeting with Gerard and Alan Mullen, some kind of urgent business he had to attend to. He said he won't be too late home.'

'Your house is lovely,' Kerrie offered. 'The garden's huge.'

'It's a lot of work. We've almost twenty acres,' explained Maureen. 'There's a tennis court and a paddock and stables where we used to keep ponies for the children when they were younger, and of course a vegetable garden, too. It leads right down to the river.'

'I'll show you it tomorrow when it is light,' promised Matt.

'Maybe you might take Kerrie out riding tomorrow, if the weather's nice.'

Kerrie blushed. She had no idea how to ride! The only time she had ever been up on a horse or a donkey was either on the beach or at some kind of fair when there were cheap pony rides for kids. Her family could never have afforded the luxury of riding lessons or a pony.

'I'm not much of a rider,' she offered. 'And besides, I didn't bring any clothes for it!'

'There are some jodhpurs and jackets, and a few pairs of spare boots, in Georgina's old room if you need them,' offered Maureen, her blue eyes steely. She seemed to be reading Kerrie's mind. 'I've made up the bed there, and also naturally in Matt's room, as I wasn't too sure what the sleeping arrangements might be.'

Matt's face reddened as if he was about seven years old.

'Mum, we're living together and getting married in a few months' time.'

'Well, you young people can suit yourselves!' Maureen said briskly. 'I must make a start on the dinner. I'm doing a nice fish pie and your favourite dessert: bread and butter pudding.'

'Great,' Matt grinned, giving her a hug.

'Why don't you show Kerrie the rest of the house and bring her things upstairs?'

Kerrie admired the large drawing room with its views of the garden, and the dining room with its red-painted walls and dark heavy furniture, and the garden room's chintz couches and wicker chairs and coffee tables strewn with gardening books and country living magazines. A small spaniel was asleep on one of the cushions. This house was a world apart from the small three-bedroomed semi-detached house where she had grown up.

As they climbed the staircase and Matt pointed out various paintings and family photographs she tried not to be overwhelmed. His bedroom was huge, and was neat and tidy, but the bed looked pretty ancient – with a heavy looking wool blanket folded over the end. There was a wardrobe, a chest of drawers, a desk and a chair. The curtains were a navy and cream stripe with a coordinating bedcover.

'This room can get a bit cold,' he warned.

'Well, you can warm me up, then!' she teased.

An hour later they surfaced.

'You look like a naughty schoolboy!' she joked.

'I feel like one,' he admitted ruefully. 'Let's hope mum was down in the kitchen and didn't hear what was going on.'

'I can smell our dinner cooking . . .'

Kerrie slipped into the next-door bathroom with its tiled floor and walls, trying not to shiver as she turned on the shower. It seemed to stop and start and spurt in the most unpredictable fashion, and the temperature of the water went between scalding hot and icy. It was a nightmare, she thought, as she wrapped herself in a towel and headed back to the room. She changed into a fitted red wool dress and black tights and pumps, going easy on the make-up but using her Mac eyeliner to accentuate her blue eyes.

'God, you look gorgeous!' said Matt, nuzzling up to her in his boxers.

'I am not braving that shower again,' she warned, dabbing her wrist and neck with a little Coco Mademoiselle. 'Anyway, I'm going downstairs to see if your mum needs a hand with anything, and you'd better get dressed quick and come down and join us.'

'Mum won't eat you! Her bark is far worse than her bite,' he proffered.

'You're her darling son . . . I'm the bad bold girl-friend who's taking you away and who you're going to marry,' she explained. 'There's no getting over that!'

When she asked Maureen Hennessy if there was anything she could do to help in the kitchen, the older woman reassured her that everything was done and would be ready shortly.

'But if you want to help, maybe you can feed the dogs.'

Jet was sitting under the table salivating, and the spaniel and a small terrier were jumping around the kitchen.

Kerrie had not been a fan of canines ever since she'd been bitten when she was six years old by next door's Jack Russell.

'There are some tins on the shelf in the scullery, and a tin opener, and they like a bit of that cereal stuff mixed in with it all. You'll see their bowls. Only give Lady – the terrier – a small portion, as she's having a bit of tummy trouble. Bobby, the spaniel, can have more than her. And no extras!' Maureen warned.

Kerrie felt queasy as she saw the three dog bowls. The smell when she opened the tin was vile and made her stomach turn. God knows what was in it. Bracing herself, she began to spoon it out. Jet nearly knocked her over as he went for his huge bowl, gulping his feed down in a few minutes. The other two smaller dogs were at least a bit slower. The spaniel wagged his tail madly as she lowered his bowl to the ground. Lady begged her for more with a pleading look in her eyes. She was kind of cute and danced around Kerrie's feet and in-between her legs, letting Kerrie pat her on the head and behind her ears.

'Here you go,' Kerrie whispered as she put an extra two spoonfuls into Lady's silver bowl, shooing the still hungry Jet and Bobby away. Satisfied with a job well done, she gave them all some fresh water.

'Thanks,' said Maureen, red-faced from checking the oven. 'Dermot will be here in a minute so I'm just going upstairs to freshen up.'

Kerrie sat in the kitchen, wishing that she could just relax, and not feel so overwhelmed about being in Matt's home. You have to get used to it, she told herself over and over. The Hennessys are going to be part of your life. You have to make the effort to get to know them better and to try to fit into their lifestyle.

Dermot, Matt's dad, came in the back door a few

minutes later and as he gave her a welcome hug she got the whiff of whiskey off him.

'Maureen phoned me to say dinner was ready,' he said, as he hung up his tweed jacket.

'She's gone upstairs,' Kerrie explained. 'She'll be down in a minute.'

'Did the woman not offer you a drink?'

'Oh, it's OK, I'll wait and have something when we're eating.'

'You're a guest in our home. You'll have a drink now,' he insisted. 'What will it be?'

'A gin and tonic, if you have it, would be nice before dinner.'

'Gin and tonic it is!' he said, opening one of the kitchen cabinets to reveal a huge selection of alcohol. He poured her a large, almost double, measure and rifled the fridge for the chilled tonic water. 'Ice?'

'Yes, please.'

They found some lemons and she added a slice to it. Matt arrived down to the kitchen as she felt the reviving shot of alcohol relax her.

'Hey, I'll have one of those, too, Dad.'

They were on their second G & Ts by the time Maureen appeared. She checked the oven and announced that the dinner was ready.

'Where are we eating?' asked Dermot.

'Let's just eat here!' suggested Matt.

'I've already set the table in the dining room.'

'I'll set here instead,' said Matt. 'It'll be more relaxing when it's just the four of us.'

'Very well,' said Maureen, 'but do it quickly.'

Kerrie was relieved that at least dinner wouldn't be too formal, and helped to put the butter dish and some glasses and napkins on the kitchen table.

'That was wonderful, Maureen.' Kerrie had to give Matt's mother her due. She had probably just eaten the best fish pie she had ever tasted in her life. Perfect fish – salmon, cod, some prawns – in a rich creamy sauce with a topping of warm buttery mash and a selection of garden vegetables. She laughed, watching Matt and his dad bickering over who would finish off the rest of the dish.

'Leave some room for pudding, you two!' Maureen warned. 'It will be ready in another fifteen minutes or so. And while we're waiting, Dermot and I want to hear all the news on your wedding plans, and find out exactly how many people we are let to invite to the celebrations.'

Kerrie cast a warning glance at Matt, who was too busy practically licking his plate to react. 'Maureen, we're having quite a small wedding,' she reminded her. 'That's why we're going to the South of France.'

'France? Are you still set on that?'

'That is where we want to get married,' Kerrie said calmly. 'Matt and I don't want a huge fuss and palaver, just close family and a few friends. We've talked about it.'

'Your sister had a wonderful wedding in Ashford Castle. Surely something like that would be more suitable for you and Kerrie?'

'That was Georgina's wedding, Mum – we want something different.'

'But Matt, think of all your cousins and relations . . . they aren't going to see you get married! And then there're some of our dearest friends . . . we've been to all their children's weddings. What are Dermot and I to say to them about this hole-and-corner-style wedding?'

'Mum, we are getting married in a very exclusive place. The South of France. It's absolutely beautiful there, and there is a lot to be said to not having miserable Uncle Clem and awful Aunt Irene, or a load of cousins that I barely see from one end of the year to the other at my wedding. Kerrie and I don't want the big hotel and the big wedding like everyone else!'

'We want our wedding to be special,' insisted Kerrie. 'It's our wedding.'

'What about your parents?'

Kerrie blushed. She knew her mam and dad had been gutted when she had told them about the small wedding in France. They couldn't understand why she wasn't going to have a big traditional wedding like her sister Martina and her brother Mike had had.

'They're totally OK about it,' she fibbed. 'I think they are both actually looking forward to having something a bit quieter and smaller without all the fuss they had for my sister and my brothers' weddings.'

'It's the young people's prerogative to have the type of wedding they want, Maureen. I'm sure Matt and Kerrie are well able to decide what they need,' said Dermot, as he got up to fetch another bottle of wine for the table. 'And that's the end of it.'

Maureen threw a despairing glance at her husband.

'Now, where's that pudding you promised us?'

Dermot gave Kerrie a wink, and she felt like hugging him. She hoped that there'd be no more discussion about their wedding for the weekend.

'That pudding is amazing.' Kerrie was not really a dessert person, but the bread and butter pudding layered with sultanas and brown sugar was absolutely yummy.

'It's been Matt's favourite ever since he was a little boy. The others would want a big chocolate cake for their birthday, and all Matt would want was "my pudding".'

'It's still my favourite.' Matt laughed.

'What kind of puddings do you make?' Maureen asked inquisitively.

'I'm not much of a pudding person, to be honest,' Kerrie admitted, flustered, thinking of the desserts her local delicatessen, Polly's Pantry, offered or the Marks & Spencer range. 'It's more just a cake or a tart when we have friends in, with some ice cream or something.'

'No bread and butter pudding?'

'No, sorry . . . I guess I'll have to start making it for you, Matt.'

'Maureen's a great cook,' beamed Dermot. 'Trained in London, you know!'

'I did a cordon bleu course there when I was about twenty. My mother sent my older sister Jane and me over to do a cookery course there for six months.'

Shit! Matt's mother would have to be a cordon bleu cook. Now Kerrie felt even more inadequate. 'That must have been fun,' she said.

'It was a lot of hard work, but I have to admit it has stood me in good stead!'

Kerrie stared at her plate. Why had Matt never mentioned to her that his mother was a trained cook? The only food he ever talked about was the awful swill he was served at boarding school. He'd told her

68

that ever since, he hadn't been able even to look at a boiled egg, let alone eat one!

'Let's take our coffee and cheese in the drawing room,' Maureen suggested. 'The fire is lit and it will be nice and cosy just to sit and chat there.'

It was warm in the drawing room, and Kerrie curled herself up on the couch beside Matt. The fire was flickering, casting shadows on the polished mahogany and sparkling glass of the sideboard. She felt kind of relaxed and drowsy after all the wine. Matt and his dad were talking about having a game of golf in the morning.

'There's the MacRory Cup Dinner on in the golf club tomorrow, if you fancy it?' suggested Dermot. 'The Mullens and the Finlays are going, and I'm sure most of the neighbours. Are you and Kerrie interested in coming along? Your mother and I have a table booked already.'

'Sounds fun!' Matt laughed. 'Thanks, Dad. It'll be nice to meet up with some of the old gang and introduce them to my beautiful fiancée. Count us in.'

Kerrie had hoped that maybe Matt and she could slope off on their own to one or two of the nice local pubs and grab a bit of food there.

'And I've organized for everyone to come here for Sunday lunch,' added Maureen. 'Georgina and

Charley say they'll come down from Dublin, too.'

Kerrie tried to hide her dismay at such a big Hennessy gathering over the weekend, with no time at all for Matt and herself to be alone!

'What about a glass of port to go with that lovely Gubbeen cheese?' urged Dermot, as he poured Kerrie a glass of the ruby red port.

The dogs were sitting at the fire. Jet, the Labrador, was panting spreadeagled on the mat. Bobby moved over to Dermot's feet, while Lady ambled over to Kerrie and jumped up on the couch beside her, resting her head on Kerrie's lap. Absentmindedly, Kerrie petted the little terrier's ears, trying to stifle her fear of dogs and pretend that it was OK to have one panting and breathing kind of funny on top of your dress.

The port was lovely, giving her a warm glow all over, and she was so relaxed that she almost managed to forget the terrier was there until it began to make a strange kind of choking noise. Ugh, what was wrong with it? Suddenly Lady began to gag, and regurgitated a pile of steaming hot brown disgusting dog vomit that somehow resembled what Kerrie had fed it earlier. Looking at the smelly pile of yuck deposited on her red dress, it was as much as she could do not to hurl herself in front of the Hennessys!

'Matt, open the French doors and let Lady out

immediately!' ordered Maureen. The little dog leapt off Kerrie's lap and beat a hasty retreat towards the open door.

'I'm sorry, Kerrie! But the poor dog must have eaten too much earlier on,' murmured Maureen. 'You didn't by any chance give her any extra dog food when you were feeding her?'

'No, of course not,' Kerrie fibbed, her cheeks blazing.

Matt disappeared to the kitchen and reappeared with a cloth and a bucket, and began to help clean the offending mess of vomit off her good dress. Yuk, the dress was destroyed. She would never be able to wear it again without feeling nauseous.

Finally able to stand up, she escaped upstairs and stripped off, throwing the ruined dress into a plastic bag. She was so upset she felt like climbing into bed and pulling the duvet over her and staying there. What a disaster of a night!

She didn't belong here, didn't fit in . . . this whole family set-up was totally out of her league! The Hennessys knew that, and so did she . . . Matt was the only one who seemed blind to it. Why did that dog have to go and ruin everything?

She couldn't . . . no, wouldn't, let a dog destroy her future, she thought as she ran into the bathroom and washed herself. She covered herself in perfume before pulling her long black knitted John Rocha top over her black leggings and touching up her lip gloss.

'You OK, Kerrie?' asked Matt, concerned, when she eventually reappeared.

'I'm fine,' she lied, sitting down on the couch beside him, relieved to see there was no sign of the dogs as she cuddled into him.

The fire was blazing and his parents were talking softly.

'Kerrie, dear, is there anything I can get you?' offered Dermot, standing up.

'I'd love another drop of that lovely port please, Dermot.' She smiled, pulling her long legs up under her.

Chapter Six

Kerrie pulled on her warm grey cashmere sweater and slipped her feet into her sturdy black leather walking shoes as she glanced out of the window. Matt was shaving in the bathroom and once he was finished they were going for a walk in the nearby woods. The rain had held off and she was looking forward to a break away from the house before Sunday lunch. She put her stylish grey suede boots back in her bag. Most of her weekend wardrobe had proved utterly useless, and she wished she had given more thought to what a few days in Moyle House would entail before she had packed.

Last night she had felt very overdressed in the golf club in her figure-hugging purple dress. The men's eyes had been out on stalks, but their wives hadn't been quite as friendly when they had had pre-dinner drinks in the bar before eating.

Matt and his dad had played golf on Saturday while she had accompanied Maureen to the village to a local farmers' market which had a huge array of vegetables, food, plants and local products on offer.

'Buy the best and use the best,' advised Maureen. She drove the stallholders crazy with her deliberations over every vegetable and pickle and chutney she bought. Kerrie had followed Maureen's advice and purchased a few things for their kitchen back home.

The cheese looked great, and there was a nutty brown bread and some pecan slices. There was red onion chutney, a damson jam, some honey, marmalade, a jar of apple sauce, mint jelly, and some delicious homemade fudge . . . one of Kerrie's weaknesses.

As they walked around the village Maureen pointed out some of the local landmarks, including Dermot's favourite watering hole, Delaneys, and the small primary school where her children had gone when they were little.

'It must have been hard for you when Matt and Ed and Georgina went off to boarding school,' Kerrie volunteered.

'Our children had to go boarding . . . it's a tradition,' Maureen said. 'The boys went to Castle Wood, where Dermot and his brothers were educated, and Georgina went to Annefield College.

You know, it wouldn't have been good for the children to be hanging around the village, like the rest of the locals. I had always known that they would have to go away. I'm sure Matt, when the time comes, will probably do the same.'

'Matt wasn't that happy in school,' Kerrie said softly. 'I think he must have missed home a lot.'

'Well, he never said much to us,' said Maureen. 'He was always a quiet type of boy . . . he needed to toughen up like his older brother, Ed.'

Kerrie said nothing. Over her dead body would any of her children be packed off to boarding school. Her childhood might have been chaotic and a lot less financially comfortable than Matt's, but she could remember walking in from school and feeling the warmth of the kitchen. Her mam would be in her apron, either cooking or cleaning or washing, but stopping whatever it was she was doing to ask how Kerrie's school day had gone, and what the teacher had said, and what she had learned. Her parents had been great encouraging them all to study and do well.

After lunch on Saturday Maureen had gone to visit a sick friend in the local retirement home. Kerrie had opted to explore the Hennessys' fields and gardens, ignoring the pleas of the dogs, who wanted to come with her. As she walked around the grounds of Moyle

House she couldn't help but be impressed by what Maureen and Dermot were doing there: there were compost heaps and organic vegetables, and even some hens scratching in an enclosure. There was an orchard with old apple trees and a pear tree, a run-down tennis court with a bedraggled looking net, an old paddock that was now overgrown, and what looked like stables and a yard in the distance. The lawn up around the house was immaculate, and the main flower beds were well pruned and neat and tidy. She couldn't help but compare it to the small suburban garden of her parents' house, with its concrete patio, patchy lawn, scanty shrubs and bushes, and her dad's attempts to grow scallions and a few heads of lettuce and carrots.

Afterwards she had made herself some coffee and grabbed one of the lovely pecan slices she had bought that morning, and curled up on the couch reading the papers in the garden room.

The sun was streaming in on her, and somehow she must have dozed off and fallen asleep as she woke to find a rug over her. Since Matt wasn't due home till 6 p.m. she realized that Maureen must have discovered her.

Upstairs she had freshened up and was blow-drying her hair when Matt returned.

'Nice day?'

She was about to moan about him leaving her on her own, but realized that she had literally relaxed most of the day, and that all the fresh air had wiped her out.

'I feel so tired.' She laughed, unable to stop yawning. 'I don't know why, as I hardly did anything.'

'I'm the same.' He laughed too. 'The old man is after beating me hands down at the golf.'

'I hope it'll be OK at the golf club. I don't know anyone, and you know I haven't a clue about golf, either!'

'It'll be fun,' he promised. 'It's kind of low key and relaxed there.'

The bar of the club had been packed, and after a few minutes Kerrie had totally lost track of all the names of the people she had been introduced to. Gerard Mullen, Dermot's business partner, and his wife Gail were at their table, plus Maureen's best friend Anne and her husband Kevin, who were great fun. Anne kept trying to find out information about Kerrie's upcoming wedding, and Kerrie tried to put her off. Anne's daughter Ciara had got married only the previous year, and she was full of wedding tips and advice. They were awaiting the birth of their first grandchild and Anne was really looking forward to being a granny.

'I'm not like Maureen,' she said, laughing. 'I'll be a hands-on granny and give Ciara as much help as I can when she has the baby.'

Kerrie wondered how on earth two women who seemed so different were even friends.

Gerard's son Alan and his girlfriend Sandy were the last to arrive and joined them as they sat down to dinner. The dinner had been fun and Sandy was, like herself, a city girl, and they teased the lads unmercifully about being from the country.

The room was a bit stuffy and hot and at times Kerrie had had to force herself to stay awake and join in the conversation.

Afterwards they had all retreated to the bar and Matt had bought drinks for everyone. Dermot and Gerard had had their heads down talking about some problem they were having with a piece of property they had invested in, and she had seen Alan was also involved in the conversation.

'Leave the men at it,' advised Gail as she regaled them all with stories of a trip to Argentina that Gerard and herself had recently taken.

It had been long after midnight before they had finally got home, and Matt had made sure that his dad, who had drunk far too much, was OK going up the stairs to bed.

'He's been under a lot of stress of late,' he confided

as they undressed, 'but I just worry that he's getting himself too involved with that Gerard. It's strange because Dad's always been his own boss!'

On Sunday morning they enjoyed their walk down through Carna Wood, with Matt showing her where he had hidden in the trees when he was kid, and where he and his brother had made a secret fort. They strolled along by the river, with Matt promising to bring her fishing there the next time they came. It started to rain and they made a run for it and got back to the house just in time.

Matt's sister Georgina and her husband Charley were already there with their little boy Henry and his baby sister Jessica. Georgina was a smaller, plumper version of Dermot, with sparkling brown eyes and a mass of curly hair. The baby was asleep in her car seat and Henry was playing with some Toy Story figures that his mother had wisely brought along.

'Glass of wine, anyone?' offered Charley.

Kerrie was unable to resist the chilled Chablis, relieved that she wasn't the one driving home later.

'Blast breastfeeding,' muttered Georgina. 'Another few weeks, Charley, and it's payback time . . . then you'll have to chauffeur me everywhere!'

'Of course I will,' Charley promised.

The kitchen was hot and there was a huge roast in

the oven. Matt's grandfather, Patrick, and his Aunt Liz were sitting in the armchairs, immersed in the Sunday papers.

Kerrie could immediately see where Matt got his handsome looks from.

'I'm delighted to meet you.' She smiled, utterly charmed. Eighty-six-year-old Patrick Hennessy might have a slight stutter following a stroke he had had two years back, but otherwise seemed hale and hearty and lively. He lived about two miles away with Liz, who was divorced and helped to take care of him.

'What a beauty, Matt! Well done!' declared Patrick. 'The next time you come down home you must bring Kerrie over to see Springfield.'

'Springfield?'

'Where I live and where young Dermot and the rest of the brood grew up. It's a fine old house, though Liz and I are rattling around it at this stage. Full of memories, though!'

'I'd love to see it, the next time I'm down,' Kerrie found herself promising.

They ate in the dining room: Maureen had cooked a large lamb roast and was just carving it when Matt's older brother Ed arrived. There were only three years between them but they looked nothing alike. Ed was big and rather stocky, and almost grey in the face, and admitted he'd been at a stag night and had only just managed to crawl out of bed.

'Poor Brian's getting married in about two weeks,' he sighed. 'It's another good man gone!'

'He takes it so personal,' teased Georgina. 'He's so immature I'm sure no girl would have him.'

'That's what you think!' he laughed.

'Sit down, everyone,' urged Maureen, getting everything out of the oven.

Kerrie gave a hand carrying the large bowl of golden roast potatoes to the dining room, while the others all took their seats at the large mahogany table with its starched linen cloth and napkins and crystal glasses.

The lamb was tender and perfectly cooked, served with honey-glazed parsnips, carrots and some creamy spinach.

'There's nothing like Maureen's Sunday roasts! I really look forward to them,' praised Patrick as he poured gravy over his meat.

Maureen was a perfect hostess, and was in her element, as she loved entertaining . . . loved cooking. In a month of Sundays Kerrie would never be as accomplished in the kitchen. She would never be able to serve a meal like this! The lamb was falling off the bone and everything was so perfect. It was a massive meal, and they all tucked in. Kerrie reckoned she must have put on at least three kilos over the weekend with all the food and drink.

'Georgina, talk to your brother about his wedding,' insisted Maureen. 'Kerrie and Matt want to have only a handful of people to some ceremony in France. It's not what people are expecting at all! Tell them about your wedding. You had over two hundred guests and it was such a wonderful day. Some of my friends are still talking about it.'

'Mum, I wouldn't dream of interfering in someone else's wedding plans,' said Georgina, giving Kerrie a sympathetic glance. 'Matt and Kerrie are totally entitled to have the type of wedding they want.'

'But it is going to be such a small affair,' Maureen continued doggedly.

'Well, when the time comes, if Charley and I are invited we'd love a few days in the South of France seeing my little brother getting married!'

'Of course we'd want you there,' said Matt.

'It's just going to be family and a few close friends,' said Kerrie, her cheeks flaming. 'That's what we want.'

'I'm not up to flying any more,' murmured Patrick, 'so I'll be sorry to miss it.'

Matt cast a despairing glance at Kerrie. She knew he was very fond of his grandfather and wanted him at the wedding.

There was silence around the table for a minute,

and Kerrie could feel a growing swell of resentment from her future mother-in-law.

'Hey, well I'll help organize your stag night!' offered Ed. 'That's the part of people getting married that I like.'

'Ed!' They all laughed, breaking the tension.

Henry was across from Kerrie, and he was such a cute little guy, with a mass of blonde curls and big blue eyes. He had just started kindergarten and was full of chat about his class. Little Jessica began to cry and fret and was obviously hungry, and Georgina reached to take her baby out of her seat and feed her.

'Georgina!'

Even Kerrie couldn't ignore the glacial glance Maureen directed at her daughter, who was starting to feed the hungry baby.

'Your father and grandfather are present.'

Dermot and Patrick were so engrossed talking and eating that they hadn't even glanced in Georgina's direction.

Kerrie was embarrassed, not by Georgina feeding the baby, but by Maureen's attitude. Georgina was among family. Kerrie's own sister Martina felt totally at home when she appeared with her babies, and had breastfed her boys till they were each about one year old.

Without a word, Georgina left the rest of her meal and got up and disappeared off upstairs with the baby in her arms. Poor Georgina, letting her mother dictate when and where she could feed her child!

They had finished dessert and coffee and Matt's sister had still not reappeared.

'We have to be leaving soon,' warned Matt.

'I'll go upstairs and get my bag,' Kerrie offered, scooting off up to their room.

Georgina was sitting on the landing.

'You OK?' Kerrie asked.

'Fine . . . sometimes I forget how bad she is. Why Charley and I so rarely come to visit. I want Jessica and Henry to know this is their grandparents' home and to feel welcome here even if they are not.' Georgina said this tearfully, trying to control her emotions.

'They're great kids,' Kerrie offered. 'And you're a great mum.'

'I thought it would be nice to have one family meal . . . to try to make the effort.'

'Thanks. Matt and I appreciate it.'

'Next time you'll come to us, and there'll be none of this shit!' Georgina insisted.

'Sounds great.' Kerrie smiled, reaching for Georgina and giving her a hug.

'And don't let Mum get on your case about the

wedding,' Georgina warned. 'Charley and I might have had over two hundred people at ours, but when I look back at the photos and the DVD I don't know half of them! Don't let her boss you around.'

'Sure.'

'Are you two packing up to leave?'

'Yeah, Matt wants to get back to Dublin.'

'I'm sure Charley is ready to go too, then.' Georgina stood up and blew her nose on a Kleenex. 'Jess is asleep. I'll gather all our baby gear, and we'll get going, too. Get out of Mum's way! There's no point hanging around.'

Kerrie stood in the bedroom trying to collect herself, to imagine Matt growing up here in this old house. OK, there were the woods and the gardens and the river, and so much for a boy to do, but there was something missing . . . something that she had had that he hadn't. Sitting on the bed, she sent a text to her mam.

I'm down in Moyle with Matt. Love you and miss you.

See you tomorrow. Kerrie

Chapter Seven

Alice had walked for almost two miles along the seafront, passing by Scotsman's Bay, the Joyce Tower, the Forty Foot and Sandycove with Lexy, her West Highland terrier, trotting beside her.

She felt like a huge weight had been lifted off her since going and talking to Hugh about quitting her job at Ronan, Ryan & Lewis's, and him promising to deal with it. Now it had all been resolved, and she was finishing up on Friday. Sinead, a junior they had just taken on, would take over her work until Maria, the girl who was out on maternity leave, came back in eight weeks' time.

'Young Sinead is chomping at the bit to move up a level,' Hugh had reassured her. She suspected he was secretly relieved that she was leaving the firm before she committed some catastrophic error and embarrassed him even more!

Despite her ropey financial straits, she was glad she could now concentrate on trying to find some other source of income to bolster her diminishing savings. She'd get on to a few of the agencies to see if there were any jobs coming up, and scour the ads in the newspaper, too. She had to find some way of making money as Liam was being tight-fisted as usual, and claiming he could barely afford to give her anything, and that she had better get used to keeping herself.

For the past two and a half years Liam had complained about the difficulties faced by a small engineering firm like his: the contracts cancelled, the constant bidding for tenders, the lack of major orders coming into the firm. She had listened and tried to support him, glad that at least they could share their worries and talk about things. That's what marriage was about! 'We'll get through this,' she had reassured him, 'and business will pick up again for Kinsella Electrics.'

Unfortunately, while she had been worrying about her husband's business affairs, Liam had been busy with a different type of affair! She had discovered totally by accident that Liam was involved with a thirty-eight-year-old called Elaine. She went over it again and again in her mind, refusing to believe, at first, that honest, reliable, straight-talking Liam would do such a thing to hurt her and damage their marriage. Sure, he was under stress, but that didn't mean he had to be unfaithful. How could he be stupid enough to betray everything their marriage stood for?

Pretty and petite and dark-haired, Elaine Power was the manager of a fancy new wine and tapas bar in the city where Liam and his business friends used to drink on a Friday after work. Alice had rarely ventured along on those nights, reckoning Liam deserved a chance to unwind with his pals while she either went to the cinema or was content to watch *The Late Late Show*. Then, one Friday evening, after going shopping with Nina in town, she had decided to surprise Liam and turn up in the wine bar and get him to take her to dinner. The surprise was on her! The minute she saw him and Elaine flirting and touching each other she became suspicious. Elaine was polite to her, but Alice sensed immediately that something was going on. She thought about the nights working late, and the business weekends away when he was supposed to be attending conferences, and confronted him. She wanted him to say Elaine was a big mistake, beg her to forgive him, say he was having a midlife crisis, but instead Liam, un-apologetic, had told her that he loved this younger woman. Now that their children were grown up Liam believed that there was no need to prolong things and stay together. Their marriage had run its course and was over, though he hoped they could somehow still be friends.

Be friends with a man who had ripped your heart out of your chest and left you reeling . . . she didn't think so! Liam wanted to turn over the page and start a new life with Elaine. What Alice did was no longer any of Liam's concern!

Everything had been a mess. A nightmare! Following weeks of crying and anger, disbelief and despair, she had finally got enough sense to look at what she still had – her three healthy adult children, her home, her friends – and pull herself together in some sort of fashion. She couldn't, wouldn't, let Liam, her unfaithful bastard of a husband, destroy her.

Alice took a few deep breaths of the sea air, watching a cormorant dive patiently again and again in the water and reappear in the foaming tide below her. No matter how hard she tried she often found herself overwhelmed by loneliness. With Liam gone she suddenly found that she had no one to share her life, her home or her bed with. It was awful to wake up day after day and have no one to chat to over break- fast, to argue with or discuss articles in the papers or the news. To plan for the future with, let alone holidays or weekends or nights out. No one to laugh or joke with, confide in or simply to hug and hold. The boring routines of married life and living with a spouse were now gone from her as she faced the cold harsh fact of being a single woman again. The bloody loneliness of it could drive a person mad, she suspected, no matter how supportive their children and family and friends were. There was no escaping the fact that she was on her own now and had to get used to it. The tide was in and she walked quickly, glad of her navy fleece and scarf as there was quite a wind out there. Then she turned and headed back towards Monkstown.

'Come on, Lexy, let's get home and get something to eat.'

Passing by the old stone Martello Tower on the seafront she turned up home, thanking heaven that for the moment she still had the house on Martello Avenue to live in. So far Liam hadn't the gall to go after that but she worried he might force her to sell the family home and move somewhere else. She loved the old red-bricked house they had bought off the busy Monkstown Road at an auction. They had ignored the rotting windows and roof problems and ancient kitchen and grumbling heating system, lured instead by the friendly neighbourhood, the long sun-filled back garden where the children could play, and the view of the sea at the end of their road. It was twelve years before they could afford to do up the house the way they wanted to. The death of Alice's generous Aunt Betty enabled her to repay their mortgage ahead of schedule and build a wonderful bright sunny kitchen extension and family room and upgrade the rest of the house. Liam had wanted her to invest her inheritance in some fancy new apartments that were being built in the city centre, but wisely she had refused, knowing in her heart that eighty-three-year-old Betty, who had been a regular visitor to their home, would have preferred the money to be invested in number 23 Martello Avenue. So nearly all Betty's money had gone into their home, and Alice had absolutely no intention of selling it or moving away, no matter what Liam and Elaine did!

She flicked on the CD player as she began to make a salad and popped her dinner in the oven to heat. She'd made a creamy cheese and ham pasta bake and it smelled delicious. She slipped off her trainers and curled up on the leather couch in the kitchen. Sean had told her this morning he'd be late home so she'd save him some. Nothing unusual in that, as like most students he practically lived on UCD's campus! His life revolved around the student bar, restaurant and the gym; although she supposed he did attend a few lectures in arts, his chosen subject, as he had passed his first-year exams with flying colours. Sean was flinging himself into the college social scene and the smell in his room some mornings would rival the Guinness brewery. With his sandy-coloured hair and lean build he was a lot like Liam, but he had Alice's manner and sense of humour and blue eyes. She liked having her youngest still living at home, even if he did drive her crazy with his constant computer games and hours on Facebook. When he was in the house there was music and noise, the phone ringing, friends calling, but once he left she was conscious of the silence and loneliness that sometimes gripped her. Tonight he was going to see some new indie band playing in town.

She glanced at the newspaper. She read a few pages and then turned to the back – sudoku or crossword? She would do one before she ate and one after. It was one of the luxuries of being on her own: being able to read the paper in her own fashion without Liam monopolizing it. She was engrossed in the puzzle when the doorbell went.

'Hey, Alice, thought I'd just call in and see what happened about the job.' Joy had been delayed at work and was only on her way home to Shankill now.

'I'm finishing up in Ronan, Ryan & Lewis's next Friday.' Alice grinned. 'And it's such a relief.'

'There's nothing worse than being unhappy in work and trying to hide it,' her friend said seriously.

'I was worried about letting them down. But Hugh says they've got someone else lined up to take over till Maria, the full-time person, comes back . . . so it all worked out fine.'

'There, I told you it would be all right.'

'Have you eaten yet?' Alice offered.

'Alice, I'm not landing myself on you for another meal. We had a meeting with the third-year parents and you know these things. They always overrun and seem to go on for ever. I just dropped in to make sure you were OK.'

'You haven't eaten yet, so stay and have some dinner with me!' offered Alice. 'You know I hate eating by myself. Sean's out, so there's plenty.'

'Smells good,' admitted Joy, taking a seat at the kitchen table.

Alice set an extra place and served up the pasta bake with salad and a helping of tomatoes and vinaigrette.

'Tastes gorgeous,' said Joy. 'Sure beats my usual baked beans and toast or a fried egg.'

Alice laughed. Joy lived in a nice two-bedroomed bungalow near Shankill. She had absolutely zero interest in cooking and her small galley-style kitchen was barely used except for the sturdy microwave.

'So what next?' quizzed Joy, as she helped herself to some more salad.

'I haven't a clue,' admitted Alice. 'I'll have to do something to make a bit of money, but I don't have any ideas yet.'

'Well, we'll all have to get our thinking caps on and see what kind of opportunities are out there for a talented woman like you.'

Alice had to laugh. Joy believed everyone had an innate talent or gift, and it was just a question of discovering it. No wonder she did so well as a career guidance counsellor in the big secondary school she worked in over in Ballinteer. The kids and their parents loved her, as she would leave no stone unturned in finding out what pupils were good at and the avenues they should explore in their career and studies.

'When did you say you're finishing up in work?'

'Next Friday.'

'Then what about a girly celebration meal on Saturday night?'

'That sounds great.'

'What about that nice Italian in Dalkey? I'll check if the others can make it and book a table in Da Vino's for us.'

'Sounds good to me,' Alice said. 'I can take the DART out to Dalkey.'

*　*　*

When Joy had left Alice returned to the solitary glory of the crossword in *The Times*, while listening to the evening news.

Chapter Eight

Lucy stood in the queue for signing on for her social welfare payment . . . the dole. She hated it. Standing there at the hatch and filling in the forms like she had to do every few weeks. It was embarrassing and soul-destroying, with everyone avoiding eye-contact and hoping that they wouldn't meet someone they knew or went to school or college with. She was grateful that her line wasn't too busy.

It was bad enough at her age being out of work and trying to find a job, but it was the grey-haired middle-aged men she pitied, and the big strong guys in their thirties. They had not only lost jobs in the construction business but in banking and law firms, and had a constant haunted expression in their eyes. They were lumbered with kids and family and mortgages and loans, and she had utterly no idea how they managed on the government payment they received. She found it hard enough to get by. It was awful not having a job, and she was embarrassed by it.

'You've been paying tax long enough, Lucy. You are only getting back a fraction of what you've paid over the years!' her dad had reminded her. 'Remember that.'

Dad was right. Since she was about sixteen she had always had some sort of job. Realizing that she really wasn't academic, she had started working at weekends and on Thursday and Friday evenings, when she probably should have been studying. She'd worked in restaurants, bars, pizza places, clothes shops – and then got involved working at most of the major concerts held in the Point and Oxegen and the RDS and Croke Park and Slane. Hail, rain or shine she'd be there, selling programmes and T-shirts and drinks. U2, Bon Jovi, the Foo Fighters, Snow Patrol, Bob Dylan, and even the Red Hot Chili Peppers; she'd seen them all perform live and loved the buzz of the music and crowds. That's where she'd got to know Jeremy, who would usually be trying to push some new upcoming singer-songwriter or small band, and she was thrilled when he offered her a job in the shop.

Phoenix Records was just such a cool place she didn't see how she would ever find anywhere like it to work ever again. Still, beggars can't be choosers, and at this stage, with a massive overdraft and large credit-card bill, she just had to take whatever job came her way.

Up at hatch 5 she filled in the form.

'How's it going, Lucy?' asked Brian, the guy behind the counter. He was from Tipperary, and being a civil servant had a cushy number, with constant breaks, a guaranteed salary and job security. The social welfare office moved at snail's pace, with Lucy and the rest of those signing on watching enviously as the staff disappeared for their regulation tea breaks and phone breaks. Still, Brian was a decent enough guy, and used to buy the odd CD from her in Phoenix Records.

'Nothing doing!' she sighed. 'Absolutely nothing.'

'Well, check in with the FÁS office and see if they have something.'

'Sure,' she promised.

The jobs up on the board across the street in the FÁS employment office were poxy, and most involved having qualifications. Employers expected degrees, or all kinds of computer and specialist knowledge, which she did not have.

There was one sign up on the revolving stand for an experienced shop assistant in a new baby and children's wear shop in Dundrum shopping centre and, taking down the code, she went to enquire about it. Maybe it was the kind of job that might suit her. She could get the bus over to Dundrum, and she liked kids and babies.

'We filled that position two days ago,' the girl at enquiries informed her rudely when she gave the code.

'Then why is it still up?'

'A mistake, someone forgot to take it down.'

Annoyed, Lucy moved away.

She was heading towards the employment office's fancy glass doors when she spotted Finn McEvoy. He'd been in college with her and played drums in a rock band that had broken up.

'Hey, Lucy, I thought it was you,' called the tall guy in the navy jacket and frayed jeans.

She coloured, then remembered that by virtue of being in the same place they were likely both in the same situation: unemployed and broke.

'Finn,' she said, giving him a quick hug. 'How are things?'

'Could be better!' he said. 'Nothing doing today, by the look of it.'

Lucy felt sympathy for him. He'd been a bit of a swot in college, from what she remembered, very focused on his studies and work.

'I've been working for Browne & Dunne, the big engineering company, for the past three years. But I was put on a three-day week last year, and now with no new jobs or projects coming into the firm I've had to sign on. They say when things pick up I can try for my old job back, but to be honest there's no sign of anything like that happening.'

'You were in that big glass building down near the docks?' Lucy asked, impressed.

'Aidan Brown helped to design it himself. Solar power, the lot. Unfortunately there are two floors of it empty now.'

'I'm sorry,' said Lucy.

'I'm just one of many,' he said, shaking his wavy black hair. 'What about you?'

'I worked for Phoenix Records, remember.'

'That was such a shame they had to shut down,' he said angrily. 'I remember they sold about two hundred copies of a CD the band and I made when we were younger. Made us feel like we were a proper band, even though we were only about eighteen.'

'Jeremy was great at that.'

They began walking through the door, and standing outside realized that despite the winter sunshine it was actually chilly.

'Do you fancy a coffee?' he asked. 'Or are you rushing off somewhere?'

'Sure, that would be nice.' She smiled. She had time to kill and it would be better than just hanging around back home.

'There's a nice place about two streets away,' he said, as they fell into step together. 'And they do a great toasted bacon sandwich. I haven't even had breakfast yet.'

Lucy watched from the corner of her eyes as Finn tucked into the sandwich, with its layers of bacon, brown sauce, cheese, sausage and tomato. It was a meal in itself, and he wolfed it down.

'So what do you do with yourself?' she asked, curious, stirring her mug of tea. 'Do you still play drums?'

'Big time!' He munched. 'The only good thing to come out of this bloody downturn is that we all have plenty of time to practise and jam and write music, I guess.'

'Is the band still called STIX?'

'Hey, you remember!'

'I saw you guys play a few times.'

'We've put a few new tracks up on Myspace and YouTube and set up our Facebook page. We've had lots of downloads already.'

'That's great!' she said admiringly.

'What about you?'

'I'm just doing stuff trying to get a job. I used to share a house with some friends, but now I've had to move back home.'

'Bummer.'

'I'm thinking of doing some kind of course, just to have something to do. Get me out at night!'

'I can't imagine that's a problem for you, Lucy.'

She thought of Josh. There had been no one since him. No dates or nights out! No one special! No one to talk to or care about! She felt suddenly awkward.

'Hey, I'd better get going,' she said, pulling her jacket back on. She didn't really want to buy another pot of tea or anything to eat.

'Maybe we'll meet up again,' Finn teased.

She looked at him. What was he saying?

'When we're both signing on again,' he added.

'Sure.' She laughed. 'And I'll check your new songs out on Myspace.'

Chapter Nine

Dublin on a wet cold rainy night. Could anything be worse? thought Alice. She pulled on a pair of sturdy black leather boots and grabbed her raincoat and hat, making a dash for the DART. The rain was coming in sheets, and so much for washing and trying to style her hair! It would be in a right frizz by the time she reached the restaurant.

Da Vino's was packed, and Nina, Joy and Trish were already there.

'Bring another glass, please,' Joy asked the waiter as Alice slid into the seat across from her.

'God, this place is hopping! I never expected it to be so busy.'

'What else can people do on an awful night like this but eat out and drink?' joked Nina.

'Here's a menu,' said Trish.

Alice skimmed lightly through what was on offer. The girls decided to share a large antipasti platter, and Alice for her main opted for the house special of Da Vino's cannelloni and spinach.

'Alice, how did finishing up in Ryan, Ronan & Lewis go yesterday?' asked Joy, curious.

'They brought me out for a lovely lunch to the Brasserie and everyone clubbed together and got me a voucher for Brown Thomas, which I didn't expect, as it's not like I was permanent staff or anything.'

'It's great they gave you such a nice send-off and that there was no bad feeling,' added Nina, topping up her glass with a good barolo.

'Hugh said a few words, and Emer Lewis the tax partner and Alex Ronan were there, too.'

'Well, I'm glad they treated you well,' added Nina firmly.

'I actually felt a bit sad leaving,' Alice admitted.

'You'll find something else,' assured Trish. 'Just wait and see.'

Alice wished that she could be as optimistic about her career prospects as her friends were, as she hadn't a clue how a woman of her age was going to earn a bit of money to keep herself going.

* * *

Another bottle of wine later they had all had a taste of each other's main courses, with Joy stealing half of one of Alice's minced-lamb-filled cannelloni.

'I should always order what Alice orders when we go out; she picks the best thing.'

'Well your veal parmigiana is great, too,' Alice said soothingly.

Refusing the temptation of desserts they all opted for more wine.

'No one's driving so we're fine.' Trish grinned.

'Here's to Alice and whatever she does next!' toasted Joy.

'Well, I just wish I knew what that was,' Alice admitted.

Here she was, with her three closest friends, who had somehow managed to get her through the past twenty months without having a nervous breakdown. And she had utterly no idea what lay ahead for her.

'Alice, don't be silly, you'll find something. You're great at lots of things.'

'I don't have qualifications like you, Trish. I wish I did.'

Trish was a nurse and had worked in St Vincent's Hospital till Laura, her second, was due. Then, when the last of her four children had started secondary school, she had gone back and done a refresher course in nursing. She now worked part-time as a theatre nurse in Mount Carmel Hospital.

'If I hadn't done that course I'd be gone mad with boredom sitting at home, waiting to do homework and make dinners and listen to teenagers fighting!' Trish laughed.

'Alice, why don't you go back to college like I did?' suggested Nina, who had taken on a part-time arts degree in UCD nearly three years ago. 'There are so many good courses.'

'What about going back into the hotel or restaurant business?' reminded Joy, her expression intent. 'It's what you know, after all.'

'It's what I grew up with, but it's a totally different environment now!'

'I remember your folks' place, it was a great hotel.'

Alice's parents Barry and Mary O'Connor had owned the Silver Strand Hotel between Wicklow and Brittas Bay. Across from the beach, it did great business during the summer and boasted large gardens and a sunny bright terrace where residents could relax and unwind with a drink or some food. Her parents ran a tight ship, with small but immaculate bedrooms and an old-fashioned restaurant with great food and service and crisp linen tablecloths and napkins. Alice had worked there every summer holiday and every school break since she was about twelve years old.

She had loved the Silver Strand, and on leaving school she had, without hesitation, signed up to study hotel and catering management, drawn especially to the cookery side, and a career in it.

She was away training in a small hotel in Brittany when her mother Mary had collapsed suddenly one morning as she cooked bacon and sausages in the hotel kitchen for the breakfast. She was dead by the time the ambulance got her as far as Loughlinstown, the nearest hospital. Alice's dad had been devastated, and despite Alice's offer to give up her course and return to help him run the Silver Strand, he'd insisted that she complete her training. Her last year was spent working in the busy kitchen of the Rivoli, one of Paris's top hotels, where Alice soaked up all she could learn from Maurice, the master chef, who had taken the young Irish cook under his wing.

By the time she returned to Ireland things had begun to change. People wanted big fancy hotels with swimming pools, saunas, en suite bathrooms and TVs in every room. The Silver Strand could no longer compete, and her dad had lost heart. Barry and Mary O'Connor had been a team, and without his wife at his side Barry lost interest in the business. He accepted a generous offer from a property developer who hoped to convert the site to an upmarket beach resort with a golf club, nightclub, and bars. Then Alice's dad had moved to a townhouse in Sandymount where he could enjoy his retirement and play golf and bridge.

Alice, with her excellent references, immediately got a job in Wilde, one of the city's finest restaurants. Here she worked alongside chef Myles Malone, as the restaurant won not only culinary awards but an impressive reputation.

She had met Liam Kinsella at Trish and Brendan's wedding and fallen madly in love with the tall skinny engineer with big plans! Before she knew it her dad was walking her up the aisle. When Conor was born she had juggled the restaurant and family life, but when Jenny, their second, came along she had reluctantly said her goodbyes to working with the wonderful Myles Malone and the staff at Wilde and settled down to raise her family. Conor and Jenny and Sean had kept her busy, and she hadn't missed it all.

'Joy's right. There're lots of new hotels springing up everywhere. Dublin's full of them!' encouraged Nina.

Alice didn't think she could bear going to work in

one of the new city-style hotels which seemed to offer tourists just a bed and breakfast and didn't even have a proper dining room. Or one of those extravagant hotels which were just massive corporate venues with bars and spas and gyms, dependent on conferences and weddings to keep them going.

'Well then, what about the restaurants?' Joy asked. 'Maybe you'd get something there!'

Alice just couldn't imagine herself coping in the kitchen of a busy restaurant at her age.

'I suppose you're right.' Joy sighed. 'It's probably not much fun turning out pizzas or steak night after night for people like us.'

'Would you open a little place of your own?' suggested Trish.

'Sure, there's bound to be a bank manager out there who thinks that bankrolling a fifty-plus retired chef who wants to open a restaurant and is not Darina or Rachel Allen or Nigella Lawson is a good idea!' Alice said.

'Then what will Alice do?' exclaimed Trish.

'What about baking more of those lovely cupcakes you used to sell?' Nina said.

'For God's sake! I had to get up at about six o'clock every morning to bake them, and then ice them, and trek them around endlessly to coffee shops and restaurants.'

'They were delicious with that frosting and soft butter icing you made.'

'It was fun at first.' Alice laughed. 'But then too many other people liked making them, too!'

'Cupcake Wars!' Nina laughed.

'What about catering, or selling some of those fancy dishes you make for people to cook at home?' Joy suggested.

'Joy, my kitchen would have to pass all kinds of inspections and regulations to do something like that, and it's still back to me trucking around like I did with the cupcakes, trying to sell them!'

'Well, what about giving cookery demonstrations or lessons in your home?' suggested Trish. 'You're a professional, and you've that great big kitchen and your Aga and the other cooker – and lots of space. Maybe you could take on a smallish group in your home and for a reasonable fee help them to learn to cook or improve on what they know.'

Alice hesitated. She kind of liked the sound of a cookery school, but she wasn't sure anyone would actually sign up for lessons with someone like her.

'I'm not a famous chef or from Ballymaloe!' she reminded them.

'Alice, for heavens sake! You are a professional. You studied and trained for years in France and here. You worked in one of the country's best restaurants ever, and with one of the most famous French chefs. Not to mention all the years at your parents' place,' Trish said.

'Plus you are a brilliant cook and always seem to make cooking seem simple and easy,' added Nina firmly.

'Let me think about it,' Alice begged as they paid their bill and ordered a taxi to take them all home.

Chapter Ten

Alice had woken early. OK, there had been a lot of drink taken on board last night – far too much red wine – but she couldn't get Trish's suggestion out of her head. *Teach cooking. Give cookery lessons. Run a cookery school.*

Set up a cookery school here in the house in Monkstown! Why, she just knew that was something she would enjoy.

It was a lot more appealing than trying to work on the computer in some boring office administration area, or sell things in a shop, or get some sort of small catering company off the ground. She walked around her large kitchen.

It was a cook's kitchen and was well-equipped with her top-of-the-range fancy Prochef cooker and the original old Aga that had come with the house, still in use. The electric cooker she'd used for years was now consigned to a space in her large utility room, but could easily be pressed into service if needed. She had her really large kitchen table, the island and her other baking area. There was plenty of room, and she had a good range of cooking utensils and dishes and baking trays. The kitchen was over-equipped if the truth be told.

If she kept it to a small group it would be manage-able. Eight, no, maybe ten people. She'd want them to not just watch her demonstrate but make the dishes themselves. From her experience, it was the best way to learn. You gained so much from your successes and even more from your culinary disasters – which were rarely repeated.

What kind of things did people want to learn to cook? What kind of people signed up for cookery classes?

As she was eating her usual bowl of fruit and natural yogurt with a sprinkle of muesli Sean appeared. He was wearing a pair of grey shorts and a brown T-shirt that had seen much better days, and she made a mental note to buy him some decent pyjamas.

'Nice night?'

'Great,' he said, sitting down with a mound of hot toast and chocolate spread in front of him and a large glass of orange juice. 'We went to Becky's place first and then headed into Howl at the Moon. It was deadly.'

'Are you in or out tonight?'

'I've got Mark's twenty-first party,' he reminded her.

This was a big year for parties for her youngest son, as he and his friends were all turning twenty-one. It was a happy, if not exhausting, time! Sean's turn wasn't till June, but they'd have to get planning something good for his birthday around then.

'How did your dinner with the girls go?' he asked.

'Great. We went to Dalkey to a gorgeous little Italian. I got a taxi home.'

'That's good,' he said, sounding very adult. It surprised her how protective Sean had become towards her since Liam had left. He watched over her a bit. Checked when she was in or out, or if she was going to be alone in the house, and made sure she was OK. He was a great kid!

'You know I finished working in Hugh's office on Friday?'

'Yeah!' he drawled, pouring himself nearly another half litre of orange juice.

'I won't miss the office and the work but I'll miss the pay cheque so I'll be back to job hunting!'

'Dad should give you more money,' Sean said angrily.

Alice hadn't the heart to tell him that his beloved father wasn't making the slightest contribution towards either of their living expenses.

'Trish said something to me last night about cooking,' Alice said.

'Are you going to start making those buns again?'

'No, Sean, not buns. I've had enough of them. No, what Trish was saying was: why didn't I give cookery lessons?'

'Cookery lessons? Where?'

'Here in the house so I don't have to go renting anywhere . . . maybe just one night a week to a small group of people.'

She could see by his expression that he was mulling it over.

'You should teach them how to make those great burgers you taught Conor and me to make. I made them for Becky the other night and she was blown away . . . I did the homemade barbecue sauce and everything to go with them and those big chips.'

'She liked them?'

Sean cooking for a girl! That was certainly a bit unexpected.

'And do that Indian buttered chicken that Jenny and I like, and your carrot cake with the icing.'

'So you don't think it is a kind of crazy idea?'

'Nope,' he assured her. 'Not at all. Lots of my

friends' mums have no idea how to cook. Colm's mum, every time I go over, only makes sausages and chips or this yucky mince thing with pasta. I don't know how he sticks it.'

'Do you think people would come to classes?'

'I don't know, Mum, but you're a great cook and you were always showing us how to make things. Colm should get his mum to come along.'

'Sean!'

Making herself a mug of coffee, she couldn't believe that Sean actually thought it was something she could do.

She spent the rest of the week checking out cookery schools and seeing what they covered and how much they charged. She had sent off for some brochures and course itineraries. There were courses all over the country, the most famous being at the renowned Ballymaloe School in Shanagarry in Cork, but there were also ones in Ennis and Dublin and scattered across the country. Otherwise those with an interest in the culinary arts could head to one of the prestigious London or French cookery schools. Locally there were a few that ran all year round, and she couldn't believe how expensive they were. Courses covered everything from basic first-step cooking to entertaining, Italian food, bread-making, vegetarian food and even barbecuing, which seemed very popular with men. Perhaps her course could be quite broad and cover a bit of everything, with the aim of putting good healthy food on the table for family and guests. She worked away on the computer, doing figures and trying to draw up a very rough guide to what she would hope to achieve if she set up her own cookery school here in Martello Avenue – The Martello Cookery School. Alice liked the sound of it.

The weather was awful, and she dragged Lexy out for a quick walk even though it was so cold the wind burned her cheeks. She was back just in time to get ready to drive to the golf club to meet her dad for Sunday lunch.

Sean had disappeared back upstairs to his room and was snoring under the blankets.

'Aren't you going to come to lunch with Granddad?'

'No.' He groaned. 'Tell him I'll call over to him after college on Thursday.'

Conor and Lisa were joining them, but she knew her dad would be disappointed that Sean hadn't made the effort to come to lunch, too.

Barry O'Connor had his usual table in the dining

117

room at the window, overlooking the eighteenth hole which, given today's weather, was deserted.

'It's bitter out there today,' he warned, as she hugged him and sat down.

'I know. I had Lexy out earlier and it was even too cold for her!'

'That dog's got sense,' Barry O'Connor joked. Alice was glad to see her father looking so well. He had been plagued with arthritis over the past two years or more, and often lately appeared stiff and sore. Today he looked relaxed in his tweed jacket and the new pale-blue winter shirt she'd bought him.

They ordered quickly, all opting for the traditional Sunday roast beef with trimmings.

'Lisa and I are going to Lanzarote next weekend for a break.' Conor smiled.

'It'll be great to get away from this cold weather,' added Lisa.

Conor and Lisa had been going out since college and they'd moved in together last year. Alice hoped that in time they would get married, as they were a lovely couple.

Conor, her eldest, reminded her at times of her dad. They both had the same eyes and dark hair and round faces, though Conor was as tall as Liam, but a totally different build. Conor was a big softy . . . he had always been like that, and bent over backwards to help people. He had studied pharmacy and now worked in the big chemist shop near Ballsbridge. He was ambitious and she knew that it was only a matter of time before her twenty-eight-year-old son eventually had his own business. Lisa was a radiographer and worked in Crumlin Children's Hospital. She was a gorgeous girl with dark eyes and dark hair, and had a great sense of humour. It was no wonder that her young patients loved her.

'While the three of you are here I wanted to sound something out with you . . . see what you think of it?' Alice said nervously.

They all looked at her expectantly, and she managed to steel herself to tell them.

'I am thinking of opening a small cookery school in the house.'

'A school?' her father repeated, puzzled.

'Yes, a cookery school . . . for people to learn how to cook! I'd give classes, show them how to make a dish, and get them to try to make it, too. All kinds of things: fancy dishes for dinner parties, and simple basic good food. Teach them about ingredients and loving food.'

'Sounds great!' encouraged Lisa. 'You're an amazing cook, and I keep telling Conor that

I'm so lucky to have a boyfriend who can cook.'

'Mum, you taught me how to cook!' Conor joked. 'So I think it sounds a good idea. How much are you going to charge, and how long will the courses go on for?'

'Those are all things that I have to work out,' Alice explained. 'I'm going to meet Hugh and have a chat and get some good financial advice. I'm not a money-grabber, but this new venture of mine has to make a bit of cash as I'm pretty skint and only living on my savings. I will start off small and see how things go . . . maybe one night a week. And then if there is enough interest I can add more classes.'

'That's wise,' said her eldest son. 'Any kind of business set-up needs proper planning and organization. But, you know, Lisa and I are a hundred per cent behind you, whatever you do.'

'Thanks,' Alice said, leaning across and giving him a big hug.

'Mary would have been proud of you,' declared her dad. 'She'd love to see you setting up a business of your own and making a go of it.'

'I know,' Alice said, trying to control her emotions.

'You've had a very rough time the past two years with that husband of yours. Near broke my heart to see what he did to you and his family,' her dad said slowly, fiddling with his napkin. 'But now you are coming into your own . . . like the little Alice your mother and I sent off to Paris long ago . . . your head filled with ideas and new ways of doing things. All I want is to see you happy again. And if you need any help from your dear old dad, let me know!'

'Dad, thanks,' she said, giving him a huge hug and a kiss on the cheek.

'To Alice,' announced her dad, toasting her with some wine. 'And this new venture of hers – her cookery school!'

'The Martello Cookery School.' She smiled, testing it out and getting used to the sound of the name. 'The Martello Cookery School, that's what I'm calling it.'

Chapter Eleven

Alice had run over everything with Hugh, the two of them hidden away in his den. Hugh got out his calculator and did all kinds of estimates and projections on the proposed cookery school.

'I actually think it could be quite a nice little business,' he concluded. 'As long as you keep your overheads low and you are the main person giving the lessons. Fortunately, for the moment you don't have to rent premises or hire staff or equipment, so your overhead costs are being kept to the minimum. So even though the class size is restricted you should still be able to earn a wage from it and also make a bit of profit.'

'So you think it can work?'

'Yes, I do,' he said, fiddling with his glasses. 'Obviously if it became more successful and you were giving additional cookery classes things would improve even more. The main thing is to be meticulous about purchases of foodstuffs, necessary kitchenware, electricity or gas. Remember to keep a record of everything, too.'

'I will,' she promised, suddenly beginning to feel excited about starting up a business of her own.

'Alice, you're sure that there is nothing that you have overlooked? Ovens, hobs, sinks, fans? Properly equipped kitchens cost a fortune, you know, and there is all that expensive cookware that Sally keeps buying!'

'Honestly Hugh, I don't think so. As you know I have my Aga and the fancy professional cooker I put in when we extended the kitchen, and my old electric one is still in the old part of the kitchen where the utility room is. It was very handy having all those ovens when I was baking cupcakes!' She laughed. 'Anyway, if I manage to get ten students, with the exception of having to buy a few small things for them to use – like some extra plastic mixing bowls and sieves and perhaps a few oven trays and colanders or knives – I think I'm pretty well set up. Despite Liam's protests at the time, I treated myself to a proper cook's kitchen with Betty's money when she died.'

'I know it's an awful time to be starting up something,' Hugh admitted, 'but this is so simple, and the kind of thing people want to do! You are lucky that you don't need to go to the bank, cap in hand, to borrow money, because at the moment they have clamped down on lending to small firms and on small projects like this.'

'I want to do something for myself, Hugh. You understand, don't you?'

'Sure. I know how hard it's been for you since you and Liam broke up,' he said gently. 'But I admire you for having the guts to go and do something for yourself. The country could do with a few more people like you who are willing to at least try something new . . . give it a go.'

'The only thing I have to lose is my time and patience, and, if it all turns out to be a disaster, I suppose my pride!'

'Somehow I don't think that's going to happen, Alice. You're a trained professional – a chef – and you are passing on your knowledge and skill to those willing to learn.'

'Thanks for the confidence boost.' She grinned, jumping up and giving him a hug. 'And as my accountant I promise you I won't go mad.'

At home, Alice looked around her kitchen and made an inventory of every item she would definitely need. People didn't mind sharing and taking turns, but there were some things a cook just couldn't do without! She was still working out a week-by-week plan of the dishes she would cook, ranging from the simplest to the more complex, all things that she hoped her students would be able to cook themselves successfully.

She had put an advertisement for 'The Martello Cookery School' in the local *Dun Laoghaire Gazette*, and also put some printed flyers up in some of the local shops and a laminated one on her gate. Already she had interest, with lots of people phoning and calling. Six were signed up to start in January.

Chatham Kitchens was one of the best suppliers of kitchen utensils and kitchenware in the country and Alice went with her list in hand to choose the things she needed. It was a glory hole of fabulous kitchenware and Alice had to steel herself not to give into temptation and pile all the wonderful range of dishes and plates, and expensive saucepans and casseroles, into her trolley. There was stunning glassware, table linen, and gadgets to help a chef do everything from crush garlic and peel apples to mix the lightest, frothiest foams.

She loved this shop. Loved the smells from its large spice section, and loved its display of kitchen fittings with smooth pull-out drawers and presses –

it had a storage range that was utterly fabulous.

She spent a glorious few hours picking exactly what she needed, determined not to stray too far from her budget. She checked and rechecked her list to make sure that she had forgotten nothing. In the linen section she added more tea towels and some extra sets of black and white striped oven gloves, and couldn't resist the gorgeous black and white and lime green striped cook's aprons which matched them. The aprons were reduced in price, and when she asked about them she was offered a hefty discount if she ordered a dozen.

'Do you want your restaurant or company name on them?' asked the assistant.

'It's not really a company,' she tried to explain.

'It only takes two days, and we'll keep your details on file in case you need to reorder.'

Before she knew it Alice found herself writing 'The Martello Cookery School' on the order form for the aprons. It would look so inviting, and, also professional she hoped.

She had covered everything on her list, and she was about to pay when, in the safety section, she spotted kitchen fire-blankets and extinguishers. Hopefully these would not be put to good use, but they were an utter necessity in the kitchen, she decided, as she purchased two of each.

*　*　*

As she drove home she couldn't believe that she was actually one step nearer to opening her cookery school. If anyone had told her two or three years ago that she would be considering such a venture she would have said they were mad, but everything in her life was so different now, and she was no longer the complacent good wife who had mostly agreed to whatever Liam wanted. She had to stand on her own feet, try to pay her own way, and develop the capacity to earn over the coming years.

Chapter Twelve

Kerrie O'Neill looked at the congealed mess stuck to the bottom of her expensive Le Creuset casserole dish. Beef, tomatoes, onions, garlic and peppers had all lost any reasonable shape and were fused together into a sludge of brown misery which was like some sort of glue. Ugh. She poked it with her wooden spoon. Nasty, nasty, nasty and nothing like the glossy picture in her Jamie Oliver cookbook. The people who wrote those books and sold them should be locked up. What did they mean by saying this load of tripe was easy and simple to prepare? Jamie and his friends, off quaffing a glass of wine in the photograph, while Armageddon happened in her oven! She'd spent a fortune on the sirloin steak and organic onions and peppers, and now all she had was a pot of rice boiling on the hob and a great big lettuce salad. What was she going to give Matt for dinner?

He was working late and she'd promised to have dinner ready when he got home. Usually he did the honours and was cooking for her when she got in . . . he was the best boyfriend ever, and living with him was perfect, but he had a right to expect her to turn out the odd meal that was edible. It was so frustrating! Everything she touched seemed just to go absolutely wrong . . . nothing she cooked or tried to make ever turned out right. She read the books. She studied the recipes, measured the ingredients exactly with the expensive kitchen scales she had invested in, and followed the method step by step, every time expecting some kind of decent result!

Nigella, Rachel Allen, Jamie, Neven Maguire, Sophie Dahl, Gordon Ramsay, Domini Kemp . . . she wasn't an idiot, but how did it happen that, despite slaving over their recipes, no meal she produced even vaguely resembled the glossy photos of their luscious dishes in the cookbooks? It wasn't fair. Matt's mum was a cordon bleu trained cook, and his girlfriend a useless one!

She tested the sludge. It tasted burnt, and on closer inspection some of the meat was tough and blackened. Maybe it was their fan oven that did it. Was it too hot and burning the bejesus out of everything? God, what a mess! Better destroy the evidence before

Matt got home, she thought, and getting the wooden spoon she began to scrape it all into the bin. She'd soak the pot, even though it looked like it could take days before the stain from the brown mess would wash off. Then she'd pop it into a bucket and throw a tea towel or two on top of it to hide the incriminating evidence. Maybe she should have phoned her mam and got her recipe for the beef stew she always made. The big pot of her mam's concoction of meat and vegetables was a constant feature on the stove in the small red-bricked house on Riverfield Grove where she had grown up. The stew tasted even better by day two or three than when it was first served. It was almost like a soup by the time they all polished it off and got her mam to make a new pot. How did her mam do it? Turn out edible meal after meal? Kerrie certainly hadn't inherited her mother's talent for cooking.

She gave a quick tidy around and retrieved the packet of beef bourguignon from the freezer. Polly's Pantry, their local delicatessen, provided a huge array of their own chilled and frozen meals that could be easily reheated.

Kerrie pulled the beef dish from its wrapper and packaging and reheated it in the microwave, turning it into one of her beautiful blue oven dishes. Then she poured in a drop of red wine from the open bottle on the counter before giving it a final touch by sprinkling on a few bits of red onion and some chopped parsley. It really looked homemade, she thought proudly, before popping it into her oven and hiding all the packaging in the bin.

She loved Matt; loved to hear the sound of his key in the door, his heavy footsteps on the floor, the smell of his aftershave, the steady rhythm of his breath as he pulled her close to him. Matt was the man she truly loved, her other half, her better half, her fiancé. He was so kind and good and intelligent, and she still couldn't believe that in only a few months' time she would be married to tall dark handsome Matt, and would be Mrs Kerrie Hennessy!

She was busy on the internet when Matt returned home.

'Hey, that smells good!' he said, smiling and kissing her.

'It'll be ready in a few mins,' she warned, 'so why don't you get out of your suit and change?'

She watched proudly as Matt tucked into the beef. Everything looked perfect: their oak table and brown leather table mats, their white plates with the ripple design and their modern glassware. The mixed leaves were in an expensive hand-turned salad bowl and the rice in a Stephen Pearse bowl.

'Thanks,' Matt said, raising his glass of wine to her as if she had performed some great feat. 'It's delish. Maybe you should cook this the next time we have Justin and Lindsey over. We haven't had anyone to dinner for ages. I'll set something up.'

'Sure.' She smiled. 'That would be fun.'

'We'll get a few good bottles of wine in, and some beers, too, since we've lots to talk about.'

Kerrie nodded. Matt's best friend Justin was going to be his best man. He and Lindsey had got married the previous year in a big wedding in the Mount Glenn Hotel in Wicklow, a complete contrast to the small exclusive wedding she and Matt were planning in the South of France, with only thirty or so people attending.

'Hey, is there any more of the beef left?' asked Matt, looking hopeful.

'Sure,' she said, scooping the last of the beef out on to his plate. As she watched him polish off a second helping, she made a mental note to cook at least five packs of Polly's Pantry beef if there were four of them eating.

'I'm such a lucky guy,' he said, snaking his arm around her waist and pulling her on to his lap. 'Meeting a girl like you, and then getting to marry her.'

Kerrie buried her face in his shoulder. She loved him. Loved him madly! Meeting Matt had been the best thing ever that had happened to her, too. He'd transformed her life . . . changed it totally.

'And you are such a good cook, too!'

She blushed. Lies! Lies! Lies! How had she got herself into this? How much longer could she go on pretending to Matt to be someone she wasn't?

Chapter Thirteen

Rob had taken great care cooking the piece of steak he'd bought in the butchers, the potatoes were almost done, and he had tilted a pack of a fancy-looking ready-made salad into a bowl. He'd have liked a few onions fried with the meat, or some of that lovely pepper sauce Kate used to make with their steaks. How hard could it be to do a few onions and make a sauce?

He was keeping a weather eye on *Sky Sports* in the next room for the rugby results when the smoke alarm sounded. He ran straight back into the kitchen, flinging the frying pan with the burning steak and onions off the hob. The small saucepan he'd put the peppercorns and flour and butter into now held an unappetizing porridgy dough.

'Shit!' he said, opening the window to get rid of the smell.

The alarm stopped. He scraped the blackened onions off the meat, and lifted the saucepan of potatoes off the hob and drained them. Overcooked! He searched to see if there was some sort of masher thing that would complete the process.

He'd been looking forward to the steak and grabbed the newspaper to read as he swallowed a few mouthfuls. It was not what he'd expected. No matter what he did, nothing he put on this confounded fancy hob and oven that Kate had chosen when they put in a new kitchen five years ago seemed to come out properly. Getting the temperature spot on was a lot harder than it looked, and Kate had made it all appear so effortless. He accurately followed recipes step by step, and yet nothing seemed to turn out the way it should. He took another bite of the dried-out toughened beef. It was disgusting and, giving up, he cut it into bite-sized pieces and went across and tipped it into Bingo's bowl. The dog lumbered over excitedly to claim another of Rob's culinary disasters.

Rob phoned the Bamboo Garden, his local take-away, and ordered his usual fillet of beef with ginger and scallions and some rice.

He was watching the golf on TV when Gary from the takeaway delivered his order.

'The usual.' Gary grinned, passing him the brown

paper bag. 'Plus you get two small tubs of ice cream . . . chocolate whirl and a toffee one.'

'I didn't order any ice cream.'

'No . . . but if you order a takeaway more than three times in the one week you get ice cream compliments of the Bamboo Garden,' Gary explained, as Rob paid him.

He sat reading the newspaper as he ate. Afterwards he polished off the two tubs of ice cream. He debated watching another rerun of *CSI* or *Law and Order* or slipping down to his local in Monkstown for a pint. The lure of his local pub midweek was hard to resist.

The first few weeks after Kate's death Rob had found himself opening bottles of wine and drinking Scotch whisky when he was alone here in the house at night. It might have numbed the pain and loneliness to sit slumped on the couch with a good malt or fine Bordeaux, but he knew it was something that could not continue. So he had set himself a maxim for the past four weeks: not to drink on his own in the house midweek. If he had someone in, some company, fine, otherwise he had to go out. Turning off the TV he grabbed his jacket and set off for Goggins. The night was chilly, and he pulled on a scarf and gloves. Kate and he used to walk regularly down to the pub to meet friends or just to have a drink on their own.

He'd taken those times so much for granted. He was passing along by Martello Avenue when he saw the simple sign attached to the garden railings of the red-bricked house with the green-painted door and the tubs of purple heather. Curious, he stopped.

Want to learn to cook?
Join our simple cookery school.
Small group. An encouraging environment.
All welcome.
If you are eager to learn how to cook tasty
and delicious food why not join
The Martello Cookery School on
Tuesday nights from 7.30 to 10 p.m.
Telephone Alice Kinsella for information.

Rob stopped and read the notice. It seemed like just what he was looking for. He wouldn't dream of attending one of those expensive fancy cookery courses advertised in the back of the *Irish Times* or mentioned by the food writers and critics, but this was literally down the road from where he lived. He put the number in his phone. Perhaps he'd phone tomorrow and find out the details from this Kinsella woman. He wasn't looking to be a gourmet cook or that kind of nonsense, he just needed to be able to cook a few dishes, learn about preparation and make something decent to eat. Cooking was a necessity, and he had to learn how to do it if he was to manage living on his own. Rob knew that he couldn't depend on the Bamboo Garden and Tesco and M&S microwaveable meals for ever. He was getting bored by the limited menu and was realistic enough to know that despite his reluctance he had to learn to cook!

The bar was quiet, only a few regulars in attendance, and Rob ordered a pint and sat up at the counter. Jimmy, the barman, made small talk with him about the weather and asked if he had been watching the golf. He noticed old Bill Deering sitting only a few places from him. He was a contrary old geezer and lived about eight doors away from Rob. Bill had been annoyed by the kitchen extension Rob and Kate had put in a few years ago, even though he was in no way affected by the bright, sunny one-storey space. He seemed to enjoy being difficult, and had lodged an official objection with the council. Kate had been furious at the time, and had invited him in for a cup of coffee so she could show him the plans and explain how little effect the extension would have on neigh-bouring properties and dispel his fears, but Bill had refused to budge. Still, he had come to her funeral.

Bill's wife Nora had died about ten years ago, and

despite regular rumours that he would sell up and downsize he hadn't made the expected move to an apartment or a townhouse. He had four children, including a daughter in Cork and a son who was married and lived on the other side of the city.

'Good evening, Bill,' Rob said, nodding.

'How are you?' asked his seventy-year-old neighbour.

'I'm fine,' Rob said, taking a slow sip of his beer.

'I'm fine, too,' said Bill. 'Fine, fine, fine.'

Alarmed by the tone in his voice, Rob glanced over at him. The barman was busy unpacking glasses from the under-the-counter dishwasher. Grabbing his beer glass Rob moved his seat down the bar and sat in beside Bill.

'Everyone says the same thing every bloody time you meet them . . . you must be finding that,' Bill said truculently.

Rob had to admit it was true. Friends, family, work colleagues and neighbours all greeted him constantly with the same concerned tones whenever he met them or even dealt with them on the phone. He welcomed their support at the moment, but it was as if he had become a new person in their eyes: a man to be pitied . . . a widower . . . a loner.

'Nora will be dead ten years in August. You know we were married forty years. Ruby, they call it, for sticking out that much time together. Nothing's the same without her.'

'I'm sorry,' said Rob.

'Your wife was a nice person,' Bill ruminated, staring into his glass. 'She made a lovely carrot cake.'

'So you tasted it?'

'Had it the day I was in your house.'

'Yeah, Kate was a great cook, a great wife,' Rob said. 'I miss her every day.'

'My Nora was the best wife a man could have. I don't know how she put up with me, to tell the truth.'

Rob burst out laughing, recalling the reputation of the puckish man with the white shock of hair and tweed jacket sitting beside him.

'Here's to the women,' toasted Bill. 'The both of them!'

Rob bought Bill another pint of Guinness and ordered another beer for himself. Bill might seem a contrary old character but he wasn't bad company, and loved to talk about the past.

'Our generation went through tough times, with emigration and unemployment. Nora and I had to live with our in-laws before we saved enough to get a home of our own. It was a little box of a place, and we lived there for eight years till we got on our feet,' Bill explained. 'Work was what it was about. No one particularly liked their jobs, or did what they wanted to do. You were just glad to be able to earn a wage, put food on the table, keep the roof over your head and pay your bills. That's what it was all about in the old days. Not like the kids nowadays, with their fancy jobs and cars and houses and holidays. They want too much! Is it any wonder the country is in the state it's in?'

'I think most people still want to be able to take care of their family,' Rob argued. 'That hasn't changed, but now they also want to work at something they consider worthwhile.'

'Jobs are scarce!' Bill sighed. 'It's a shame to see the best educated lads and lassies in the country all bound for Canada and Australia, and the like. Reminds me of the fifties and sixties: my three younger brothers went to Liverpool and Manchester. Settled there, and never came back except on holidays. I had to stay put, as Nora and I were starting a family and she wanted us to get a place of our own.'

'My two boys are both overseas.' Rob found himself telling Bill about Gavin and Luke. 'To be honest, I'm not sure either of them will ever come home.'

'What a shame!' said Bill sympathetically. 'At least our four might be a bit scattered, but I get to see them regular enough. The girls boss me no end. Grainne wants me to sell up here and move down to Cork where she lives. What would I be doing in Cork, I ask you! She means well but I've no intention of leaving my home. Emer is into wholefood and has me plagued with feeding me nuts and lentils and beans and bloody muesli. It gives me wind! She's a teacher living in Wicklow, and she and her husband are big into healthy living. The two boys are married: Eamon's in Clontarf and Kevin's in Waterford. I've twelve grandchildren so far. Nora, Lord rest her, would have been chuffed with them all.'

Rob, holding his glass, felt envious of the other man, who at least had his family and their offspring around him, compared to the awful loneliness he was presently enduring.

'People say it will pass. That time heals,' said Bill. 'I tell you . . . they have no bloody idea. No bloody idea at all.'

Rob swallowed hard, recognizing the understanding in the older man's eyes.

'Here, let me get you another pint,' offered Bill, calling the barman over. 'One for the road!'

Chapter Fourteen

Lucy was fed up. She'd met Finn a few times lately, and they had got on brilliantly, and she had waited and waited for him to be the one to phone or text her and ask her out properly, not just the two of them hanging out like they did. She really liked him, and she thought maybe he felt the same way, too, but he was doing nothing about it. Maybe he already had a girlfriend!

Phone me! Phone me, phone me! She willed for Finn to contact her . . . but there was a great big nothing.

At least she had managed to get a temporary Christmas job four days a week wrapping gifts in the Avoca Store, but on 24 December she would be back to being broke and unemployed as she faced into the New Year.

'Well, if you want to do something in the New Year, why don't you go and sign up for Alice's cookery class?' advised her mum as they began to put up the Christmas decorations.

'Learn to cook?'

'Yes, go and learn how to cook properly. I wish I had learned when I was younger. Alice, as well as being one of my best friends, is also an amazing cook. She's a total professional,' explained Nina Brennan, 'and she is running the cookery course at home in the house. Why don't you phone her?' Nina, her face serious, sat down on the side of the bed. 'It might be fun. Alice says it'll only be a small group, and she really is a great cook. She worked as a chef in one of the top restaurants ever when she was younger. She gave it all up when she had the kids. But each time we eat over at Alice's it's like going to one of the best restaurants. She's only taking a small group to teach, but maybe it's something you might enjoy. You'll definitely use it.'

Lucy had to admit her culinary skills left a lot to be desired. Her repertoire of meals was limited. She usually stuck to pasta in a homemade tomato-type sauce or curry with rice and salads.

'Alice is nervous starting off this venture, worried she won't get enough people wanting to learn to cook and join her cookery school, so it would be lovely to be able to support her a bit.'

'Can I think about it, Mum?'

'Of course. Your dad and I would make a contribution towards it, but with the proviso that once you started you would be expected to finish it. It is only one night a week, after all.'

Lucy flushed. She had abandoned the expensive nail-care course she had signed up to last spring, bored beyond reason at filing and polishing nails all day. Her dad had ranted about the money she'd wasted. She had never given cookery the slightest consideration.

'Why don't you call over to her?' urged her mother, looking for the fairy lights. 'I'm sure Alice can fill you in about what kind of things she intends teaching people to cook.'

Lucy thought about it. It was rather appealing, the idea of being able to cook something that involved more than a pot of boiling water and a non-stick pan. She'd probably be hopeless, but maybe tomorrow she'd drop in on Alice and ask her all about it.

Alice was trawling through her extensive collection of cookbooks and cookery notebooks, trying to build up a selection of recipes and dishes that she could use to demonstrate to and teach a class. They would only have two and a half hours together on a Tuesday evening, so anything too complicated or time-consuming, no matter how delicious, was ruled out. She had decided to teach them how to make one main course and either one starter or dessert per class. That would be enough for most people to take in; obviously she would add some accompanying vegetable or salad dishes if there was time.

Trying to whittle down her favourite recipes was a task in itself after a lifetime of cooking. Chefs, like most people, had a handful of signature dishes they cooked over and over again, and it was easy to get stale. A top chef should know it was good to introduce something new, something unexpected, and hopefully with a completely fresh taste sensation. She was determined not only to teach them how to cook some classic dishes, but also to encourage them to stretch themselves a little!

Reading back through some of her notebooks from the time she trained in Paris and from her days cooking with Myles Malone in Wilde, she had to admit her writing was hard to read. Even now she struggled to decipher some of the words as she began putting all the recipes up on the computer in a special folder she had set up for her cookery school. She was rereading a recipe for a cassoulet of beans when the doorbell went.

'Hey, Lucy!' She smiled, inviting her friend Nina's daughter inside. She had always had a soft spot for

Lucy, who seemed different from her sister and brothers. She was big into music and bands, and had lost her job and her boyfriend, and now was back living with Nina and David – which had to be awful for her, and a bit of a strain for everyone else.

'Mum was telling me about the cookery classes you are going to give, and I wanted to find out more and talk to you about maybe joining.'

Alice led her down to the kitchen.

'I was just about to make some coffee, would you like a cup?'

'Yes, thanks.'

Lucy was a pretty little thing. She had the same grey-green eyes and perky nose as her mother. Alice got out the biscuit tin, hoping that Sean had had the decency to leave a few of the chocolate chunk and peanut cookies she'd made only two days ago.

She watched as Lucy studied her shelf of cookbooks and the notebooks lying on the table.

'I'm just going through years of recipes to find ones to use for the class. Other people collect silver or glass or perfume bottles or teddy bears, while I collect cookery books! I hadn't realized just how many I'd amassed. This notebook here, with the pictures of cats on the front . . . I began that one when I was a little girl, cooking in the kitchen with my mother. See that stain? That was from the sponge cake we were mixing together. I'd dip my finger in the mixture and eat it,' Alice said, remembering.

'Wow!'

'Do you like cooking, Lucy?'

'Yeah, I suppose so. I've always liked making stuff, and seeing it turn out all right. I get a kick out of it. Though there are only a handful of things I cook. I usually end up sticking to the same old recipes: like pasta and curry for my friends, or burgers, fried chicken or sausages at home. I wouldn't mind learning how to make some new things, and how to do them properly.'

'My aim is to take some wonderful dishes that are tasty and well-presented. And teach a selection: ones that are simple to cook and others that are a bit more complicated, but definitely have the wow factor. Especially if you are having a dinner party. Good food is really what matters, whether you're cooking for one or for fifty people!'

'Are you just going to demonstrate how to make things?' Lucy asked.

'Oh no. I'll show everyone, but then they've got to turn around and make the dish themselves. It's the only way to learn.'

'I guess so, because Mum and I are always watching *MasterChef* and all those kind of programmes, but we can't really make any of the things.'

'Cooking is hands-on.' Alice laughed. 'And that is what these classes are all going to be about. The course will start after the New Year and run for sixteen weeks, and costs 320 euros which works out at twenty euros a night.'

'It sounds great. I'd love to do something different. I don't know if Mum told you, but the music store I worked in closed down.'

'Yes, I was sorry to hear about it,' Alice said gently. 'There seems to be so much changing at the moment, and your generation is taking the brunt of it. It must be hard for you.'

Lucy nodded.

'Change is always awful. We humans aren't very good at it. Most of the time we want to curl up and hide and pretend it's not happening to us, get our lives back the way they were . . . though sometimes that's just not possible . . . we can't go back . . . can't turn back time no matter how much we want to . . . we have to go forward.'

Lucy was thoughtful, nibbling at a circle of biscuit.

'So, Lucy, that's what I'm doing . . . with this school . . . going forward. Trying something new, and hoping that the people who come along to learn will enjoy it, too.'

'Sounds great,' said Lucy. 'I'd love to give it a try, if that's OK, Alice.'

'I'd love to have you.' Alice laughed. 'You're the seventh person on my list.'

'Can I pay you by the week?' Lucy asked. 'I'm not working at the moment, and I don't want Mum or Dad forking out for this. I want to pay it myself, if that's OK with you?'

'Of course, Lucy, love, whatever suits you.'

As Alice watched Lucy walk down the path she had to admire the young girl. It would be a pleasure to teach Nina's daughter how to cook.

Chapter Fifteen

Alice could feel the tension slip away from her after only twenty-four hours in Wexford, staying in Joy's house near the beach. The place was practically deserted, and Alice loved to sit in the big cushioned window seat watching the constantly changing seascape. Joy and Malcolm had bought the house only twelve years ago, and nowadays Joy spent as much time as she could there. There was no traffic, no crowds, no stress, no rush, only water, sand, fresh air and lots of quiet – which was exactly what Alice needed.

'Come down and chill out after Christmas ... you're welcome to spend New Year in Curracloe with me if you want,' Joy had offered.

This Christmas had been a lot easier than the

disastrous one last year, when Alice and the kids had toughed it out at home. She had spurned offers to go to her brother's house for Christmas Day. She wanted to keep the bloody tradition, even if it made her miserable. She'd cooked the usual huge turkey and ham and all the trimmings, and remembered feeling she would choke on the turkey meat as she tried to pretend everything was normal, when it totally wasn't! She had spent St Stephen's Day sobbing upstairs alone in the bedroom, cursing Liam and blaming him for destroying her life, destroying Christmas!

This year had been very different: she and Jenny and Sean had spent Christmas with her brother Tim and his wife Patsy and Erin, her dad Barry joining them there, too. Conor and Lisa had gone down to Cork to Lisa's parents. Alice had brought along a baked ham and a pudding and her Christmas sherry trifle, and had never imagined that she could have had such a relaxed and easy Christmas Day. The day had started with Christmas drinks next door at Molly and Jack's, with no worries as she wasn't on duty cooking, then her dad had collected her, Jenny and Sean, and driven them to Rathgar, where Tim and Patsy had served up a fabulous Christmas feast. They'd stayed over that night and she hadn't got to bed till all hours as Tim and herself and her dad had reminisced about their childhood. The next day

Jenny and Sean had been invited to have dinner with Liam and Elaine in their apartment.

'Go!' she had told them. 'I'm fine here with Tim and Patsy and Erin. We've a mound of food to get through.'

Joy had invited her to come to Wexford after Christmas.

'Beth's on duty all over the New Year in St Vincent's Hospital. You know what it's like – the young trainee nurses get all the worst shifts – so I've no intention of staying on in Dublin on my own.'

Alice had accepted, glad to escape to the seaside. The kids had their own post-Christmas and New Year plans, catching up with friends that were home from London and Canada for the holidays. Jenny was heading back to Galway for New Year, and Sean and a few of the lads were renting a house in Lahinch.

So Alice had packed her bag and brought the dog with her, looking forward to the lazy days ahead and long walks on the beach, and the utter heaven of being away from it all. Lexy had jumped out of the car the minute they arrived and run down across the sand to the water's edge, barking at the tide.

'Well, she's happy to be here.' Joy laughed, welcoming them both.

* * *

The beach house was bright and cosy. The logs in the wood-burning stove gave great heat, which warmed the pine kitchen and snug sitting room with its stunning view of the whole bay. Joy and she were content to read and relax most days, watching the changing colours of the sea below, the shifting tides and water birds and the small boats that skimmed along.

Going out for a walk along the sand, they muffled up with fleeces and woolly hats and scarves as they braved the chill winds and cold and enjoyed the bracing sea air. They walked for miles.

'Joy, thanks for being such a good friend, especially since the whole thing with Liam.'

'Any contact with him over Christmas?'

'Not a word. Though he made the kids have dinner with him and Elaine on St Stephen's Day.'

'Awkward?'

'He is their dad, and they have to get over this and keep their relationship with him, and, I suppose, maybe build one with Elaine – whether I like it or not.'

'Men are so bloody odd!'

'Talking about men, what about Fergus? What's happening between you? How come you're down here on the beach with me instead of celebrating the New Year with him?'

'Fergus is great. Honest, he's a good man, probably one of the most decent that I've met. But he's gone to Brussels for Christmas. His daughter and her husband live there, and he's spending the holidays with them. They just had a baby boy, so he was dying to see his new grandson. He'll be back next week, and we'll get together then. Just because he's divorced doesn't mean he hasn't family commitments. It's good to see that he's close to his kids and is on pretty good terms with his ex-wife, which is kind of freaky.'

'Well, I'm dying to meet the guy who has put a sparkle back in your eyes,' teased Alice, the wind catching her as they walked a further few miles.

Over the next few days there were late breakfasts-cum-brunches and simple, uncomplicated meals.

'No one is wasting their time cooking!' warned Joy. 'You'll be sick of it when you're trying to teach your new students how to cook.'

'I'm nervous about it,' Alice admitted, 'but I'm also excited! Teaching a group of strangers how to cook is a bit of a challenge, but if I can pass on my love of food and making it and creating dishes, I guess I'll be happy! I can't believe that already I have nine people signed up. I just need one more to have my ten.'

'You don't start till the nineteenth of January, so I'm sure you'll have somebody signed up by then,' assured Joy as they walked the beach.

*   *   *

'Joy, I can't believe that I've actually got through a second Christmas and almost a second New Year without Liam,' Alice said. 'This time last year everything was so fecking awful, and I was so scared about everything, thinking: how could I possibly face anything without him? I was so depressed. Some days I wished Liam had died. Being a widow must be easier than just getting dumped. It drives me crazy to think of Liam not only living about three miles away from me with bloody Elaine, but the two of them in bed, or watching TV, having breakfast or shopping; his life just going on.'

'That will pass,' Joy promised, 'honestly it will. Eventually you genuinely start to forget about him. And he'll mean less and less to you.'

'I hope so!'

'The New Year after Malcolm and I separated Beth went to stay with him in London for a few days. It was awful. I was on my own. I came down here and sat and moped and felt really miserable. I got utterly pissed . . . drinking on your own is never a good idea, and I remember this desperate urge I had to stop everything that was going on . . . I wanted to swim. The beach was deserted.'

'Joy?'

'I know . . . I swam out and it was bloody

156

freezing . . . I went out as far as I could up to my neck . . . I just wanted the pain of it all to end . . . I was up to my neck with water . . . I could taste the salt water in my mouth and nose and my throat, and then suddenly I thought of Beth . . . Beth having to live in England with Malcolm and Linda. And of my mum, and my sister and brother and their families, and I bloody well got sense and turned around. I remember a wave catching me and throwing me off my feet, and thinking . . . I'm going to drown! And panicking, and frantically trying to get my breath back and stand and save myself. Somehow I managed to wade in. I was so cold, I thought I'd die of hypothermia. Somehow I must have crawled back up to the house, and I was crying and blubbing and so happy that I was OK. I remember stripping off and wrapping myself in the duvet and sitting in front of the fire, and even though I was alone, thinking: this is the best New Year ever . . . I can begin again.'

'I'd no idea,' Alice said, stopping in her tracks and hugging Joy. 'Absolutely no idea.'

'I suppose I didn't want to talk about it. I remember I almost got pneumonia out of it. I told everyone I'd got the flu. And you all fussed about me, and my sister Maria insisted on coming to stay and minding me till I felt better.'

'Promise me, no more crazy swims!' said Alice, a

157

shiver going through her as she took in the strength of the waves and the isolation of the beach on a cold winter's day.

'Alice, I love life too much . . . every day is special . . . and I know it. Now, come on, let's head back and heat up some soup . . . I'm flipping freezing and my toes are going numb.'

'*The Sound of Music* is on TV this afternoon.'

'Well, we can't miss that!'

On New Year's Eve they debated walking to the local pub for a few drinks and some pub grub, but instead opted for staying in and feasting on Joy's legendary spicy chicken curry with all the trimmings.

'Alice, go and check . . . I'm sure there's a packet of poppadums in the cupboard, and some chutney in the back of the fridge from Halloween! Let's hope that they've not gone out of date!'

'Two weeks to go, so we're fine.' Alice beamed as she set the table and tried not to interfere with what Joy was doing.

'Wow, that's hot,' she declared thirty minutes later when they sat down to eat, two candles setting their shadows dancing on the wall, the sound of the sea outside in the darkness. Thank heaven for the chilled beer they'd bought in the local off-licence. The curry was hot . . . really hot . . . Joy had been a bit heavy-handed with the chillies and curry spices, but it was good.

'That's the way I like it,' Joy insisted, wiping her eyes on her tea towel as she filled two huge glasses with iced water for them.

Afterwards they curled up on the two armchairs with a bottle of wine, happy in each other's company, while Lexy snored softly on the floor.

'Did I tell you Malcolm is getting married again?'

Alice didn't know what to say. Joy rarely mentioned her ex.

'Apparently he's dumped the lovely Linda and his two boys, and is now madly in love with a Russian girl called Sylvia. Poor eejit to get involved with the likes of him!'

'I'm sorry, Joy.'

'Don't be! Malcolm's ancient history! As far as I'm concerned the only good things Malcolm ever did were to father Beth, and, I suppose, agree to buy this place.'

'It's a great house,' said Alice, raising her glass.

'I fell in love with it the minute I saw it, even though it was pretty trashed, with peeling paint and broken windows. And it was a horrible yellow-beige colour with high windows and a disgusting bathroom and grey concrete patio. Malcolm kept saying he wasn't sure we needed a holiday house, but I talked him into it, insisting it was a bargain, and would be a great place for the summer and weekends, as it was only an hour and a half from Dublin. I suppose I imagined long hot sunny days here on the beach with my husband and a few kids around, my own mini-Kennedy compound.'

'You were lucky to find it!' laughed Alice.

'OK, I didn't exactly get the rounders team on the lawn and the happy family set-up, but it's always been such a special place to me. I guess that's why I dug my heels in and refused to let Malcolm sell this place when we split up. It was bad enough having to give up that lovely old house in Ranelagh and down-sizing to Shankill with Beth.'

'You've a nice house,' soothed Alice.

'I know, it's fine, but having this place to escape to is my sanity saver. OK, I need to rent it out during the holiday season to pay the mortgage, but the rest of the year it's mine, my retreat from the big bad world and what is going on there.'

'And mine, too,' agreed Alice.

'You know you can always come down here if you want to get away, Alice . . . just hop in the car and drive here if things get too much for you. I'm serious.'

'Hey, it's getting late!' warned Alice, noticing the clock. 'We're coming up to twelve.'

'I'll open another bottle of wine. We're not going

to sit here with empty glasses ringing in the New Year.'

'Looks like someone is having a party in the big bungalow further down the beach.'

'That's the Reynolds. I saw some of the kids earlier today around the place. They always have great parties.'

'Hey, they've got fireworks.'

Alice and Joy went outside to watch as the fireworks banged and lit up the darkness, rockets and Catherine wheels and giant snakes of vivid colour flashing and whizzing across the sky. They hugged each other when the local church bell rang out midnight and some of the ships at sea began to sound their horns.

'Happy New Year!' said Joy. 'Here's to us!'

'Happy New Year!'

Alice texted all her family, wishing them good things for the year ahead, and Beth managed to sneak a phone call to Joy, while the ward sister was busy with a patient.

'Poor Beth, the hospital casualty is already full of drunks!' Joy laughed.

'She's a wonderful nurse, so like you, and good with people.'

'But with a strong stomach. You know me. I faint at the sight of blood, whereas Beth is always cool and calm in a crisis. I suppose she gets it from Malcolm!' Joy paused, noticing Alice was reading a text. 'So what's Liam doing for the New Year?'

'The kids say he and Elaine have gone skiing to Austria.'

'I thought he had no money?'

'I don't know.' Alice shrugged. To be honest she didn't really care too much what Liam did any more.

As the fireworks died down they went back inside.

'Resolutions?' quizzed Joy. 'Have you got any?'

'Well, obviously I really want to make a success out of my little cookery school, perhaps even grow it!' Alice admitted. 'The other thing is to try not to bad-mouth Liam in front of the kids. What about you?'

'I'm certainly not giving up bad-mouthing Malcolm, because he so deserves it! No, my New Year's resolution is to try to be kinder to everyone and to slow down and listen before I jump in to talk.'

'What about Fergus?' pressed Alice.

'Well, I suppose I need to give him a chance. He gets on great with Beth, which is the important thing, and it's nice to have someone in my life again . . .' Joy raised her glass. 'Enough about me. Here's to you and your cookery school,' she toasted.

'And here's to us!'

Chapter Sixteen

'Are you going to be OK, Mum?' Tessa asked, fussing around Florence Sullivan upstairs in the bedroom before she left. 'I won't be too long at my cookery class, and if you need me my phone will be on.'

'Honestly, Tessa, will you stop all the worrying and go and leave me in peace? I want to watch *EastEnders*, and then that new detective programme on BBC. I'm quite capable of being left on my own at night, you know!'

'I know,' Tessa apologized, giving her elderly mother a hug while secretly checking that the portable phone was beside her bed, and that her personal alarm was on, and that she had a drink nearby, and that there was nothing that she could fall over underfoot.

Outside, as she pulled on her jacket and grabbed

her car keys, Tessa Sullivan asked herself how she had become such a fusspot, constantly worried about her mother and what might happen to her! It had been two years since her mother Florence had suffered a heart attack and fallen down the stairs here at home. She'd given them all such a fright, and Tessa could remember racing through Heathrow Airport's Terminal 1 with tears racing down her face as she tried to catch the last Aer Lingus flight back to Dublin from London that night. Her brother Donal had come back from San Francisco, and her sister Marianne had arrived from Hong Kong.

For a week the three of them had sat beside their mother's bedside wondering if Florence could possibly survive such a massive heart attack. But their eighty-year-old mother was made of strong stuff, and a week later was sitting up in her hospital bed sipping a mug of tea, thrilled to see her three children together for once and back in their home town. She'd given them all a right fright, but the doctors and nursing staff made it quite clear that the next time she might not be so lucky, and that in their opinion Florence would no longer be able to live on her own.

It had come as a shock to them all, as up to now their mother had stubbornly defended her independence. They all knew that it was difficult for her, being a widow and having all her children living overseas, but she had become an intrepid traveller and loved visiting them: spending a few weeks in the US with Donal and his boys, or with Marianne and her young family in their luxurious home in Hong Kong. She loved her regular trips to London, too, and she and Tessa had travelled all over England: from the Lake District to the beautiful Regency town of Bath, from Cornwall to the home town of the Beatles in Liverpool. Florence Sullivan was interested not just in the places around her, but also the people. Now Florence faced two choices: she could go into an old people's home, or one of the family would have to return home to care for her. Confining their mother to an old people's home, they all decided, was not an option.

They had argued and reasoned and weighed up the implications for all of them. Donal had only just been made a professor lecturing in bio-chemistry at Stanford University in California. He couldn't just go and throw up such a position, as it would be impossible for him to get a similar one back home. Also, since his divorce from Leigh Anne, if he wanted regular access to his two sons he needed to be in the US where he could see them regularly.

Marianne's husband had a big job working for Goldman Sachs in Hong Kong. They had a great house and lifestyle, and with a thirteen-year-old, a ten-year-old and an eight-year-old there was no question of Marianne being the one that could come home. So it had fallen on Tessa to volunteer to give up her job as a human resources manager at Bridgetown & Murrow and return to Dublin.

In her late thirties, Tessa was still single and childless and not even in a relationship, so it made utter sense as far as everyone was concerned that she throw her life up in the air and return to Dublin. She had sublet her pretty garden flat in Notting Hill Gate, and loaded up her cream and black Mini Clubman, and taken the car ferry back to Dublin to mind and care for their mother. With no dependants, the onus was on her to be the one to do the decent thing and put her own career and life on the back boiler. That had been almost two years ago, and somehow she had fallen into a dull pattern of routine and caring. She had managed to find a part-time job three mornings a week in a small recruitment company off Baggot Street. Two of those mornings Lilly, their Moldovian home help, came in to do a bit of cleaning and to care for Florence, while on Wednesdays Florence went to the local community centre's over-seventies club, where there were activities organized and the old people got a three-course lunch. Minding her mother involved a fair bit of juggling but, with kind-hearted Lilly's help and willingness to do a few extra hours the odd evening, Tessa somehow managed it.

She loved her mother – but she had sacrificed so much of her career and her freedom and financial independence by moving back to Ireland. She had tried to reconnect with many of her old friends from when she was younger, but most of them were married and busy with families of their own. She knew they pitied her. Some days she ached with regret for all the lost and wasted opportunities.

'Mum, I won't be long,' she called, closing out the hall door.

It was raining slightly, and she put on the wind-screen wipers as she reversed the car out of the driveway. She was rather nervous about tonight, and didn't know why she had signed up for cookery lessons. It was hardly as if she was entertaining madly while living back home in the four-bedroom 1950s home in Mount Merrion where she grew up. Still, cookery had always interested her, and being able to produce good food with a bit of a twist was a skill she would really like to learn.

In London she had given a few small dinner parties but her repertoire of dishes was very limited, and now she had the chance she really wanted to change that.

Bored and lonely, Tessa had never imagined that at thirty-nine years old she would be back where she started! Back in Dublin, with no man in her life, no child and very little to show for the past fifteen years of her life except for some savings in the bank, a few designer clothes and shoes and a whole heap of regrets.

The traffic was awful – any kind of wet seemed to bring out the worst in Irish drivers – and she snailed along the Stillorgan dual carriageway and took the left lane and turned off for Blackrock and the Dun Laoghaire area. Seeing the round Martello Tower on the seafront at Seapoint, she turned immediately right and pulled up a few seconds later in front of the large house on Martello Avenue where the cookery class was being held.

She sat for a few minutes trying to get her courage up, watching her fellow students arrive . . . it was not quite as bad as she feared. Then, grabbing her handbag and notepad, Tessa took a deep breath and got out of the car.

Chapter Seventeen

Alice stood nervously in the kitchen, watching the clock. In fifteen minutes her cookery school would open its door to its first students. The kitchen was gleaming and clean and polished, with all the equipment she needed ready. The ingredients she would be using to demonstrate to the class were already prepared and divided into bowls and plates, and she had gone over and over the recipes for tonight's class so there would be no mistakes. Her heart was pounding and she had only managed two slices of grilled cheese on toast for tea as she was feeling so stressed.

What if nobody showed up for her class? Maybe they'd all changed their minds about coming along to cookery classes. She considered a whole heap of possible disasters, and prayed that nothing would go wrong. She had opted to wear a simple pair of grey trousers and white top with her apron on to protect her clothes. Conor and Lisa had sent her a big bunch of brightly coloured flowers to wish her well, and she had placed these in a glass vase on the sideboard, as she wanted to keep the island and table free. All day she had been getting texts and messages and cards wishing her good luck from her friends and family.

Sean had surprised her by making her breakfast and carrying it up on a tray to the bedroom.

'What a treat!' She had laughed and kissed him.

'It's a special day for you, Mum, I know that,' he had said. 'I won't be back till later tonight, but I'll be dying to hear how it all went.'

'Fingers crossed.' She had laughed again.

She had put on the oven to heat and was just checking it when the doorbell went and her first student arrived. She ushered the stylish young woman into the kitchen.

'Wow! What a kitchen!' Kerrie O'Neill said, taking in the top-of-the-range Prochef cooker and massive Aga. A few minutes later a young couple called Gemma and Paul Elliot had joined them and were equally impressed by Alice's kitchen.

'Our apartment is a bit of a dive, and the gas cooker is absolutely ancient, but it seems to work OK.'

Within minutes the rest of the group had all arrived

and taken their seats around the kitchen table as Alice introduced herself.

'I love cooking . . . making food that is good and great and delicious, meals that you remember! Cooking has been my career, my life, my passion, I suppose, and over the next sixteen weeks I hope to pass on some of my knowledge and expertise and passion to you. Every night we will be using the freshest and best ingredients available to us to create some pretty interesting dishes. I'm so pleased that you are willing to give up your time and come along to my school here on Martello Avenue and learn about cooking and food!'

The group clapped, and looking around the eager faces and the ten very different people listening to her Alice began to relax.

'Now will you all please introduce yourselves, and just tell us a bit about why you are here and what you are hoping for.'

The young couple, Gemma and Paul, had got married the previous year and 'wanted to share everything, and that includes learning to cook together'.

Tessa Sullivan told everyone that she loved cooking and welcomed the opportunity to perhaps expand her range of dishes. She had returned from living in London and was settling back into life in Dublin, and it was nice to become part of a group with similar interests.

Emmet Ryan, an architect, admitted that the last thing he had thought of doing was cookery classes, but even though he was only in his mid-thirties his cholesterol level was through the roof, and his stress levels were equally high. He couldn't face the thought of another session in the gym or doing yoga, and had opted instead to join Alice's class, as ever since he was a kid he'd enjoyed cooking. It relaxed him.

'I'm temporarily out of work and unemployed,' Lucy Brennan explained, to sympathetic noises from everyone. 'So I decided to improve my skills and learn something new.'

Sisters Rachel and Leah said they both were mad on cooking and entertaining but were fed up cooking the same boring old things for their husbands and families.

'Everyone on the road knows Alice is an amazing cook,' praised Rachel, who lived at the top end. 'So when I heard about these classes, I persuaded Leah to come along, too.'

'Every year I sign on for an evening class,' admitted sixty-four-year-old Kitty Connolly, her cheeks reddening. 'Gets me out of the house . . . gets me trying out something new. Last year I did furniture upholstery, and the year before that flower arranging. I thought cooking classes might be a bit of a change. I'm fed up cooking the same food day in, day out. A person needs a bit of a change.'

'Of course,' said Alice, secretly wondering how on earth she was going to balance out the needs of such a diverse group. She turned towards the exquisitely dressed young blonde woman with the false nails.

'Well, I came along because basically I just need to improve my cooking skills,' Kerrie said calmly, 'and I need to brush up a bit as I'm getting married in September.'

'Congratulations,' murmured everyone.

The tall distinguished-looking man with the grey hair went last. He seemed ill at ease. 'My name is Rob. I'm a bit older than most of you here. I signed up for this because I need to learn how to cook, plain and simple . . . My wife Kate died about seven months ago and it's been pretty tough without her. She was a great cook, and I guess I always took her . . . took food and meals for granted, but of late I've learned that man cannot live by takeaways alone, so I'm here because I basically need to learn how to cook . . .'

Alice felt such a rush of sympathy for him. The poor man! She wasn't at all surprised when Lucy stroked his shoulder and Rachel, Leah and Kitty all clucked over him like a clutch of motherly hens.

'Well, we have a wide range of skill-levels here, I suspect.' Alice smiled. 'But it doesn't matter if you are a beginner like Rob, or a more experienced hand like Tessa, as you are all here to learn. Each night we will cook something a bit different from a range of recipes that are well tried out and tested and can be relied on not only to be tasty and delicious, but also to be part of a very good, wholesome healthy diet, and fairly easy no matter what level you are. The ingredients we will be using are mostly readily available from your local supermarket and a good butcher and vegetable supplier. I prefer if possible to use local produce.'

They were all listening to her intently, and she realized that they were a great group, a group she could really work with.

'I would like to give you each a small gift from the Martello Cookery School.' She passed each of them a striped cotton apron, and as they all pulled them on and tied them she suddenly felt that this group were her students, her class.

'As I've told you when I've talked to you previously when you phoned and joined up, the structure of the class will be a demonstration from me of one main course and either a starter or a dessert from the list I am giving you. Then you will work with a fellow classmate and cook these yourselves, with me there to advise and support you and answer any questions and deal with any problems that arise along the way. The menus I've chosen over the sixteen weeks are not set in stone, and if any of you have a special dish you really would like to try I'm sure we can accommodate you.'

'Sounds great,' said Kitty approvingly.

'Now, tonight we are going to start off with a basic . . . something most of you will cook at some stage or want to know how to cook: a tender fillet of beef with roast vegetables and fondant potatoes. For dessert I am making a pear and almond tart. Good food, restaurant quality, but suitable for any decent cook to make. So I'll start you off, and then you'll all have a chance to try it yourself.'

Alice stood at the island, showing them how to tell a really good fillet of beef from one that was less perfect. She trimmed eight large potatoes to an oval shape, browned them in a heavy-based pan with oil, adding a splash of vinegar, some garlic, herbs and rock salt and two hundred millilitres of chicken stock, and then transferred the potatoes with their sauce into the oven to let them cook for about forty minutes. She kept turning them so the potatoes developed a lovely glaze from the stock. As they were cooking she showed her students how to season the meat and turn the large piece of fillet on all sides to brown it before letting it rest, and then putting it in the pan and into the oven for anything between twelve and twenty-five minutes to finish cooking through.

'Keep an eye on your oven temperature,' she advised, 'and remember all ovens are different, so get to know your own. Forget exactly what it says in books, as you could have a very hot oven or a cool one.'

'Mine's got a mind of its own,' joked Rob, 'it just burns everything.'

'Turn it down, then,' she advised. For the vegetables she did a mixture of carrots and parsnips and turnips seasoned and tossed in a little oil and popped in the oven.

'Smells gorgeous,' echoed Paul and Gemma approvingly.

The tart was a light pastry base using a mixture of flour and ground almonds, which she baked blind and then filled with the pear and custard mixture, sprinkled with some more almonds and popped back in the oven.

'This is a very useful pastry base for everyone,' she explained, 'and the fillings can be changed. Apricots, cherries, rhubarb, apple, and, of course, in the summer raspberries and even blackberries. Serve it with whipped cream or ice cream, or even plain yogurt.'

They all gathered around when she took the tender fillet of beef and the vegetables out of the oven.

'I wish mine would turn out like that,' said Kerrie wistfully as she took another taste of the almost melting potatoes that had absorbed all the liquid stock.

The pear and almond tart was cooked to golden perfection, and Alice served it with a little cream, giving Rob an extra-large slice to sample.

'Now it's your turn,' she cajoled. She had sorted them into pairs, and was going to see how they all worked together. Gemma and Paul were obviously a couple, as well as Rachel and her sister. She had hesitated about who to put Rob with, and after much deliberation had paired him with Kitty, who, being a bit older, would probably be more patient with him than the rest of the group. Tessa and Kerrie seemed about on the same level experience-wise, and that left Lucy and that guy Emmet. Anyone would get on with Lucy; she really was an asset to the group with her easy smile and ways.

Alice tried not to smile as they all produced their ingredients from the list for tonight's menu that she had sent them last week. She knew that it was one thing to watch someone give a demonstration and a totally different matter to shop and buy the right ingredients and then prepare them and cook a dish yourself . . . this was where they would learn. Two groups were on the long kitchen table, two at the island and Gemma and Paul were happy to use what she called her spare table, which is where she mostly preferred to sit and relax and read.

She walked around answering questions, noticing that some of the class had opted to buy less expensive cuts of beef than fillet. Good fillet of beef was expensive but usually worth it for the taste, or a piece of sirloin or strip loin would work well too. Kitty was patiently showing Rob how to peel his potatoes properly and explaining to him how to crumble up a stock cube.

Kerrie looked white in the face as she browned her beef, and Alice couldn't help noticing that her vegetables were cut far too thick and would take too long to cook.

'Kerrie, if you slice them a bit thinner they will cook easier,' she said, showing her how to do it. Tessa, on the other hand, seemed to have got well organized, and was already popping her tart base in the oven to bake. Emmet was taking an age, and she could see that Lucy was trying to give him a gentle hint that he needed more liquid with his potatoes. Rachel and Leah were working in tandem and seemed to have everything under control.

A sigh of relief went around the class as the food finally went into the ovens, and Alice was able to brief them on the next week's dish, which was to be a chicken breast cooked with mozzarella and wrapped in Parma ham, served with baby spinach and potatoes, with Maryland crab cakes to start.

'Wow! That sounds great,' cheered Rachel and Leah together.

Tessa's fillet came out first, and was cooked to absolute perfection, the meat almost melting and her potatoes and vegetables exactly right. She certainly had a natural ability to cook. Lucy's sirloin was also cooked perfectly but there was a difference.

'Tessa's meat looks like it could melt in your mouth,' Lucy admitted, a bit disappointed. 'Though I don't know if I could eat such a big bit of meat. I prefer smaller steaks like this.'

Rob's massive fillet was still pretty rare when he served it but it was just the way he liked it.

'I don't like my meat too overdone,' he said proudly.

His tart had burned slightly, and his custard-type filling was a bit too thick. Still, it was a great effort. Kitty, like Lucy, had selected cheaper meat, and it had affected the taste and quality. She had also scrimped on the ground almonds, so her pastry was a bit different from everyone else's.

Rachel and Leah had cooked everything beautifully, and Emmet was proudly cutting into his beef. His tart was the perfect consistency and he had substituted tinned apricots for his filling as he hated pears.

Kerrie's potatoes were done fine, but her vegetables were too chunky and undercooked to serve. Her tart filling was lumpy, and she hadn't cooked her base enough, so the filling had leaked through and made it even soggier.

'You have to let the base cook really well before you fill it,' advised Alice. 'Don't rush too much.'

'But my beef is fine,' Kerrie said proudly. 'I can't believe it. The fillet turned out OK!' They all had a taste of each other's dishes, and Alice had to say she was delighted with the results. Everyone had something good enough to eat in front of them. It was a real confidence-builder on their first night, and they were all chatting excitedly about what they had made.

Rob sat down at the table, and without any fuss began to eat his straightaway, while some of the others packed up their dishes to take home. Gemma and Paul sat in beside him and ate their own fillet of beef and the vegetables.

'Seriously good,' remarked Paul, tucking into his beef. 'I'd have usually just flung my meat under the grill.'

*   *   *

Half an hour later they'd all gone. Lucy and Rachel had helped Alice to load up the dishwasher, and she had slipped off her shoes and poured herself a glass of red wine. She was helping herself to some beef and potatoes when Sean and his friend Dara O'Loughlin appeared.

'Wow, it smells great. How did it all go?' asked her son, automatically grabbing some extra plates and cutlery. She served the boys with a small portion of the fillet and popped potatoes on their plates.

'It went really well. They are a great bunch. I'm sure over the next few weeks we'll all get to know each other better . . . there's nothing like working in a kitchen to see what people are really like. But I have to admit I'm very pleased with the class.'

'This beef is really good . . . and what kind of potatoes are these?' asked Dara, tucking into what was left.

Dara had been eating at their house since he was about seven years old, usually turning up with Sean at mealtimes. He lived about five minutes away, and he and Sean were almost inseparable. They had gone to the same primary and secondary schools and now were in college together. Dara was studying commerce in UCD, and Sean studying arts. Dara was a great kid and a hard worker, and had been a

181

real support to her son over the past year or so.

'They're called fondant potatoes,' she explained. 'And there's some tart left, too, if you fancy any. I'll take a sliver with my coffee.'

'So there's going to be food every week after the class?' Sean laughed. 'A late supper for us!'

'Honestly, you two!' She smiled, and answered her phone, noticing that Jenny was on the line to find out how it had all gone.

Chapter Eighteen

Kitty couldn't believe how the time had flown. Their teacher, Alice Kinsella, really knew what was what about cooking. A pretty woman, she had a nice way about her, spoke slowly and clearly, and explained everything very well. The class was a bit of a mixed bag: that pretty girl with her make-up and false fingernails, and those two sisters who seemed to spend their whole time laughing and joking about their husbands, and as for that poor widower! The poor man hadn't a clue! The *crater* could barely peel a potato, let alone cook one! Well, it certainly was interesting, and a bit different from the other classes she'd done over the years.

The last cookery class Kitty had attended had been when she was about sixteen and was part of her home economics course when she was in school. She could still remember the greasy mutton stew Sister Patricia had made them all cook, and the brown bread, scones, potato soup and gammon and cabbage. Sister Patricia, red-faced and sweating, told them she was preparing them for their lives ahead. God be good to the poor old nun!

Martello Avenue was very nice, an old-fashioned kind of road, and the Kinsella woman certainly had a fine big house. Kitty couldn't imagine what it must be like to work in such a bright modern kitchen with those big windows overlooking the garden and comfy chairs and big table and island. It was another world compared to her old kitchen, she thought, as she locked the Ford Fiesta and came in home. She'd put some of the meat and potatoes in the microwave and reheat them. She passed the sitting room. Larry was sitting watching *Sky Sports* on TV, his feet up on the footstool she had worked so hard on upholstering last year. The newspapers were scattered around the floor. He must have fallen asleep. It drove her mad, and she resisted the urge to go in and switch off the TV and headed for the kitchen instead.

She sighed as she looked around. It was a good size. They'd raised five kids in this kitchen. All had sat around the big pine table, eating and doing homework and school projects. Now they were grown up and gone, all living relatively close by, and Larry and herself had their three grandchildren. Jack and Roísín were usually dropped in with barely a moment's notice for their granny to mind, and on a Thursday she took little Danny for the day, as her eldest daughter worked in the laboratory in Beaumont Hospital. Caroline, their daughter-in-law, was due in about ten days, and then there would be another new baby in their family. Kitty had a high chair in the corner, and a basket of toys for the kids to play with downstairs, and the old cot set up upstairs.

She put on the radio and divided up what she had cooked. The rest could keep till tomorrow. It smelled great, and she set the timer on the microwave. OK, so there were no fancy ovens or cookers in this kitchen, and the lino was worn through on the floor, and the doors on three of her kitchen presses were loose. Also, you had to stand at the sink to look out of the window at the back garden with its washing line and shed and patio, which she supposed was the old way of doing things.

Larry, when he retired first, had talked about fitting a new kitchen, doing a bit of redecorating around the house, but it had never gone any further than looking at a few brochures. She was all up for it, and then Larry had stopped . . . sat in front of the TV and done nothing, like he always did. The two of them had had all kinds of plans for when the kids were finally grown up and independent and Larry was retired from his job in the civil service – forty years working in the Department of Health – on a good pension. They were going to visit her sister in America, go to Rome and see the Vatican, spoil themselves and eat out once a week, buy a new car, take trips, go on some of those special midweek deals that the hotels were always advertising, hire a boat, cruise the Shannon, and learn to play pitch and putt.

So many plans they'd had, and in the end she had given up raising things with Larry as it annoyed her so much when he told her he was too tired, and he wasn't going wasting his hard-earned retirement fund on some stupid thing or another.

All Larry wanted was a few drinks on a Saturday night in the local pub, and to spend the rest of the time watching sport. Didn't matter if it was football or GAA or the racing or even golf, he would settle himself on to the couch and not budge till 11 p.m. most nights. Two birthdays ago the kids had bought her a small TV of her own to use in the kitchen, as she never got to see any of her programmes any more, and last May she'd gone to Rome with a group from the parish. She had had enough of waiting around for her husband!

* * *

She grabbed a place mat and sat down at the table to eat the beef and some of those nice potatoes. She'd have a slice of the pear tart with her cup of tea after.

Larry came in.

'Are you making tea?' he asked.

'In a while.' She kept eating.

'That smells good,' he said, curious, looking at her plate. She'd left him a chop and some mash for his dinner earlier.

'Bit of fillet of beef and some potatoes . . . it's very tasty,' she said. 'Made it at the cookery school I've joined.'

'Cookery school?'

'Larry, I told you I was doing another night class . . . something useful . . . you just didn't listen to me. We made a lovely pear and almond tart for dessert. You can have a piece of it with your cup of tea if you want.'

'That would be nice,' he said, scooting back out. 'I'm in the middle of watching the snooker. Will you bring it in to me?'

She wanted to say, 'I will not bring it bloody well in to you,' but wasn't in form to have a fight with him. Larry was never going to change, and she just had to put up with it. She took out her recipe sheet from the night.

Not bad at all. On next week's ingredient list

chicken breast and that crab thing were on the menu. Sounded good!

It was strange doing the classes on her own . . . every year she had done night classes with her best friend, Sheila O'Leary, both of them glad of a night out and a chance to escape their stick-in-the-mud, stay-at-home husbands. Poor old Martin suffered with chronic arthritis in his back so at least he had some excuse compared to Larry! She and Sheila were a right pair, and had been friends since they had their first babies, Clodagh and Melissa, around the same time. Sheila was always up for everything. She'd restored a whole mahogany sideboard last year. She laughed, thinking of Sheila with a mask on, injecting all the woodworm holes with some kind of chemical, and the two of them wondering where the woodworms would escape to. They'd had a great few days in Rome in the spring with the rest of the parish group. They'd seen the Coliseum, the Vatican, and the Trevi Fountain, but now poor Sheila was laid up in the hospital. They'd diagnosed breast cancer, a small lump, last year and removed it – but now it had spread. Sheila was in having her treatment. Kitty hated seeing her sick. Sheila was strong, a big woman. The medicines would work, and she'd get better, and the next time the two of them would go to

Paris. Climb the Eiffel Tower. See the Mona Lisa. Go to mass in Notre Dame. She'd bring Sheila up a bit of tart tomorrow – the hospital food was awful – and tell her best friend all about the new class and what she was missing.

Chapter Nineteen

Lucy waited near the film centre in Temple Bar for Finn. They were going to see a great French film that had got brilliant reviews in the *Ticket*, and that she had texted him about.

'Hey!' he said, surprising her, and brushing his lips against her cheek. She liked it, and lightly kissed him back.

In the darkness they held hands, and she rested her head against his shoulder, listening to the rhythm of his breathing. Afterwards they went for a pizza and a drink.

'Like your T-shirt.' She smiled when he took off his leather jacket and revealed the pale-grey T-shirt with white stars and the words 'Busy Stargazing'.

'Nothing much else to do when you're on the dole, so I put it on a shirt,' he said sheepishly. They spent the next hour shouting out other busy things people like themselves on the dole could do.

'Busy Cooking,' she suggested. 'Since I've just started my cooking course.'

'Busy Sleeping.' Finn laughed.

'Busy Daydreaming.' She added, 'We all do a lot of that!'

'Busy in Bed,' he teased. 'Well, some people might be.'

'Busy Busking,' she roared.

She really liked Finn, and was thrilled at the end of the night when he suggested meeting for lunch again in two days' time and maybe hanging out for a few hours.

'Busy Queuing,' he called out as she stepped on the DART and headed for home.

'Busy Hanging Out,' she texted him five minutes later.

Lucy tossed and turned during the night, thinking of Finn and his T-shirt. He was so relaxed and easy and good fun, so different from Josh. She was more herself with him. He could accept her for who she was; there was none of that shit she had got from Josh. Things would get better, and in time she and Finn would have jobs and careers or whatever, but now when they both had nothing was a pretty good time to see if you liked a person or not or maybe could fall in love with them.

191

'Love it,' she yelled when she saw the familiar dole hatch and the words 'Busy Queuing' on Finn's black T-shirt.

'A guy on the bus asked me where I got it.' He grinned.

They went to the Chinese on Dame Street for a shared lunch special, and then walked up to St Stephen's Green and hung out there till it got too dark and cold.

'We could go back to my place?' he offered.

Finn was sharing a gaffe in Ranelagh with two old college friends, and they were busy playing Mario on an ancient Nintendo when she was introduced to them.

'This is Duggy . . . he's a film editor, and this is Karl. He's a photographer.'

The guys greeted her warmly and then returned to their gaming as she and Finn disappeared to the kitchen and made a big pot of tea.

'I've got free tickets to see the Bunny Crew in Whelan's on Saturday night, if you fancy it,' she offered.

'Great, I saw them playing in the Mezz last year and they were brilliant.'

Lucy couldn't believe it . . . they even liked the same bands.

'I was thinking about you the other night when I was in bed,' she said.

'Well, that's good to hear,' he said, grinning lecherously.

'No, Finn, I don't mean like that . . .' She blushed, embarrassed. 'Well, I do, but I was thinking about your T-shirt. And then, seeing this new one today, I think they are kind of hot . . . like right on the button. You said that guy on the bus asked you about it . . . well, maybe other people would, too. Be interested, I mean.'

'What the hell are you talking about, Lucy?' Finn laughed.

'Everyone thinks when you are on the dole that you are just dossing and bored out of your tree, which let's face it, is partially true, but we all are trying to keep busy . . . doing things even if they are kind of stupid. We do keep trying things. We keep, as you say, busy. I just think that with so many of us on the dole that maybe there might be a bit of a market for your T-shirt.'

'Sell my shirt?' he said, pulling at it.

'No, I mean print and make more of them, and see if we can sell them at one of the markets or on the internet. People like shirts. We used to sell loads in the shop. Some of the bands sold more T-shirts than CDs!'

'People on the dole don't have much money for buying T-shirts.'

'You've had two new ones the last few days I've seen you.'

'I suppose they . . . they're a kind of statement.'

'Exactly, Finn . . . that's what I mean.'

'You're some girl,' he said, pulling her towards him and kissing her.

'I'm serious,' she said, looping her arms around his neck and pulling him even closer.

'Same here,' said Finn, taking her hand and leading her into his room and closing the door behind them.

Chapter Twenty

Lucy and Finn and Duggy had got up early and driven into town in Duggy's ancient green Peugeot. They had three boxes of printed 'Busy' T-shirts, and Lucy was determined they were going to get a good place to set up their stall in the bustling Temple Bar market. Early birds get the worm, and she'd had to cajole the boys with a hot cooked breakfast of pancakes and bacon served at 6 a.m. to get up and get moving.

'We don't want to be at the back end of the market,' she warned.

'We'll probably be first, cos we're so early,' yawned Duggy, pulling a fleece hoody on over his 'Busy Bonking' T-shirt . . . trust him.

The market was already buzzing when they got there, with Duggy dropping them off with their boxes, fold-up table, stools and the display board for their posters – and then going off to find a car park.

OK, so they didn't get a premium location, as they were already taken by experienced marketeers, but they set up their T-shirt stall beside a guy selling great-looking leather boots and someone selling doggy-print cushions, and there was a Mexican hot food stall just across from them.

'Mexican food stalls are always busy.' Lucy grinned, satisfied with their location.

Finn and herself laid out a load of the T-shirts, and pinned up a display of the four designs they had got printed. They had also done sample graphics for a few more, and people could order these if they wanted.

'Looking good!' yelled Duggy, appearing back with three hot cups of coffee for them.

They each took a turn to wander quickly round the market and see how much competition there was for their product.

'Saw a girl with pretty fairy T-shirts near the entrance,' sighed Finn, 'and did you see the two guys at the back selling Guns N' Roses and Metallica ones?'

'Different market to us,' Lucy said confidently.

Duggy slipped off and came back.

'That stall with the jeans has a few T-shirts for sale,

too. There's a cool kind of Japanese print one and a Kung Fu one and one with James Dean on it.'

Lucy went off and checked them all out, and prayed another T-shirt stall wouldn't set up today.

The first hour was quiet, and they all tried to stay upbeat, and talk as if they were having great fun and a lack of customers didn't really matter. Suddenly people began to arrive at the Mexican stall to get a breakfast wrap, looking around while they waited for them to cook.

'Take off your jacket,' she bossed Finn as she pulled off her own grey sweatshirt and Duggy dumped his, too.

Within a few minutes they had sold four black 'Busy Stargazing' T-shirts and one 'Busy in Bed' one. Two guys with guitars came and bought 'Busy Busking' ones, and they couldn't believe it when they sold a dozen 'Busy Queuing' ones in only a few minutes. All morning it continued, with quite a crowd collecting around the stall and reading what they'd written about how being on the dole had inspired the T-shirts. Some people suggested more ideas, which Finn diligently wrote down.

Duggy had to split around lunchtime, as he was doing a bit of editing in Filmbase for a friend of his.

'Give me a shout when you need me to pick up your stuff,' he offered.

By three o'clock the market had started to wind down, and Finn and Lucy realized that they had sold over fifty 'Busy Stargazing' T-shirts and had eight orders for them. Twenty people had bought 'Busy Queuing' and there were only three left, and they'd cleared out all of their 'Busy in Bed' ones. 'Busy Busking' had sold well, too.

Lucy couldn't believe it, but they had sold over a hundred T-shirts! Finn was incredulous – and glad that Lucy had insisted on keeping the prices low.

'Everyone's broke at the moment, and so twelve euros for a T-shirt that is original and different is a fair price. If we can keep getting them made up and printed for five euros it's a good mark-up for us once we've paid for our stall and our overheads.'

'I just can't believe it.' Finn laughed. 'A hundred people walking around Dublin in something I designed . . . it's kind of cool.'

'You're kind of cool.' Lucy grinned, and kissed him.

That night they ordered in a celebration takeaway from the Balti House and drank some beers. It had been some day, and they were pretty knackered.

'We've booked the stall for next week,' announced Finn.

'Great!' approved Duggy, helping himself to some

naan bread. 'You know, I was thinking maybe we should put the T-shirts up on the internet and sell some that way ... well, try it out, anyway. Set up a "Busy ..." website.'

'That would cost a fortune,' worried Lucy. 'But we could definitely do Facebook and Twitter!'

'Yeah, great, but my friends and I are always setting up web stuff and sites like that for the film projects we work on, but this would be different as you would be selling, and people would have to pay online, and you'd send them T-shirts ... I'm not sure how that works.'

'I'll ask my dad,' Lucy offered. 'He works in a bank, he'd probably know about that kind of thing.'

'Well, here's to Busy,' toasted Finn, wrapping Lucy in his arms.

'Here's to a business that might actually get us all off the dole!' Duggy and Lucy laughed in unison.

Chapter Twenty-one

Alice was busy down the garden clearing out the old leaves and rotting debris of last summer's bedding. The crocuses were up, and the first of the daffodils were beginning to appear under the sycamore and lilac trees. It was damp and chilly, but with her fleece, woolly hat, gardening gloves and sturdy boots she was well-equipped for the occasion. She'd been out since mid-morning and had only taken a short break for a bowl of soup, and with the temperature beginning to drop was about to call it a day when she heard the doorbell go. No point going through the house; she'd go down the side passageway and see who it was.

'Alice!'

'Rob! How are you? Is everything OK?' she asked, surprised to see Rob Flanagan standing on the foot-path in his coat and a business suit.

'I was on my way home from work, and decided to call in for a minute as there was something I wanted to ask you about.'

'Oh, fine, come round this way, please.' She smiled, took off her gloves, and led him around to the back garden and the back door. There she kicked off her muddy boots, took off her hat, and led him into the kitchen.

'Is everything OK about cooking on Tuesday?' she asked, concerned and hoping that Rob didn't feel too overwhelmed by the class.

'Alice, the class is fine. To my great surprise I am really enjoying it, and it's exactly what I need.'

'Well, that's good,' she said, relieved. 'I was about to have a cup of coffee, would you like one?' she asked.

'That would be lovely,' he said, settling his large frame on to one of the tall stools at the kitchen island.

'I've some homemade peanut cookies. Sean is addicted to them, would you like one?' she said, opening the biscuit tin.

'Thanks.'

'Everything going OK with cooking at home?' she asked.

'Yes, couldn't be better. I had an old neighbour, a widower like myself, over for dinner on Sunday and I did the fillet of beef. It turned out perfectly, and as for those potatoes done in the stock, we ate far too many of them.'

'Well, I'm glad that you are putting it all into practice.' She laughed. 'That's what I like to hear.'

She watched him over her coffee. He was a good-looking man, with an expensive suit and shirt, well-turned-out. He looked after himself.

'The biscuits are great,' he said, taking another one from the tin.

'I must put them on my class recipe list,' she teased.

'Alice.'

'Yes.'

'The reason I called over was nothing to do with the class, and I didn't want to ask you with everyone else around. I was wondering if you would be interested in coming to the opera with me next Friday. They are staging *La Traviata* in the Gaiety as part of the opera season. Kate and I used to go regularly, and I suppose I am still on some priority booking list or other. I have two tickets.'

'The opera!' This certainly was a bit of a surprise, but if he had two tickets it would be such a shame to waste them, and it was years since she had gone to the opera. It would be fun, and Rob, from what she knew of him, was good company.

'That sounds very nice, Rob. I'd love to come along, thank you for thinking of me.'

'There is a pre-opera supper in two or three of the restaurants close by. Kate and I always used to grab a bite before the show started. They all make sure to have you out in plenty of time before the curtain goes up.'

'That sounds great!' She laughed.

'I'll book Peploes, then, for about 6.00 p.m,' Rob said, sounding very pleased with himself.

Walking him to the front door in her socks, Alice suddenly realized that she had agreed to go on a sort of a date, her first date with a man since Liam had left her.

Was she gone mad?

'Calm down! Calm down!' Joy advised her when she phoned her that night. 'It's just opera and a bit of supper . . . he's not taking you off on a sexy dirty weekend!'

'Ugh,' said Alice, 'don't be so disgusting. It's nothing like that. He's a very nice man who also happens to be one of my cookery students. It's just two friends having a night out together. Do you think I am breaking some code of ethics by dating one of my students?'

'For God's sake, Alice, you are both over the age of consent. Anyway, I thought you said this was just a night out with a friend,' Joy teased.

'I suppose he's very lonely.'

'Lovely,' said Joy. 'You should suit each other!'

'You know I haven't been out with anyone but Liam since I was twenty-three,' Alice worried. 'It's just so weird going out with someone.'

'You go out with me all the time,' teased her friend. 'So just relax and enjoy your date with that very eligible man, and don't think too much about it. I believe the opera is totally sold out, so you're lucky he got tickets.'

Chapter Twenty-two

Alice decided to take a taxi into town to meet Rob Flanagan at Peploes, the busy city centre restaurant on St Stephen's Green. He greeted her warmly when she arrived.

As she sat down the waitress hurried along to take their order. They both opted for the smoked duck starter and for her main Alice went for the hake on a bed of chive mash.

Rob ordered some wine for the two of them.

'If we don't finish this bottle before we leave for the theatre we can come back for the rest after the performance,' he explained.

As she sipped her wine and ate, Rob entertained her with stories of previous operas he'd seen.

'I'm not much of an opera buff,' Alice admitted,

'but I did get to see *Aida* performed in the open in Verona. It was such a magical night, and Liam and I brought the kids along. I remember about halfway through the performance we heard a sound like thunder, and thought it was special sound effects at first, until we saw the flashes of lightning in the sky. Then it began to rain, and we all had to make a run for it and go to the little bars and cafés around the amphitheatre for shelter.'

'What happened then?' he asked, laughing.

'We waited and waited, and had a few drinks, and the kids had some ice cream, and then the rain cleared and the orchestra started up again and we all made our way back up into our seats. It was well after midnight before the performance ended. I don't think any of us will ever forget it.'

'Verona is beautiful. Kate and I went there a few times.'

'That was our only family holiday in Italy, and I haven't gone back,' Alice said.

They had just finished their main course when they noticed a huge exodus as their fellow diners began to head for the theatre.

'Come on, we'd better get going, too,' urged Rob.

Looking around the foyer of the theatre Alice was glad she had put a bit of effort into dressing and worn her oyster-coloured silk shift dress, as some of their fellow opera-goers were in full evening dress, and it was quite a swanky affair. They had wonderful seats only a few rows from the stage, and Rob was so attentive and kind to her that she could feel herself relax and be taken up by the music and story.

Rob knew the opera well, and patiently explained some of its intricacies to her during the second and third acts.

'Rob, thank you so much,' she sighed as they watched the last act, with Violetta dying in the arms of her lover. 'Why are opera stories all so tragic?'

'That's what opera's about, and what brings people to it: life's tragedies!' he said quietly, as they went back outside. 'Will we polish off the Merlot, or would you prefer to go for a nightcap somewhere else?' he asked.

'Another glass of the wine would be lovely before we head home,' she agreed, as they walked back up on to the Green.

The restaurant was quieter now, and some of the tables were empty. They sat in the corner and talked about their families. Rob was very proud of his two sons and their careers, but Alice felt it must be hard for him having them live away.

'You must miss them both so much,' she said.

'I go and visit them, and they try to get home once a

year,' he said, putting a brave face on it. 'You raise sons to be bright and intelligent and strong and then you can't really complain when they want to go and live somewhere else and take on new challenges.'

'I'm so lucky,' reflected Alice. 'My gang are still around so far, and they've been brilliant since Liam and I split. I don't know how I would manage without them all.'

They shared the taxi home, and when the driver pulled up outside her house Rob got out and gave her a big hug.

'Alice, thanks for coming along tonight.'

'Rob, it was lovely,' she said. 'More fun than I've had in a long time.'

'Then we must do it again?' he said softly.

She gave a wave at the front door as she opened it and let herself in. Lexy rushed out past her to the front garden.

It had been a lovely night and Rob had been far better company than she had expected. At first she had felt a bit awkward and ill-at-ease being out with a man, but Rob was so nice he had made her feel relaxed, and it had been such a treat to dress up a bit and go to the opera. Liam had hated theatre-going and opera and the like, and had only ever gone under extreme duress.

Letting Lexy back in, she was about to go upstairs to bed when she got a text message on her phone.

Are u home yet?

Honestly, Joy was such a curiosity box! She'd make herself a cup of tea and get comfortable on the couch in the kitchen before ringing her best friend who would, no doubt, demand a blow-by-blow account of the night.

Chapter Twenty-three

Kerrie sipped at the red wine. Everything had gone perfectly: the prawn cocktail starter, the beef bourguignon with baby potatoes and a salad, and another of Polly's Pantry's specials – a chocolate tart, which she served with cream and ice cream.

'Sinful!' praised Justin, asking for another slice.

'I'll give the chef a rest,' teased Matt, getting up to make the coffee for everyone.

There really was nothing like having a perfect dinner for friends, Kerrie thought, as she sipped on the Burgundy.

'The beef was great,' remarked Lindsey. 'Is there a lot of wine in it? You must give me the recipe.'

'A glass or two of what we're having,' Kerrie smiled. She had absolutely no idea how Polly's Pantry made their beef dish, but hopefully some of the ingredients were listed on the back of the packet. There was bound to be some wine in it, and truthfully she had tossed a glass of red into the beef herself while she was heating it up.

'How are all the wedding plans coming?' quizzed Lindsey. 'Weddings are so exciting. There is so much planning, but I had such fun organizing mine. You and your mum must be busy with getting everything done!'

Kerrie nodded. She knew her mum was still annoyed with her about wanting to go away. She was making most of the arrangements herself over the internet, which made it all feel distant and unreal.

'Have you got *the dress*?'

'No, not yet,' Kerrie admitted. 'It will be hot in early September in France, so I just want something white and light and summery. I've seen one or two nice ones. I went to that designer Rhona Coleman on Merrion Square, and she's got some really great dresses that are perfect for France and kind of simple and classic, just the thing I'd like.'

'Sounds lovely. Though she's meant to be expensive,' continued Lindsey. 'Will you get your bridesmaids' dresses there, too? How many are you having?'

'I'm having just one bridesmaid, my friend Ruth, who was in college with me.'

'I thought you had a few sisters, don't they mind?'

'Well, they understand we are keeping it small,' Kerrie explained. 'It's going to be quite an intimate affair. Just a few close friends like you and Justin, and our families.'

Kerrie had given no thought to her sisters being bridesmaids, and all the drama and shopping that it would have involved.

'God, when I think of my crowd! Remember? I ended up with five bridesmaids.'

Kerrie remembered five girls of various sizes and heights in layered pink ballet-type dresses all cluttered together up at the altar and later around the reception and in the photographs.

'There was my best friend Vicky, and my three sisters, and Justin's sister. It was mad, and we were months trying to get dresses that would fit everyone. Talk about arguments!'

'Well, at least I won't have that problem. Ruth will probably wear some kind of summery cocktail dress.'

'Aren't you having any flower girls or pages? Do you remember how cute little Ella and Ruby and Oisin were at our wedding? They were such cuties.'

Kerrie thought of her little nieces and nephews. They were a wild lot, and even Matt's little nephew Henry could throw a right strop at times. There was no way anyone was bringing kids to their wedding.

'Well, being away in the South of France it's a bit difficult,' she explained. 'Probably best the kids are left at home.'

'I'm sure your mum is all busy getting her mother-of-the-bride outfit, getting something to suit a *très chic* French wedding! I know it's going to be in France, but she is still going to be the mother of the bride!'

'Mum's not really into that much style, but we'll go shopping nearer the time.'

'God, it all sounds so simple and organized compared to our wedding. Poor Mum went on a diet trying to drop two dress sizes and ended up putting on half a stone with the stress of it all, and my three sisters went on the Atkins diet for months before and were cranky as a bag of cats. I spent more time worrying about their outfits than my own.'

'Lindsey, your dress was amazing, and you looked beautiful.'

'Thanks, Kerrie, that's what happiness does.' Lindsey laughed. 'All I wanted was to be married to Justin. To start our life together surrounded by all our family and friends, the people we love.'

'It sure was a big wedding!'

'It was a hooley! I don't think there was a cousin or an auntie left out. What a family! But they are a great bunch and it was such a huge party. Justin and I had such fun.'

Kerrie remembered the big hotel outside Dublin, the food and dancing and long wandering speeches, loud music and everyone tucking into the midnight feast of sausages and sandwiches. She'd slipped away to bed at around 2 a.m. while Matt had stayed up singing and talking and hanging around with Justin and his pals till almost breakfast time. He'd been bleary eyed and hungover when they'd finally checked out of the hotel after lunch.

'Your wedding was brilliant, Lindsey, but ours is going to be a lot smaller! I can't wait till you and Justin see the church and the restaurant overlooking the harbour of Villefranche and the Mediterranean. It's so romantic and a bit different.'

'We're both looking forward to it.' Justin smiled. 'I'm working on my best man's speech already! Afterwards we're going to hire a car and drive around Provence for about a week.'

'Are you sure you two won't mind having only a few people at your wedding?' Lindsey asked, taking another sip of her wine. 'If it was me I'd probably miss everyone!'

'Not everyone wants a big lavish wedding with all the frills, and crowds of people,' said Kerrie tartly.

'Listen, if Kerrie had her way we'd be saying our vows all on our own on some far-flung beach in Mauritius or the Maldives.' Matt laughed nervously.

'Kerrie wants to keep everything as simple as possible. I've had a hell of a job to convince her even to have our families and a few friends there, believe me!'

'Kerrie, maybe you're just not into weddings?' offered Justin kindly. 'Lindsey, on the other hand, as you can tell, is obsessed with them. Even though we are well and truly married now she still just loves talking about weddings, and finding out about them, and cries when she sees wedding photos and videos and magazines. She's such a wedding junky!' he teased, leaning over and kissing his wife gently.

'Hey, I love weddings, too!' protested Kerrie. 'I loved your wedding, but it's just that ours will be different.'

Kerrie tried to stifle her annoyance with Lindsey. They were lucky! They'd been going out for years, and both families were friends and not only lived near each other but had so much in common. Theirs was a totally different situation! If she'd had her way neither the O'Neill family nor the Hennessy family would be at their wedding. She could already see Matt's mum being her usual snobby self and turning up her nose when she met the few members of Kerrie's family that would make the trip to France. After a drink or two her dad would get on his high horse, his pride wounded, and God knows how they

215

would all get through the day without some kind of row!

'*Vive la difference!*' toasted Justin, a little drunkenly. 'And here's to my best friend and his beautiful bride!'

'Hey, do you two want to come to dinner at our place in a few weeks' time?' Lindsey asked. 'You've made such a big effort having us to dinner tonight, I'll cook something special. This whole doing-a-dinner-party thing is kind of nice, especially when Kerrie and I are foodies and both so into cooking. It'll be fun. Maybe we'll ask Grace and Ritchie too, and what about Emily and Aongus?'

'Count us in,' agreed Matt, passing her the coffee pot. 'Kerrie and I would love to come and have dinner with everyone, great!'

Kerrie felt sick to her stomach. She couldn't imagine anything worse than getting involved in having rounds of dinner parties. She had only just started her cookery classes in Monkstown, and was only a beginner, and in no way ready to start entertaining their friends yet. Trying to cook for a few couples would be a nightmare! She could kill Matt for agreeing to it.

'Matt, I know it sounds fun . . . but remember the next few weekends are very busy, as we've a lot to do with the wedding!'

'Hey, but you guys have just told us you are keeping the big day low-key and having a small wedding,' reminded Justin.

'We are,' she explained, 'but, even so, there is a lot to do and organize with setting things up in France. So maybe we can leave having dinner together for a while?'

'Sure,' said Lindsey, looking disappointed as Matt got up and opened another bottle of wine.

'Why did you shoot down Justin and Lindsey's dinner party idea? It might have been fun,' asked Matt as they were getting into bed, the kitchen tidied the way she liked it, with the dishwasher on.

'It didn't sound like fun to me, getting into a round of having to cook for people.'

'They're our friends, Kerrie! Don't be like that.' He groaned.

'Lindsey was so annoying tonight,' she complained. 'It's none of her business what kind of wedding we want.'

'Justin is going to be my best man,' Matt reminded her. 'He's my best friend, and we've been friends since we were twelve. They spent a fortune on their wedding. Lindsey's folks paid so much, but he told me that they had to take out an extra bank loan to cover it all.'

'Well, that was stupid!'

'Honestly, Kerrie, sometimes I just don't get you,' said Matt. 'I've known Lindsey since she started going out with Justin and she's a sweetheart. She hasn't a bad bone in her body. Tonight she was genuinely interested in what we're doing about our wedding, and you just had to keep putting her down!'

'I didn't.'

'You did! They're our friends. It was embarrassing!'

Kerrie felt tears prick her eyes.

'We've both been to so many weddings over the past few years, and the one thing we know is how important everyone's wedding is to them. We just turn up and have a good time where they might have been planning it for years and spent a fortune. I know we are doing something a bit different, but I still feel guilty that we're not inviting most of the people whose weddings we've been to, and that my granddad won't even be there!'

She said nothing.

'I'm tired, Kerrie,' he said, unbuttoning his shirt as she climbed into bed. 'I don't want to fight with you, ruin a good night, but you have to lighten up! The past few months you've changed. I don't know what's got into you. Some days it feels like I don't know you at all.'

'Matt, I'm sorry,' she admitted. 'I'm just tired and stressed with the wedding and work and everything. I'll phone Lindsey tomorrow, tell her we can go to dinner. You're right, it will be fun.'

'Good.' Matt grinned, leaning across the bed and running his hand along the bare skin of her shoulder and neck. 'Look, can we forget about Justin and Lindsey and think about other things . . . ?'

'Other things?' she teased as he began to fling the rest of his clothes untidily around the room. Leaning against the pillows, she watched as he stripped off before flinging himself on to the bed to join her.

Chapter Twenty-four

'Tonight is our "fishy" night,' laughed Alice as she looked around her group and started to lay out her ingredients.

Tessa was ready with her notepad, as was Rob, who really was trying so hard.

'We are an island nation and yet it is a sad fact that so many of us rarely eat fish, let alone cook it. We have some of the best fish going, but most of it is exported to overseas markets!' Alice couldn't help but vent some of her frustration at the poor uptake of what should be an Irish staple. 'Tonight's dishes include a favourite of mine: prawns done with garlic, butter, wine and the sweetest of cherry tomatoes, which is a wonderful starter or can be served as a main course. And for mains I'm doing a lovely blackened salmon served with a creamy spring onion mash and asparagus in balsamic vinegar. First off I want to show you how you can tell if the fish you are buying is fresh. Come closer and I'll reveal all.'

As they gathered around Alice showed them how to study the skin of the fish, its flesh and its eyes, and then to lift it up and smell it.

'It should smell like it just came out of the sea, slightly salty. Any other bad type of whiff and it means it's a bit older than they are telling you. If it is pongy, walk away. Then, with the prawns, look at the colour, smell them, and also feel if they are still firm. If they're too jelly-like and soft, say no . . . Then to clean a fish . . .'

'Yuk,' said Kerrie.

'Well, most of the fish you get will have been cleaned, unless you are catching them fresh yourself, but boning them is often necessary. For some, when you cook them, the bones will lift off fairly easy if you run a sharp knife under the skin, but for others you need to take out a bit before you cook them. Always check for bones before you serve your fish.

'Now, to the prawns. These raw ones can be boiled quickly, and you will see the colour change. Then I tend to peel and top and tail them, and then remove that little black line you see that runs down the centre.'

'I hate it when they give them to you in a

restaurant in their shell with their feelers and claws and everything.' Kerrie grimaced. 'And then you are trying to eat them, and it's so messy!'

'That's the way I like them.' Emmet laughed. 'With the garlic butter or oil running down my fingers and my chin.'

'Well, the ones I'm using tonight I've already peeled and cooked, and we are just going to heat a nice few spoons of olive oil and some chopped garlic and then throw in the prawns. Try not to keep stirring at them or they may start to break up a bit.'

A few moments later, Alice continued. 'OK, as you can all see the prawns are beginning to cook, so now I'm adding some of the halved baby cherry tomatoes and you will see the juice from my tomatoes is mixing with the prawns. As they cook a bit more I'm adding about half a glass of white wine. It's good to taste at this stage, in case we need another drop of wine. Everything is looking good, but now as the final flourish I'm adding a large knob of butter. This gives the sauce a rich, almost creamy, feeling and a sort of gloss. You must let your sauce thicken up a little bit, but also make sure you have plenty to serve with the prawns. For a starter, I am going to serve this with a little bit of rocket leaf or mixed green salad, and some nice crusty bread, but if this were a main course for

Gemma and Paul or someone I would probably serve it with rice or baby potatoes.'

They were all delighted to sample the piping hot prawns, and Alice left the dish on the counter as she began to show them how to pan-fry the salmon and how to make a proper creamy mash without any lumps and that wasn't too watery.

Now it was their turn.

Paul and Gemma, a great young couple, were a pleasure to watch in action as they divided the work equally. It was funny that Liam had never given a hand in the kitchen, or lifted a finger to cook a meal for her or his children during all the years of their marriage. Cooking was Alice's business and she had let him get away with it.

She must have been daft! She'd made sure the boys could cook, but had never tried to get Liam involved. She wondered whether Elaine was making the same mistake; or maybe Liam was somehow different with her.

Lucy's face was intent as she cut the tomatoes and added them to her prawns. She might need a little more oil. Emmet was already preparing his potatoes for the mash. He was an instinctive cook and clearly enjoyed food and eating out.

'Lucy, you need more oil in that!' he advised, as if reading Alice's mind.

Tessa's prawns had turned out perfectly, and her fish was almost ready.

An attractive woman in her late thirties, she always seemed slightly tense to Alice, but then it couldn't have been easy for her to give up her career and independence and come back home to Dublin to look after her mother.

'Alice, Mum loved the chicken with mozzarella. She made me make it again the other night when her friend Annie came over.'

Florence Sullivan seemed to be a great character, and was enjoying all the meals Tessa brought home to her.

'Well, I hope that she enjoys the fish, too!' Alice said.

Kerrie was hunched over her frying pan trying to salvage the salmon, which was far blacker than intended and breaking up into pieces. Her potatoes were undercooked, which had made them almost impossible to mash, and her prawn starter seemed to have far too much liquid and needed a bit more reduction.

'I hate fish!' she said. 'I'd never cook it at home.'

'Kerrie, why don't you use this to lift out your salmon,' suggested Alice, passing her the plastic fish slice. 'Hopefully you will be able almost to get it out in one piece to put on your plate.'

Before her eyes Alice watched the overcooked salmon disintegrate in the pan, with Kerrie trying to spoon it out. The mash looked lumpy, and Kerrie was near to tears when Alice suggested adding some milk and a little butter to it and popping it back in the pot. Alice didn't know what was going on with Kerrie, but she certainly did not appear to have any understanding of cooking or feel for it.

'It's crap!' Kerrie said. 'Absolute crap! I'm just a crap cook, and no matter what I touch it goes wrong. I'll never learn how to cook properly.'

'Listen, Kerrie, we all have a few disasters.' Alice laughed. 'Don't worry about it.'

'I'm getting married in a few months' time, Alice, and I cannot cook. Cannot cook anything! I've managed to fool my boyfriend into thinking I'm some kind of Rachel Allen because I can heat up the best ready meals ever and make them look good on the plate, but I can't keep it up for ever. I'm such a fraud.'

Alice stood there stunned. Kerrie was simply trying too hard, expecting too much of herself. It was funny, but people who were, like her, afraid of food and not relaxed and comfortable with it, and needed to do everything too precisely, were often awful cooks. While others, who just flung things together and never needed to bother to check recipes or amounts, just cooked instinctively and were brilliant.

Lucy had darted over and was being very solicitous while Tessa wordlessly took over the mash.

'My mum's a pretty crap cook!' confided Lucy. 'So at the weekends or if there is anything special on my dad usually does the cooking. He loves it. It's his secret hobby. Kerrie, it doesn't really matter who cooks, does it?'

Alice smiled. Nina was a fairly good cook but she'd always suspected it was David who was the adventurous chef in the Brennan household!

'But I should be able to do it.' Kerrie sniffed. 'Cooking is simple, pretty basic. Surely anyone can learn?'

'Of course they can!' said Alice matter-of-factly, glad that the drama was over. 'Now, I have some extra fish in the fridge and here's a nice fresh pan. How about you give the salmon another go? One of the most important rules for any good chef is always to have extra ingredients around, just in case they need them. Never ever leave yourself short!'

Twelve minutes later, under her watchful eye, Kerrie had produced a perfect piece of blackened salmon, which she served with the creamy mash that Tessa had managed to whip into shape.

'Your boyfriend will love that!' said Rob reassuringly.

Kerrie O'Neill drove home and pulled up into the basement car park. She opened the silver foil container and ate a bit more of the warm blackened salmon and mash. It was nice, and she really liked the asparagus which had been quickly roasted in the oven with a little balsamic vinegar. She finished off the asparagus and then got out of the car and walked over to the big communal bin and tipped the remainder of the food in its container inside. Then she grabbed her bags and laptop from the car and, locking it, took the lift to their eighth-floor apartment.

Matt was stretched on the couch watching TV.

'How did your class go?' he asked.

'Intense. We were looking at various comparisons in the global markets.' She smiled.

'The company work you far too hard,' he said. 'How much longer does this course go on?'

'A few more weeks,' she said, rinsing her hands in the kitchen and pressing on the Nespresso machine as she secretly studied next week's menu.

Chapter Twenty-five

'What about a walk and lunch on Saturday?' suggested Sally, as the three friends left the Monkstown parish fundraising coffee morning. 'Hugh's off playing golf most of the day.'

'Well, I've nothing on,' admitted Nina. 'What about going to Powerscourt?'

'I haven't been there since the autumn,' Alice said.

Alice certainly liked having something to do on a Saturday, and the old Powerscourt house and estate in Eniskerry, with its magnificent Versailles-type gardens, waterfall and pet cemetery, had some great walks. During the summer months it could be very overcrowded with tourists and overseas visitors, but this time of year it would be a bit quieter.

Sally collected them at ten o'clock, and they went for

a brisk two-hour walk around the grounds. They laughed as they watched a crowd of young scouts trying to set up their picnic near the waterfall. In the Japanese garden the early spring blossom had begun to appear and, like snow, clung to the branches of the trees, and along the rest of the woodland paths the ground was covered with dainty snowdrops, their pretty heads bowed. Sally, who had taken up digital photography, tried to capture them on camera.

'I'm starving!' said Nina, as they headed back to the old house, part of which had been restored and converted into a busy café and gift shop, with a great garden centre housed separately outside.

They managed to get a nice table near the window with wonderful views, and all opted for the lamb hotpot, which looked great with its pastry topping.

'Good, warming, hearty fare,' declared Alice, as Sally entertained them with the antics of her beloved little granddaughter Ava.

'You're such a granny!' Alice joked.

'I love being a granny!' Sally admitted. 'Though Hugh keeps saying he wants the baby to call him Hugh when she's older, not Granddad! Did you ever?'

'I cannot believe Hugh being vain like that!' teased Nina. 'David would love to be Granddad except that our two somehow got the words mixed up, and call him "Gandy"!'

'Gandy?' shrieked Nina and Alice in unison.

'I know! Poor David, as no matter what he says they will not budge from it, and no doubt he'll be Gandy for ever!'

Alice told them about her cookery school.

'I just can't believe it's going so well, and that I'm enjoying teaching so much.'

'Lucy says she really looks forward to Tuesday nights,' confided Nina. 'She says you are so interested in what you are doing that you are passing that enthusiasm down to them.'

'That's nice to hear.' Alice smiled. 'Lucy's great, really bright, and a natural at cooking!'

'She's testing all your recipes on us and her new boyfriend Finn.'

'Well done,' said Sally. 'We're proud of you, Alice.'

'I know, a few months ago I was so nervous about it. But now, I can't believe it, I've so many people wanting to join that I'm starting a new group after Easter on a Thursday night.'

They had all picked out a cake for dessert and Alice offered to go up and get the coffees.

She was walking down with the tray in her hands when she almost did a double take . . . oh no . . . don't say bloody Liam and Elaine were here, too! She had spotted Liam in the distance, and he seemed to be carrying food for two on a tray.

Don't let them be sitting anywhere near us, she prayed silently! She really did not want to ruin a good day by bumping into her ex and his girlfriend.

'Here's the coffee,' she said, almost flinging the scalding mugs at her friends. 'Nina, change seats with me!' she ordered.

'What?'

'Change seats!'

'What is it? Alice, what's up?' Nina questioned, standing up and moving to the other side of the table.

'I want to have my back to the rest of the restaurant. There is somebody I don't want to see.'

'Somebody?' they both asked, curious eyes darting in all directions.

'Stop it, the two of you!' she bossed. 'He'll see you.'

'He'll . . . you don't mean Liam, do you?' asked Sally.

'Ssshh!'

'Where is he?' asked Nina, spinning around and earning a sharp kick under the table.

'He was walking over to the far side with a tray,' Alice whispered.

'Is she with him?' quizzed Sally. 'I've never seen her. I'd love to see what his girlfriend looks like.'

'Feck off, Sally!' Alice hissed. 'I don't want to meet them. Hopefully Liam didn't see me.'

Alice tried to concentrate on eating her slice of carrot cake and forget about her ex-husband's presence. The restaurant was long and quite spread out, and as usual was very busy. Hopefully with any luck he'd be gone before they finished. Liam was a real eat-and-go person, while the three of them were out to relax and were happy to chill here for the rest of the afternoon chatting and having more coffee.

'He's coming,' whispered Sally, pasting a smile on her face. 'He's coming over this way with Elaine.'

'Shit!' thought Alice, wondering if she could make a sudden bolt for the Ladies.

'Sally, how are you?' asked her ex, stopping at the table. 'How's Hugh? I haven't seen him in months.'

'He's fine, Liam. Off playing golf today, so we said we'd treat ourselves to lunch.'

'Hi, Nina! Alice,' he said, looking uncomfortable.

'What are you doing here?' quizzed Nina, peering at him over her expensive designer frames.

'Elaine and I stayed over in the Ritz Carlton last night, and decided to stroll up here for a bit of lunch.' He sounded slightly embarrassed.

'The hotel is meant to be gorgeous!' said Nina. 'I haven't been in it yet.'

'It's lovely, with a great restaurant and some spectacular views from the terrace,' offered Elaine. 'And of course the rooms are enormous.'

Alice clenched her fists under the table. The utter bastard! Her ex-husband and his girlfriend were swanning off to one of the most expensive hotels in Dublin for a night when he kept moaning to her about how tight things were financially, and how the kids needed to cut back and economize!

'Everything OK with you, Alice?' he asked, almost as an afterthought.

'Fine.'

She had absolutely no intention of having any form of conversation with Liam in front of the girls. She had seen Elaine only once before briefly, and that was on the night two years ago that she had decided to surprise her husband in his regular wine bar. As soon as she'd seen the anorexic-looking Elaine she had got a strange sense of foreboding. OK, it had taken almost another three months for Liam to come clean about the affair, and admit that it was Elaine that he was seeing and phoning and texting constantly. It was only when he told her that he loved Elaine that Alice had finally begun to accept the inevitable break-up of their marriage.

It wasn't her fault! She hadn't done anything wrong! Yet somehow she blamed herself for letting Elaine steal her husband away.

'Well, Elaine and I are going to go look at the fountain and walk down by the lake. Tell Hugh and David I said hello!' Liam said, leaving their table and exiting by the large glass door that led out to the open-air terrace.

'Phew!' said Sally when they had disappeared. 'That was awkward.'

'I thought you said she was really good-looking, Alice,' accused Nina. 'She's totally different from what I imagined.'

'I saw her very briefly,' Alice reminded her. 'She was just a skinny brunette with long legs and high boots, who, when I saw her, was wrapped around my husband, for God's sake!'

'Definitely anorexic,' Sally said sagely.

'Very harsh-looking . . . hatchet-faced,' added Nina.

'Great body, great legs, great hair,' Alice admitted. 'Very stylish. Did you see those boots she was wearing? And her jacket? Though maybe she is kind of hard-looking. Her face is so thin and kind of . . .'

'Botox?' suggested Sally bitchily.

Alice burst out laughing. Sally was not only loyal but hilarious.

'Liam looks well,' Nina blurted out without thinking.

'Sex and Botox!' laughed Sally.

'What?'

'Shut up, you,' said Sally and Alice in unison.

Chapter Twenty-six

'Butterflied leg of lamb' was a bit of a challenge, but Alice believed that the majority of the class would rise to it. And there was spinach and rosemary soup to start.

'My mouth is watering already,' admitted Rachel, as she sat down waiting for Leah to arrive.

Alice checked the temperatures in the ovens, and that she had enough of everything to begin cooking.

'A good butcher is essential,' she advised as she showed them how her butcher had deboned the meat and shaped it, making it quicker and easier to cook. Then she explained how to make the marinade that she had used for her lamb.

Once the lamb was in the oven she prepared a tray of gratin potatoes to serve with it, and then demonstrated how simple it was to make the light spinach soup, blending a little rosemary in the oil used to fry the onion and potato, before adding the stock and finally the fresh spinach.

It was a bit of a squeeze in the ovens, and it worked out well that tonight Rachel and Leah were cooking the lamb between them, as were the Elliots, and that Kerrie had asked Lucy if she'd mind sharing the cost of buying the lamb, as her boyfriend Matt wasn't around and she would never manage to cook, let alone eat, it all on her own. Lucy was delighted as this week she was extra-tight on funds as she had to leave her old boots in to be repaired as the stitching was going on the toes.

Lucy was busy making her soup, tasting it, herself and Emmet chatting away easily. Alice felt Emmet was a bit of a dark horse, but he was a very able cook, had a relaxed way in the kitchen, and never got het up.

Everyone kept checking their ovens, and the lamb was melt-in-the-mouth when it was finally ready. The gratin potatoes were hot and bubbling as Rob and Gemma and Paul and Kerrie all decided to sit down to enjoy the meal while it was still piping hot.

Alice, hungry herself, joined them.

'Well worth all the work and the wait!' was the verdict, as the meat was carved up and served.

'The rest will heat up beautifully tomorrow,' Alice promised.

As she tidied up, Alice noticed that Rob had stayed behind.

'You know me, I hate eating on my own,' he explained, packing away the remainder of the lamb and potatoes to be taken home.

'Rob, when I was training we'd all devour everything we made almost the minute it came out of the oven. The head chefs would be furious with us, but it all tasted so much better than reheated later!' Alice laughed. Then she said, 'Will you have a cup of coffee before you go? I'm having one.'

'Decaf, please.' He nodded, putting the bag down.

Twice during the past few weeks Alice had gone out with Rob again. Sunday lunch and a walk in Glendalough two weekends ago, and last Saturday they'd gone to a jazz session in the Killiney Court Hotel, where he had introduced her to his brother and his wife and a few of his friends. It was nice to have a bit of male company, but she wasn't sure about where it was all going. Rob had been a perfect gentleman. He had held her hand, and even given her a polite goodnight kiss on the lips, but that was it.

'Alice, I wanted to ask if you are free to come to

dinner on Saturday?' he said as he helped her to load up the dishwasher and clear away a few things. 'I'll book somewhere nice.'

'Rob, that's so kind of you, but actually I can't – I'm going to Galway this weekend to see Jenny.'

She liked Rob, he was such a nice man, but she wasn't ready to fall into another relationship so quickly. She didn't want Rob to presume that just because they were both on their own she was ready to get entangled romantically with him!

'Then what about the following weekend?' he persisted.

'Yes, that would be great.' She laughed, giving in. 'Something I'll look forward to!'

Rob and herself were chatting away about the class when Sean and Dara arrived back.

'Rob's one of my students,' she said, introducing them.

'One of the more mature ones,' Rob added.

'What was cooking in the kitchen tonight?' Dara asked, sniffing around the kitchen.

'There's some lamb and potato gratin left, if you fancy them.'

Sean got up to sort it out. The two of them helped themselves to the leftovers and sat down again beside Alice and Rob.

'They're like vultures,' Alice teased. 'Honestly, they'd eat me out of house and home.'

'Look, I'd better get going,' said Rob, gathering his things. 'I'll see you next week, Alice.'

As the boys filled Alice in on the big plans for Dara's upcoming twenty-first in two weeks' time, with his folks giving a dinner in his house first and then going on to a nightclub in town, she thought of poor Rob returning alone to his empty house.

Chapter Twenty-seven

Alice had enjoyed every minute of her weekend with her daughter. Galway was a great city, and it was easy to see why Jenny was so happy to be up here at university. They'd gone for walks along the Corrib and out along the Salthill promenade.

On Saturday morning she'd enjoyed visiting the Galway market with all its artisan foods. There were wonderful smoked fish and cheeses and some dressings and marinades which Alice couldn't resist buying. It was a real 'foodie' heaven of a town, with its fantastic range of little restaurants: from lunch in the Old Mill to dinner in Bia which was just off Shop Street. Jenny dragged her along to meet some of her friends in Hanley's pub afterwards. They were a great crowd, and it was lovely to see her daughter so happy and settled. As she ordered a round of drinks Alice couldn't help but notice the tall skinny guy with the beard who seemed to be constantly at Jenny's side.

Dylan seemed very pleasant and nice to her, and it was only when she was going to the train station that Jenny admitted that the quiet fourth-year medical student was her boyfriend.

'Well, I really like him,' Alice said, hugging Jenny goodbye, 'and you know Dylan's very welcome to come home to Dublin whenever you want!'

Sitting on the train she laughed and texted Joy.

You were right! His name is Dylan.

The Tuesday class had gone really well, and Alice had shown her pupils how to make a simple duck confit with juniper berries and individual chocolate pudding pots.

Rachel and Leah had surprised her by turning out an almost professional-looking meal.

'Our husbands don't know what's hit them,' they joked. 'We're both having friends around to dinner next weekend, so fingers crossed that we remember everything and that it goes well.'

'I'm sure everything will turn out perfectly,' said Alice. 'Just remember to do as much preparation beforehand as possible so you can both enjoy yourselves. There's nothing worse than the hostess slaving alone in the kitchen!'

*   *   *

'Are you still on for our dinner on Saturday?' reminded Rob before he left.

'Yes, of course!'

'Then I'll pick you up about eight on Saturday night. We're eating in a nice little place overlooking the sea.'

'Sounds great. I'm looking forward to it.'

Alice had raked through her wardrobe trying to decide what to wear, opting in the end for a little black wool dress that had a cinched-in waist. She hadn't worn it in quite a while, but now, since she'd dropped another five kilos, it made her feel young and attractive. Her hair was very gradually going up a tone, and the sprinkle of light-blonde highlights that her hairdresser had introduced had given her a lift. She slipped her feet into the expensive pair of new black strappy high-heeled shoes that Jenny had insisted she buy in Galway, saying that they were an investment. Giving a twirl, Alice had to admit she was pleased with her reflection in the mirror.

I'm happy! And I look it!

The past few months had been great. She really looked forward to the Tuesday night classes; not just the cooking and giving lessons, but the planning and organizing and just being busy and having people around. She couldn't believe it, but her new Thursday night class was already full.

Rob was punctual collecting her in his Volvo. She wondered where they were heading, was it Sandycove or Dun Laoghaire? Or maybe they were going to dinner in Howth on the far side of Dublin Bay, where there were some really good restaurants.

To her surprise they only drove a few minutes and Rob pulled his car up outside his own house on Clifton Terrace which had an amazing view of the seafront and bay.

'We're having dinner here tonight!' He laughed and opened the car door for her.

'You're cooking dinner?' she asked, really surprised as he led her into the house.

'Well, I've had a very good teacher,' he explained, as he showed her around.

The house was beautiful, fabulous tall ceilings with perfect cornices and magnificent decorative centre-pieces that dated from when the house was built in the 1800s. The sitting room was upstairs on the first floor, and overlooked the whole of Dublin Bay. Alice took a glimpse through Rob's expensive telescope at Howth Head as the sun began to dip in the sky.

Although the room was huge it was warm and comfortable, with big couches, an ottoman and heavy brocade curtains, one wall lined with books and a collection of family photos. Rob poured her a gin and tonic as she had a look around.

There were lots of photographs of his sons – one slight and fair, the other tall and dark like Rob – and photos of Rob and his wife Kate. A pretty petite woman with dark hair and laughing eyes, there were photos of her everywhere: on holidays, on the beach, holding a baby, dancing with Rob, the four of them on bicycles.

'She's beautiful,' said Alice, 'really beautiful.'

'Thanks.'

Rob had set up a small table and laid it for dinner in front of the window.

'I told you we'd be eating overlooking the water.'

Alice couldn't believe that he had gone to so much trouble: silver, candles, crystal and a vase of freesias.

'I'd better go and check on things in the kitchen,' he said, leading her downstairs to the basement with its ultra-modern pale-grey and ivory SieMatic units, and finger-touch hob. 'Kate had it put in four years before she died,' he explained. 'She'd put up with a dark basement kitchen with oak units and green tiles, which she hated with a vengeance, for most of our married life! Finally we decided to do a job on it, and replaced the narrow back window with French doors to the garden, and decided on a new window and door to the front, too, so we have light from both ends.'

'It's an amazing kitchen. You'll be the envy of everyone in the class.'

'To tell the truth, Alice, I spend very little time here. I cook and then live in the other parts of the house.'

'What are you cooking tonight?' she asked, curious.

'Well, a wonderful chef I know always recommends keeping it simple, so I have taken her at her word and done just that.'

'Can I do anything to help?' she offered.

'No, I think everything is under control,' he said confidently, checking the oven.

'That smells good!'

'There's fillet steak and creamy gratin potatoes and a crumble for dessert.'

'Hey, I'm not doing a crumble for dessert for another two weeks,' she teased.

'I cheated and took one of the photocopies of the meal plan you'd left lying around two weeks ago, and followed it step by step.'

Rob was really full of surprises.

'Come on, let's go back upstairs, enjoy the view, and open a nice bottle of wine, as we are just about ready to eat.'

Rob had made prawn cocktail, and served it with slices of lovely warm brown bread.

'That bread was my mother's recipe. I found it in an old box of photos and school reports she had kept.'

'It's got a lovely, almost nutty taste to it,' Alice said, helping herself to another slice.

The steaks were perfectly cooked and tender, and worked beautifully with the potatoes and tossed green bean medley.

'Rob, you really can cook!' Alice said, praising him. 'You've come on so much. I'm impressed!'

'It started off as a necessity, but now, I suppose you're right, I'm beginning to think about food more and enjoy preparing it.'

As he went back downstairs with the plates she took in the magnificent view of the lights around Dublin Bay, and the beam from the lighthouse cast its glow over the shore and the marina and the yachts moored in the harbour below.

'Rob, what a view! It must be so relaxing after a long day at work to come home and just sit here and stare at the sea, watching the waves going in and out.'

'I suppose it is very soothing,' he said, bringing in the dessert and putting it on the sideboard. 'There is always something to watch and see. Sometimes I just sit here for hours.'

'Hey, this looks good!'

'Apple crumble,' said Rob with a flourish, as he served her the dessert with a scoop of whipped cream.

'I feel so guilty letting you do all this work,' Alice admitted afterwards, as he poured them some coffee.

'Me . . . cooking . . . it used to be a pretty rare event!' He laughed. 'I suppose I just wanted to see if I could do it!'

'Well, you certainly can! If the rest of the class have learned half as much about preparing and serving a perfect meal like you've done, Rob, I'll be so pleased!'

He blushed, slightly embarrassed, though she could see he was delighted with the praise. Funny how men rarely got praised about things!

'Let's take our coffee over and sit down in front of the fire,' he suggested, throwing another log on.

Alice felt so relaxed after the food and the Bordeaux they were drinking. She curled up on the couch beside him, and found herself telling him about her trip to Galway.

'It's one of my favourite places, too; maybe some time we'll go there together?' he said.

'Sure.' Alice laughed, suddenly feeling self-conscious.

Rob brought the remainder of the wine over and topped up both their glasses.

Go easy! she warned herself.

Rob told her about his childhood growing up on a large dairy farm in Tipperary.

'They were great times and good fun, but milking cows day after day held no appeal for me, so I came to Dublin to study law.'

'What did your dad say?'

'I suppose in hindsight he was very disappointed, as I was the eldest. My brother Johnny, who's a dentist, had no interest in the place either, but at least my younger brother Alan was mad about farming, and Dad made it all over to him years ago. Alan has built it up and increased the herd and is a real farmer; he hates leaving the place!'

Alice told him about her parents' hotel and the summers there.

'It was kind of magical, I suppose, with the beach and the guests, and working along with my mum in the kitchen. It was such a happy time!'

'Then?'

'Then, like you, I came to Dublin to study, to do a course in catering, and after two years I went to Brittany to get work experience but had to come home when my mum died suddenly. I suppose, like you, I didn't know if I wanted to stay and run the family business. But my dad made me go back to France. There I trained under a fantastic chef called Maurice Aubert in the Rivoli, which was one of

Paris's best restaurants. The hours and the pay were crazy but I learned so much. Eventually I came back to Dublin and worked in Wilde with Myles Malone, which was a great experience.'

'It's funny the way fate interferes in our lives,' he said seriously, taking hold of her hand. 'Alice, if I hadn't seen the note about your cookery school I would never have joined, and then we might never have met.'

'We might have bumped into each other, anyway,' she teased. 'We do live very near each other.'

'Both of us losing someone . . . and the loneliness of it!'

'Rob,' she said softly. 'Kate dying must have been awful for you, but Liam's alive, and though he's an utter rat, he's still around.'

'What I'm trying to say . . .' Rob laughed, 'is that I'm glad we met. I thought when Kate died I'd never meet anyone again, and then suddenly you came along!'

His expression was serious, and before she knew it Alice was in his arms, and he was kissing her. His lips were strong and his mouth tasted of wine, and she found herself responding to him kissing her. It was so long since a man had wanted her, and she found herself lowering her inhibitions and needing to be closer to him. Rob's hands touched the line of her breasts as he kissed her. Suddenly she looked in his eyes and could see the loss and loneliness and lust in his eyes. He wanted a woman, maybe any woman, to make him feel better, to wipe away the memory temporarily of the woman who stared out at them from the photographs. She had drunk a lot of wine, but somehow her head felt clear. He'd been expecting too much tonight . . . she should have seen that.

'Stop, Rob!' she shushed, taking his hand in hers. 'Stop. Slow down. I'm not ready for this yet.'

He groaned, pulling away from her. Alice got up.

She went down to the kitchen and made them more coffee. Rob sat on the chair with his head in his hands.

'Have I blown it?' he asked.

'No,' she said, serious. 'You're a lovely man, Rob Flanagan, but it's just that I'm not sure about this yet. We've had such a great time together, and I really enjoy being with you, but I don't know that either of us is ready to start another relationship.'

Chapter Twenty-eight

Lucy poured herself a glass of chilled orange juice and put a slice of brown bread in the toaster.

'I was thinking I might cook dinner for us all again tonight,' she offered. 'Alice showed us a great chicken dish with Parma ham a few weeks ago, and I could try that.'

'Sounds good,' nodded David Brennan, putting down the *Irish Times*.

'That would be lovely, darling,' said Nina, relieved that sending Lucy to Alice's cookery school was actually paying off. 'Do you want me to get some things in the supermarket?'

'No, Mum. This time I'll get the food.'

Lucy found the fact that her mum and dad were still keeping her embarrassing. She hated that she still needed her parents to bale her out at her age, but at least she had some funds now that she'd made some money from the T-shirts they were selling.

'And if it's OK with the two of you I've invited Finn along,' she said. She added, 'Dad, Finn and I need to talk to you about something.'

Lucy could see the dart of anxiety that flashed between her parents, and laughed.

'Nah, it's nothing bad . . . just good. The T-shirts we've been selling in Temple Bar are doing great, and we just need a bit of business advice, Dad.'

'Sure,' said David, unable to hide his relief that Lucy was not involved in some catastrophe or other.

Lucy shopped carefully, choosing free-range chicken breasts, mozzarella cheese, asparagus and all the ingredients for the chocolate pudding pots which she knew her mum would love. A bottle of really good wine which was luckily on special offer in the off-licence and she was set. She had warned Finn to be on time at her parents' home no matter what happened. Everything went smoothly in the kitchen, and she had the table set. The only way to keep her mum from interfering was to offer her parents a pre-dinner gin and tonic in the sitting room.

'Hey, you look great,' she said when Finn arrived in perfect clean jeans with his black boots and a 'Busy Stargazing' T-shirt under a grey and white striped shirt. Even his long hair was freshly washed and shampooed, and he had shaved.

'You look pretty hot yourself,' he said, hugging her and lifting her off her feet.

She was glad that she'd worn the cute red ladybird-print skirt with her black leggings and a little black cardigan.

She brought Finn in and introduced him to her parents, and Finn was so relaxed and nice they were all talking together in only a few minutes.

Finn helped her serve dinner, and the food was just delicious, and she could tell her mum was dead impressed by what she was learning. She even begged Lucy to give her a copy of the recipe so she could make the chicken dish for her friends, too. Her dad cleaned his plate and actually wanted a bit more . . .

The chocolate dessert was yummy, and turned out even better than the first time she had made it, and her mum and dad loved the wine.

Finn was winning them over, and they were intrigued when he told them all about the different design things he'd worked on over the years and some of the awards he'd won.

'Disgraceful, that a talented young man like you is forced on to the dole queue,' muttered David Brennan angrily. 'It's no wonder the country is the way it is when they won't give young people like you and Lucy a chance!'

'Well, that's why we're making our own chances,' Finn replied.

'And setting up a business of our own.' Lucy smiled.

'But you've no experience of business!' worried her mother.

'Mum, I've been working in businesses and shops selling stuff since I was about sixteen!' Lucy reminded her. 'I'm used to getting people to buy things, and finding out what works and what doesn't, especially for people our age.'

'What kind of business are you starting?' David asked, interested.

'T-shirts,' explained Finn. 'We've been selling hundreds of them over the past few weeks and have lots of new orders.'

'Finn is so talented and creative, and doesn't really realize how good he is at designing things,' Lucy explained. 'Simple things like T-shirts that are a kind of statement.'

'In our day we had the Che Guevara ones and the peace ones.' Nina laughed. 'Everyone had them, and the posters up on their wall, too . . . they were everywhere.'

'Well, I'm not sure we're as big as that.' Finn grinned. 'But there is a bit of a buzz about them.'

'The thing is, we can only handle one market stall,' explained Lucy, 'and be in the one place, but there are markets everywhere, and Finn and I are hoping to take a stall at Oxegen and at Electric Picnic, and some of the other big music festivals in the summer, to see how they go.'

'Sounds exciting for the two of you.' Nina Brennan smiled.

'Duggy, one of the guys who helps us, says he thinks we should set up a website to sell them so that people can check them out online and see and buy the new T-shirt designs,' Finn continued.

'Sounds exactly what you need,' said David Brennan. 'Is that what you want a bit of advice about?'

'Yes,' said Finn. 'This is all new to us. I can design the website but setting up the whole ordering and business end of it is different.'

'You know most of the business loan applications that pass my desk in the bank nowadays have to have some kind of web-based plan to work. Just depending on shop trade is almost a thing of the past, as even if a person doesn't actually pay and buy online they will often make the decision about the item they want to purchase there, and then go into a shop to pay for it. Business is changing, and they reckon in another ten years most purchases will be online.'

'Incredible,' Nina said. She had no intention of

ever giving up her lovely shopping trips.

'You may do a lot of the design work yourself, Finn, but you will need to pay something for a good website, especially one with a secure payment facility. And then you will need some working capital to cover manufacturing and storage and distribution of your T-shirts,' David Brennan said.

'I know,' said Finn. 'Lucy and I have been talking about it. At the moment we have the boxes in my bedroom in the apartment, which is OK, but I might run out of space.'

'No, that's all got to be sorted,' advised David. 'You can try a small bank loan, though I know credit committees aren't great when they see that applicants are unemployed. Otherwise, you could maybe talk to the local enterprise board and see if they would give you a bit of backing. They have some office spaces and low-cost small business units available, and offer a pretty good advisory service for young entrepreneurs like you two. I know Colm Higgins, and if you want I could give him a call and see if we could set up a meeting with him.'

'Thanks, Dad, that would be great!' Lucy enthused, delighted by his support.

'I've some designs for a website on my laptop, if you want to have look, Mr Brennan?'

'David, please,' insisted Lucy's dad, clearing the table so they could all take a look at some of Finn's web ideas.

Chapter Twenty-nine

Florence Sullivan walked slowly through Dublin's Botanic Gardens. All the spring bulbs were out and the place was a mass of colour. Red and yellow and pink tulips were everywhere!

' "A host of golden daffodils, beside the lake, between the trees" . . . aren't they just like the ones in the Wordsworth poem?' Florence Sullivan smiled as they strolled up along by the riverside. Tessa had known her mother would love this outing to one of her favourite places. It was great to see the public gardens as the seasons changed, with their magnificent floral displays and beds created by the gardeners, but probably the best part of the Botanic Gardens was the woodland, filled with trails, that bordered the river. They stopped to watch the swans and their young cygnets on the water and a clutch of

257

young ducklings following their mother further down. Out of the corner of her eye Tessa spotted a little boy on his own coming towards them, his father trying to race after him, as he'd clambered out of his buggy and was stepping dangerously near the water's edge in his determination to get to the 'duckies'. Tessa scooped him up and, ignoring the two-year-old's surprised protests, handed him back to his dad.

'Thanks! He's an utter devil! We need eyes in the back of our heads to keep up with him!'

She stifled a pang of envy as she noticed the heavily pregnant young woman rushing to join them.

Over near the gazebo some of the white and purple magnolias were starting to come into bloom, and, taking a rest on one of the park benches, Tessa and her mother laughed, watching the antics of a pair of squirrels who were racing up and down a beech tree.

'Mum, let's have a look in the glasshouses,' Tessa suggested. 'And then we'll have some lunch.'

The glasshouses had been restored within the last few years and were magnificent, with their array of hothouse flowers and orchids and lilies. Florence Sullivan picked out some favourites and read up about them from the information provided. After a quick wander around the impressive Palm House they made for the restaurant.

'Soup and a sandwich for me,' ordered her mother, as Tessa went up to join the queue.

'Thanks,' said Florence, as they sat at the table eating.

'Mum, it's just some carrot and orange soup and a roll.'

'No. I don't mean that,' continued her mother, her pretty face serious. 'For this . . . for everything.'

'Mum, it's a pleasure coming up here on a day like this. You know I've loved the Botanic Gardens ever since I was a little girl, when you and Dad used to bring us.'

'No, Tessa, it's not just coming here to the gardens, it's everything you do for me. I appreciate what you have done so much. You have given up so much to come back here,' Florence said, folding her napkin in half. 'You were always the kind one and the big-hearted one! Now it is you that has given up your career, given up that lovely flat of yours in London and your busy life, to come back to Dublin and spend most of your time with a foolish old woman.'

'I wanted to, Mum. Nobody forced me,' Tessa said evenly. 'You have been so good to all of us. We all had such a great childhood and time growing up, and that was down to you and Dad. I wanted to come back to be with you.'

'I just worry about you,' Florence said softly. 'This is not what I planned.'

'Mum, I messed up some of my life on my own, so don't go blaming yourself! I was the one who wasted almost eight years with Grant, thinking that we were going to end up getting married, and that once he got over his divorce everything would be fine. I thought I'd have a house in Surrey, a place in Spain and a great life, and that if Grant didn't want more kids then that was OK! I was so bloody stupid.'

'I'm sorry,' said her mother, squeezing her hand.

'I'm sorry, too . . . for not listening to you and my friends. I should never have believed him, wasted so much time with him. It just gets me mad when I think of him. Married now, with a new wife and a daughter! No problem about having kids now . . . apparently he loves being a mature dad! Sarah in the office keeps me posted on the goings on,' she said bitterly.

'Oh, Tessa!'

'I know. I've been so stupid . . . such a fool. So coming back home away from Grant and all the office intrigue and gossip was maybe not the worst thing in the world, Mum.'

'I just worry about you . . . I can't help it. You are a beautiful intelligent young woman!'

'Mum, I'm thirty-nine . . . and probably at this stage set to be the spinster in the family!'

'Tessa?'

'No, Mum, it's OK. At my age you have to accept things and put them behind you.'

'You need to get out more . . . see people,' fussed her mother. 'You should be socializing. I'm sure that there are plenty of decent nice men out there.'

'Mum, for heaven's sake.' Tessa laughed. 'I've given up on meeting someone! And I do go out . . . I have my job, my lunchtime Pilates class on Wednesday, and my cookery class on Tuesday nights, and I regularly go to the cinema with Cass and Naomi if they are around.'

'Exactly,' said Florence. 'You never go to parties or dances, or whatever you young people do!'

Tessa could see the genuine concern on her mother's face. She was still a very beautiful woman. She had married at twenty and been adored by Tessa's father, Christopher, right up till the day he died ten years ago. Florence Sullivan had no experience of heartbreak and deceit or disillusion! How could she?

'Well, Mum, you'll be glad to hear that I'm actually going to a party tomorrow night.'

'A party?' her elderly mother seemed surprised.

'Yes,' Tessa said brightly. 'Paul and Gemma, a lovely couple in my cookery class, have invited us all to their house-warming party this weekend. It should be fun!'

* * *

261

As they walked back to the car and her frail mother stopped to admire the bright pink camellias, Tessa decided that maybe she should really go to the housewarming. She'd presumed that Gemma had only invited her out of politeness, but to her surprise most of the class had said they would go. The crowd were good fun. She'd text Gemma and let her know she'd changed her mind.

Chapter Thirty

Kerrie debated going to Gemma and Paul's house-warming party. On Tuesday they had invited everyone round to their new flat.

'If you are free on Saturday night we are having a bit of a party, as we've just moved into the garden flat in an old house on Booterstown Avenue. It's quite close to the pub, so if we run out of drink we can get fresh supplies there,' Paul had joked.

'I'm going to cook some tasty nibbles,' tempted Gemma. 'And we really mean it. We'd love you all to come along.'

'Count us in,' said Rachel and Leah.

'But can we bring our husbands, Nick and Pete?' asked Rachel. 'We'd like everyone to meet them!'

'Of course you can! The more the merrier!'

'Finn and I'll be along too.' Lucy smiled. 'I'm dying for you all to meet him.'

'My boyfriend's off at a football weekend in Barcelona with some clients,' explained Kerrie, relieved that Matt was not around to meet her friends from the cookery school. 'But if you don't mind I'll come along on my own.'

With Matt out of the way for two days, Kerrie had the opportunity to spend most of the day cleaning and tidying the apartment. Matt was so messy compared to her, and she had sorted out his sock drawer, his underwear drawer and his sportswear drawer. She had stripped and remade their bed. Cleaned out the fridge, washed the floor and polished the windows. Looking at their expensive grey leather couches and polished wooden floor and display of Mark Trubridge's simple black and white prints, she thought the living room looked so perfect with nothing out of place, just the way she liked it. The kitchen was absolutely spotless, as was their bathroom, and the whole place looked like a show apartment now that she had jettisoned all Matt's old newspapers and magazines and put all his DVDs and messy games into a black storage box which fitted behind the plasma TV.

Pleased with herself, she hopped in the shower and then blow-dried her hair.

Unsure of what to wear, Kerrie opted for black leggings and boots and a floaty pale-green tunic that she had barely worn. Gemma and Paul were hardly stylish dressers, and probably their friends were the same. She grabbed two bottles of Prosecco in the off-licence and got a taxi to their new address.

A good crowd was already there, and Gemma gave her a quick tour of the place. They had a massive sitting room which opened off the hallway. There were three different couches in the room, one red, one black and a kind of black and white big daisy print one. There were candles and snacks laid out on a collection of small tables, and on one wall there was a display of charcoal sketches and some paintings and wonderfully decorated plates.

'They're mine,' said Gemma modestly. 'I just love working with ceramics and paints and seeing what happens.'

On the other side of the hallway Gemma showed her their bedrooms.

'We get all the morning sun in here,' she said. 'It's such a relaxing room.'

There was an enormous brass bed with a colourful throw, and a big wardrobe, a writing desk and a wickerwork chair, along with a range of blown-up photographs of Paul and Gemma on their travels.

'That's in Goa, it's really tranquil and beautiful

there, that's Brazil . . . spectacular country, and that's us diving in the barrier reef in Australia.'

'Wow, you two sure have seen the world!' said Kerrie.

'We took two years out and explored. We wanted to do it before we settled and got married and started having babies!' Gemma giggled. 'Though we're still working on the last bit at the moment. We got the bedspread in Indonesia, and that carving is from Peru, and that old saggy baggy elephant is Barnaby, and I've had him for ever.'

'Kerrie, you can leave your coat in here,' Gemma offered, opening the door of another room.

The bed was already covered with a pile of coats, and two of the walls were stacked with bookshelves and bric-a-brac.

'Come on, and I'll get you a drink!'

'I've brought some Prosecco.' Kerrie grinned.

'Well, let's get it open then!'

Paul was being barman in the kitchen, which was a big long room with windows and a door out to the garden. Gemma had something cooking in a pot on the cooker, and the kitchen table had been turned into a bar with a range of glasses and drinks. The units were ancient, but they had been painted a dusky blue and it was a lovely bright room.

'Hey, Kerrie!' yelled Rachel, introducing her to her

husband Pete. 'Leah should be here soon – their little boy Sam had a bit of an earache, so she wanted to get him asleep herself before they left.'

Kerrie helped herself from one of the bottles of Prosecco and popped the rest into the fridge. The kitchen was pretty crowded, and Paul introduced her to a few of his friends.

'This is another one from my cookery-class gang,' he said.

The party began to swell and swell as more people arrived, and some of the group spilled out on to the patio, where Chinese lanterns and fairy lights had been strung up.

'Great house!' said Emmet, who had brought along his friend Steven.

'What kind of a cook is he in class?' asked Steven.

'Great! Why?'

'I'd always figured him for an instant quick-frozen pizza and frozen-lasagne type, and now when I call over he wants to make three-course fancy dinners! He seems to have chilled out a bit, which I suppose is a good thing.'

'We all have,' Kerrie admitted.

She smiled when she saw Tessa had arrived. Tessa was wearing jeans and boots and a pretty pink shirt and looked younger. She had brought along some food.

'They're spicy meatballs, and there's a yogurt dip to go with them!'

'Great,' said Gemma, giving her a big hug.

'Is everyone else here?' Tessa asked, looking around.

'There's a few more to come, but it's pretty crowded,' said Gemma, passing her a large glass of red wine and steering her to the rest of the gang.

'Hi, everyone!'

'Wine's good,' said Rob. 'Very good.'

Kerrie left Tessa and Kitty chatting with Rob, who was busy explaining to them about how to tell a good red wine from a bad.

She escaped back outside to Emmet and Paul, who were comparing the merits of the Xbox and the Playstation; it was a debate she'd heard Matt regularly discuss, and was happy to join in even if she was crap at playing both of them.

'Hey, here's Lucy and her new boyfriend!'

Lucy looked amazing in a long maxi dress, and Finn was wearing a 'Busy' T-shirt under his combat jacket.

'What does it say?' asked Paul.

'"Busy Partying"! What else?' joked Finn, downing a can of beer.

'I want one of them,' said Emmet.

'Me too!' said Steven.

'That's brilliant,' said Kerrie. 'Nearly every guy in Dublin is going to want one!'

'That's what we're hoping,' admitted Lucy, her eyes shining.

'He's so cool and so nice,' Kerrie whispered under her breath to Lucy as the guys went to get more beers from the big plastic basin filled with ice on the patio.

'I know,' said Lucy. 'He just makes me so happy!'

Twenty minutes later Gemma announced that there was some food in the kitchen, and everyone thronged in as Leah helped her to serve plates of chilli and rice. There was also a selection of salads and breads, meatballs, chicken and vegetable kebabs.

'Where's Alice?' asked Kerrie, surprised that she wasn't there.

'It's her dad's birthday so she couldn't make it,' confided Kitty, who had, as usual, come on her own.

Once the plates and bowls were put away, Paul turned up the music volume and everything seemed to get louder. Salsa music pumped through the flat.

'Won't your neighbours mind?' asked Kerrie.

'No.' Paul laughed. 'Because they are all here! See that gang over there in a huddle knocking back all our wine? That's them . . . and that tall grey-haired man with the lady with the big earrings – they live upstairs. Tom and Rowena had us up for supper a few days after we moved in. They're great. Why, what are your neighbours like when you have parties?'

Kerrie knew hardly any of their neighbours. Because they were on the eighth floor of their building, they only really saw people getting in and out of the lift or in the car park. Besides, Matt and herself had never had a party! They'd had friends for dinner a few times, and once Matt had organized to have some people for drinks before they went to a concert in the O2. But she would hate to have people in messing up their place and spilling wine and beer everywhere!

'It's a bit different than this,' she said, slightly envious.

About midnight everyone got up dancing, and Kerrie found herself swinging around between Emmet and Steven and wishing that Matt was here with her.

Tessa and Rob were up dancing, and Finn had Kitty in his arms, with Lucy taking photos on her phone camera.

'You will send them to me, Lucy love?' shouted Kitty.

'Of course,' said Lucy.

'She wanted her husband Larry to come,' confided Gemma, 'but he's such an old stick-in-the-mud he just wanted them to go to his local as usual, so Kitty dressed herself up and came on her own.'

'She's such a character!' said Kerrie, who had found Kitty very helpful the past few weeks in class.

At two o'clock the party was beginning to thin out, and Kerrie decided to leave. She'd drunk far too much, and was ready to go home and collapse into bed. Tessa was a bit drunk, too, and she and Rob were sharing a taxi home. As Emmet and Steven were heading into a nightclub in town they agreed to drop Kerrie off en route.

Gemma and Paul were still going strong when they said their goodbyes, with Paul and his brother Dave playing their guitars and singing with a crowd in the kitchen.

At home Kerrie fell into bed. She was too exhausted to think about anything, and just wished that Matt was home with her. When she woke she felt awful, dehydrated and nauseated, but didn't have the strength to get herself a cup of tea or a mug of coffee.

She had dozed off again and was drifting in and out of sleep when she realized that there was a warm body in the bed with her.

'Mmm.' She sighed, curling in against Matt, enjoying the feel of his naked skin against hers.

'I missed you,' Matt said, kissing her.

'I missed you, too,' she said. 'What time is it?'

'Lunchtime.'

'How did the match go?'

'Brilliant, Barcelona was great. Everyone enjoyed it.'

'Good,' she said snuggling against him.

'Where did you go last night?'

'Just out with the girls, we ended up at a bit of a party. But it wasn't the same without you.'

'Well, I'm here now,' he said, Kerrie feeling his arms wrap around her. She pulled the duvet up over the two of them.

Chapter Thirty-one

Rob Flanagan hadn't been sure what type of gift to bring along as a house-warming present to Paul and Gemma, and had gone into Brown Thomas and bought them an expensive casserole set like the ones Alice used, as he knew they hadn't anything like that.

'Oh, Rob, that is so kind of you, so generous.' Gemma hugged him when she opened the box. 'It's just what we need.'

He hadn't been at all sure about coming along to this house-warming party in Booterstown; he was a different generation after all, but Paul Elliot had been very persuasive. And he had come along a little in trepidation as to what Alice's reaction might be, but hoping that meeting in the relaxed atmosphere of a party might be just the thing.

It was a fine old house, but a bit gone to rack and

ruin, and Paul and Gemma had the total run of the ground floor and also the use of the garden.

'I've been clearing it a bit, and I'm just starting to plant some things,' confided Paul. 'And we hope to have some of our own vegetables by the summer.'

Rob looked at the cans of cheap beer on the table and in the fridge, and opted to drink wine for the night.

'Would you like a glass of wine?' he offered Kitty, who was slightly upset that her husband Larry hadn't come along. To Rob, Larry Connolly sounded a bore of a man, stuck in front of the TV all day and night, and he wondered how such a nice woman as Kitty stuck him.

'What about you, Tessa? What would you like?'

'I could murder a double vodka . . . but I'll have a glass of white wine instead.' She laughed. Tessa looked good. Different . . . She'd changed her hair, and instead of her usual black or grey trousers was wearing jeans which showed off her long legs.

Rob asked where Alice was, and was a bit disappointed when Gemma told him that she wasn't coming because she had a previous dinner arrangement.

He hoped that she wasn't trying to avoid him. He realized that he had tried to rush things too much . . . made too many assumptions . . . putting two and two together and getting it totally wrong. Just because they were both of a similar age, and both on their own, and shared a lot of common interests, that didn't mean he had the right to a relationship other than friendship with her. He'd been talking to Bill Deering about it, and Bill had reminded him that sometimes it was much harder for those that had lost their partners through unfaithfulness and deceit and disloyalty than those who had lost their partners through death.

'They often have more baggage of anger and hurt than we have,' he explained. 'Our loved ones are gone from us, whereas their loved ones may be only living half a mile away and with someone new!'

Rob spent a while talking to Paul's neighbours, discovering that one of them was Frank Gallagher, who had been in school with him since he was twelve. It was nice to reminisce.

Gemma served up a great chilli and Rob had two portions of it, and also some of the lovely meatballs that Tessa had brought along.

'Really tasty,' he said, paying Tessa a compliment. Afterwards when the dancing started, Gemma pulled him up on the floor. Then he danced with Kitty and Leah and Lucy and Rachel, and eventually managed to persuade Tessa to get up.

He ended up dancing with her and chatting to her for most of the rest of the night, surprised by how easy she was to talk to. Like him, her background was in business, and she had her own theories about the current economic climate and the way various governments were handling it. She had worked in Bridgetown & Murrow for many years in London, and when he mentioned he was friendly with one of the partners there he could see she was a bit uncomfortable and changed the subject.

They danced a bit more and joined a few people out on the patio chatting, moving inside into the big sitting room where they talked to Leah and Rachel and their husbands.

'God, look at the time! We'd better go as we've both got babysitters in,' Leah said suddenly.

Rob hadn't realized the time either, and decided to get a taxi home. The young crowd were singing in the kitchen, and he offered Tessa a lift as he knew she was living fairly close by in Mount Merrion. The two of them had definitely had enough to drink and said their goodbyes to their hosts.

'Lovely party,' he said, as he helped Tessa into the back of the cab.

They were almost there when he realized Tessa had

gone asleep, her head against his shoulder. He wasn't exactly sure which road her house was on, but luckily she woke.

'Sycamore Grove. Here it is, Rob,' she said, waving madly and pointing out the white pebble-dashed 1950s-style house with the neat garden.

'Will you be OK going in?' Rob asked. 'You do have your key?'

'I'll be fine.' She giggled.

The taxi man threw his eyes to heaven.

'Do you want to come in?' she asked, hiccupping.

As she got out of the cab she nearly stumbled and Rob jumped out and grabbed her arm, paying the taxi driver. She was just like Kate, couldn't hold her drink. He didn't want to frighten poor Florence. So he'd make sure Tessa got in safe and then walk back down to the main road and grab another taxi.

He put on the kettle and made Tessa coffee, two big cups of it, and then settled her nicely on the couch in the sitting room with some cushions and a rug over her. Tessa would be fine in the morning, right as rain. It really had been rather a good party, he thought, as he closed out the door gently behind him and went home.

Chapter Thirty-two

'Tessa, Tessa!'

Tessa groaned as she heard her mother calling her. Turning around, she realized that she was not upstairs in her bed but . . . hold on . . . she was on the couch, wrapped up in her mother's big red and green check Foxford rug, lying in the sitting room. She was mortified as she suddenly remembered the previous night. Gemma and Paul's party had been so much fun. She recalled drinking wine, and talking to Emmet and his friend, and dancing with Rob, and Paul finding a bottle of vodka near the end of the night and having two glasses of it in the kitchen, with everybody singing, before leaving and getting the taxi home with Rob.

She tried to piece the journey together, and realized that Rob must have brought her in home. She took a sip of the big glass of water left on the coffee table, and saw that her black boots had been placed neatly near the couch. Shit . . . what had she done? What had she said?

Florence Sullivan appeared in the living room in her pink dressing-gown, concern on her elderly face . . .

'Are you all right, Tessa? I was worried when I woke up and saw that your bed hadn't been slept in.'

Groggy and nauseated, Tessa sat up, praying the sitting room wouldn't spin.

'It's OK, Mum. I was out very late, and just didn't want to wake you up by clattering about upstairs, and I must have come in here and sat down and fallen asleep.'

The last time she had done this she had been sixteen, and she and Suzie Corrigan, her best friend, had got drunk in Suzie's parents' house testing out bottles of gin and vodka and whiskey from the drinks cabinet. They had both been violently ill. She had managed to crawl home and on to the couch before the rest of the house had woken up, and had lain there for hours praying for death.

'Was it a good party?' Florence asked.

'The best,' Tessa said.

'I thought I heard voices downstairs,' murmured her mother, 'someone in the kitchen.'

'One of my friends came in briefly, we'd shared a taxi.'

'Would you like some breakfast, pet? I'll make it.'

If she was paid a thousand euros, Tessa couldn't have cooked her mother's regular Sunday breakfast of bacon and scrambled egg and toast today.

'I'm not very hungry.'

'Then I'll make you a nice cup of tea before you go back up to bed for a proper sleep.'

It was two o'clock when Tessa woke up. She felt so much better and jumped in the hot shower to freshen herself up. She scrubbed herself with a revitalizing blue shower gel and got dressed into her navy track-suit bottoms and her white zip-up jacket. She needed to get out, go for a walk and get some fresh air.

In the kitchen she poured herself a glass of orange juice and ate a slice of plain toast and butter, recalling Rob Flanagan making her coffee and getting her to drink it. He'd been so kind.

She was tidying up when she noticed he had left his expensive mohair scarf on the back of the chair. She would return it to him when she saw him at class on Tuesday. Suddenly she realized that she didn't want Rob thinking badly of her, and phoned him to thank him for what he had done. She had the number as Alice had given everyone a list of their fellow class-mates' numbers, in case they wanted to text about a recipe, or share ingredients.

'Hey, Rob, it's Tessa. I just wanted to say thanks for last night, for looking after me.'

'Are you OK today?' He laughed.

'Thanks to you, yes. And I guess I've slept the worst of it off. And I just need to get a bit of fresh air.'

'Me too,' he admitted. 'I'm just going to bring the dog for a walk.'

'You left your scarf. I'll give it to you on Tuesday.'

'I'm heading down the West Pier in Dun Laoghaire,' he said. 'If you fancy it.'

'Give me about twenty minutes and I'll bring the scarf.'

Her mother was asleep on the couch having her after-lunch snooze. *Casablanca* was on the TV later this afternoon, and Florence Sullivan had put a big ring around it in the TV section of the Sunday paper. She loved planning her TV viewing.

Tessa parked her Mini near the old ferry terminal and walked briskly. The day was bright and sunny, and as usual crowds of walkers and families had descended on Dun Laoghaire to enjoy the seaside. She was trying to see if she could spot Rob, and was just about to phone him when she noticed the man with the big golden Labrador on the lead waving at her.

'Down, Bingo, down.'

Tessa loved dogs and the big Labrador was excited to meet someone new.

'Bingo likes you,' said Rob, as they fell into step together, talking mostly about last night's party as they walked the pier.

At the end they got a bench and sat in the sunshine, and Tessa found herself telling Rob about her time in London.

'Rob, last night you mentioned you knew one of the partners in Bridgetown & Murrow, the firm I worked in. Well, I was involved with another of the partners, Grant Armstrong. I met him when I started working there. He was divorced and charming, and I suppose we fell in love. We'd all kinds of plans to marry, but it always seemed not to be the right time. Grant worried that it would upset his teenage kids and that we just needed to wait a bit longer till they were older ... less jealous ... gone to college. Because I loved him, I went along with what he wanted. I kept working, and at weekends we went down to his place in Surrey, and for holidays went to the villa he had in Majorca. I was happy, and if time was passing I didn't really make a big deal of it. Grant had made it clear that he already had his kids, and when we got married he wouldn't want any more!'

'What about what you wanted?' Rob asked, puzzled.

'I suppose what I wanted didn't really come into it!' she admitted, staring out at the waves. 'I loved him, I was happy with him. Then the company opened another office in New York. Grant was involved in setting it up, and was away more frequently for longer and longer stints. I guess our relationship had run its course, because he didn't miss me the way you should miss someone you love. I didn't know what was going on for a while. Office politics: no one likes to tell you these things, but he was seeing one of the junior associates. Pretty little thing! She was involved in the set-up, too. Suddenly he was openly involved with her. They moved in together, and got married about six months before I came back home to Dublin. Louisa had a baby last year ... so the irony is that Grant, despite all his protests, is back to being a family man again. Why I ever listened to him, I don't know,' she said, staring out angrily at the water and the small dinghies flying by. 'How could I have been so stupid?'

'I'm sorry, Tessa. It's awful losing someone you love. But maybe coming back home is a good thing. It gives you time to think, do different things . . .'

'Too much time . . . too many regrets,' Tessa said, patting Bingo.

'Everyone keeps telling you time heals,' he said slowly, 'I'm not sure how much time it takes. It seems an eternity when you are caught up in it . . . when you lose the person you love the most in the world and are left on your own.'

'Tell me about her,' said Tessa softly, and Rob haltingly told her about losing Kate and finding himself alone for the first time since he was nineteen years old.

'I met her the first day I started college. We both signed up to join the debating society. I know people say it's crazy to fall in love with the first stranger you meet, but that was exactly what happened, and Kate was part of my life for every day after that! That is, until last May when she just collapsed while she was shopping and died. They did an autopsy – the report said Kate had some kind of aneurysm in her brain and that nothing could have saved her. It was like a small balloon burst and Kate was gone! Taken from the boys . . . taken from me.'

Tessa could see he was fighting to control his emotions.

'It's been so hard without her. The first few weeks I could hardly get out of bed. The physical ache for her was so painful. I know life has to go on . . . Kate would want that . . . but it is so bloody difficult.'

Tessa automatically found herself reaching for his hand and squeezing it. It was so hard for Rob. Her loss was nothing compared to his.

They both sat in silence for a while as people walked up and down the pier, Bingo barking at one or two dogs; he was bored and wanted to continue his walk. Getting up, they began to stroll back, stopping for a coffee and a bagel on the open-air terrace of the Pavilion. Bingo sat with his head on his paws under the table as they chatted. Tessa was glad she had made the effort to come for the walk with Rob.

'I'd better get going. I don't like leaving Mum on her own for too long,' she explained, standing up. 'Anyway, I'll see you in Alice's on Tuesday.'

'Maybe we can do this again,' he said.

'What?' Did he mean her getting drunk and disgracing herself?

'I mean the walk.' He grinned, laughing. 'I've enjoyed your company.'

'Me too,' she said, surprised by how easy she found Rob to talk to. 'Any time.'

Chapter Thirty-three

'Great film,' teased Joy. 'Husband has an affair, husband and wife break up, husband and mistress break up and husband and wife get back together again! Honestly, as if that is ever going to happen!'

'Never. Agreed,' said Alice. 'Unless you are Jennifer Aniston; it always works out for her on screen.'

They both had ordered frothy cappuccinos in Coffee Heaven, the coffee ⬚shop near the cinema, and were trying to decide about sharing a portion of cheesecake.

'Half the calories!' promised Joy, as they got two forks.

'How is it going with you and Fergus?' quizzed Alice.

'Great. I can't believe that we are still going out, and still loving being with each other. He wants me to go to Italy for a week with him during the summer. Travel around a bit.'

'Are you going to go?'

'Yeah, I guess. Fergus is such a great guy . . . so different from everyone else I ever went out with. It's such a change to have him around. He makes me feel safe and wanted and loved, and besides that, Beth really likes him.'

'So he passed the Beth test?'

'Yeah, with flying colours!'

'Joy, I can't believe it . . . you back in love again.'

'I know . . . because I thought it might never happen again for me, and then Fergus came along and changed my mind. What about you, Alice? What about that nice widower in your class? He sounds perfect!'

'Rob is great. A real old-fashioned gentleman, but he still misses his wife so much. I can't be a stand-in for another woman. I enjoy his company and being with him, and he can be very charming, but there is something holding me back.'

'Is it Liam?'

'I don't know. Maybe! Or maybe it's too soon.'

'For God's sake, Alice, Elaine's got her claws into Liam,' reminded Joy, 'and this is no Jennifer Aniston movie.'

'I know, Joy, don't worry. I have no intention of

287

ever going back in that space. Maybe Rob just isn't right for me. You know, he cooked the most wonderful meal for me in his house, and it was so romantic with candles and music and the two of us on his couch, and then, I don't know why, but I just knew it wasn't right.'

'What did you say to him?'

'I told him it was too soon; too soon for both of us.'

'Poor guy.' Joy laughed.

'Hey, you're supposed to be on my side!'

'OK, OK.'

'But you know, afterwards, when I was back at home, I kept wondering what it was that had stopped me. I think that deep inside I know that even though he's the nicest man ever and we are both on our own it's just too simple, too obvious. Oh, I don't know!'

'Don't tell me you want heartache and heartbreak and drama!'

'No . . . I don't know . . . maybe.'

They were just about to pay their bill when Alice's phone went.

'Hey, it's Conor!' she said, picking up.

'Mum, where were you? I've been trying to phone you for the past few hours.'

'Joy and I went to the cinema and I had my phone off.'

'Sean's been in an accident. He's in hospital.'

'Which one?' Alice asked, feeling a mounting sense of panic.

'He's in the Mater Hospital. Lisa and I are here, and Jenny's on her way from Galway.'

'How bad is it?' she asked.

'Bad. He's in a coma.'

'Oh my God!' she said, feeling like she had been punched in the ribs, trying to think. 'What happened?'

'He was with Dara in the car, and they crashed on the M50. It's pretty bad, Mum,' Conor said, trying to control his own voice.

'I'm driving you straight there,' said Joy. 'This hour of the night there will be hardly any traffic.'

Alice felt numb as she sat in the passenger seat of Joy's car. The drive into the city centre hospital was a flash of traffic lights, street lights, and road signs.

'Sean is going to be OK,' said Joy, mantra-like, over and over again. 'Sean is going to be all right.'

Alice didn't trust herself to speak – to say anything. She closed her eyes, thinking of Sean heading off to college that morning. What T-shirt had he had on? Had he been wearing the new zip-up black Oakley sweatshirt she'd bought him? She couldn't remember. What did he say to her? Did she kiss him? Had she been too busy doing the crossword? He'd had orange juice and toast and hot chocolate for breakfast because she could remember putting the plate and glass and cup in the dishwasher . . . but she couldn't remember what they had said to each other. Where had Dara and he been going?

'Alice, Alice. We're here,' said Joy, parking as close to the large hospital entrance as possible.

Sean was up on the third floor and Alice spotted Conor and Lisa sitting in the corridor straight away.

'Where's Sean?' she asked, breaking down, just wanting to see him, to be able to touch her son, talk to him.

Conor took her in his arms. His face was red and blotchy and she hugged him. He and Sean were such buddies, even though there were almost eight years between them. They were very close. Sean had always looked up to his big brother.

'Mum, he's in the ward across from here, but you need to talk to the doctor on duty first.'

'Well, where is he, then?'

'Come on, and I'll bring you over to the nurses' station.'

* * *

290

'Your son has suffered a significant head injury,' the young doctor explained. 'And he is in a state of coma. We are closely monitoring his condition, and keeping an eye out for any further internal bleeding or swelling of his brain. We have him on a ventilator to help his breathing and protect his airway. Should his condition seriously deteriorate he will be transferred to Beaumont Hospital, which liaises closely with our neurology department, but for the moment he will remain with us. He has a broken collarbone, broken ribs, a broken ankle, a broken nose, and a few other injuries. We will examine him further in the morning to assess his condition.'

'Will he wake up, regain consciousness?' Alice demanded.

'We hope so, but at this stage it is too early to tell. We are just trying to keep him stable and watch for any other changes.'

'Can I see him?'

'Of course, I'll bring you down to him myself.'

Alice held her breath as the doctor opened the door to the intensive care unit, passing her a gown and mask to put on.

'We have some very sick people here,' he explained.

Sean's bed was literally inside the door, and a young Indian nurse was sitting beside his bed. Sean's eyes were shut, his face swollen and bruised like he had been in a prize fight, the ventilator tube attached to his mouth making a strange whooshing sound.

'Is he in pain?' Alice asked, trying to control herself. 'Can he feel it?'

'We have him sedated, so he's pain free,' the doctor reassured her.

She leaned over and kissed Sean. Her poor boy, what had happened to him? She touched his arm and hand, stroking them, wondering if he could sense she was there.

'How is he?' the doctor asked the nurse.

'The same,' said the nurse, passing him a chart.

'This is Sean's mother.'

'Alice Kinsella,' Alice said, introducing herself.

'He's in good hands, Mrs Kinsella, I promise,' said the doctor, excusing himself. 'They need me on the second floor. Nurse Assaf will look after you, and I'm on duty all night.'

'Would you like to sit with him for a few minutes?' offered the nurse, getting up off her bedside stool. 'I'm sure Sean would love to know that you are here.'

Alice sat beside her son. She felt like crying and breaking down, but instead told him about her visit to the cinema with Joy and the film they had seen, and going for coffee after. She held his hand, stroking his palm and fingers and wrist, wanting to feel the pressure of his fingers, a movement, anything. Instead her son seemed to be in a deep, deep sleep, in a place where she could not reach him. Sometimes when Sean was a little baby, she would stand at the side of his cot and watch him slumber, his two arms above his head, his face so peaceful as he slept so deeply, lost to the world and the rest of the household around him.

'Leave him be!' Liam used to tease her. 'You'll wake him.'

It was only when he stirred or drew a breath or moved that she could relax and go back to her own bed, knowing that her baby son was OK.

Now she watched, too, for a sign, a movement to show that he was going to be fine.

A few minutes later she went back outside. Lisa handed her a cup of coffee, and Alice filled them in on what the doctor had said.

'We just have to wait,' said Conor. 'Sean's a tough kid . . . he'll get through this.'

'Have you phoned your dad?' she asked.

'He's in London on business, but will get a flight home first thing in the morning and come straight here. He'd missed the last Aer Lingus one from Heathrow and the Ryanair from Stansted.'

'Poor Liam, I'm sure he's in a right state.' She could imagine how she would feel if the situation had been reversed.

'What about Dara? What's the news on him? Were they brought in here together?'

'Dara's been transferred to St Vincent's Hospital,' said Conor, his eyes welling with tears. 'He's got a ruptured spleen and they think he might need a liver transplant.'

Alice closed her eyes, thinking of the two best friends, always together, praying that the two of them would survive.

Joy refused to go home, and insisted on keeping vigil with them.

'Alice, do you honestly think I'm going to get a wink of sleep all night if I do go home?' she said. 'I'd far prefer to be here with you, instead of worrying about you.'

Alice had to admit she would feel the exact same way if Beth had been in an accident.

There was a small waiting room for families, and they made themselves comfortable there. They took it in turns to check with the nursing staff how Sean was doing. Alice felt such relief when she saw Jenny and Dylan arrive.

'Dylan was great, he just put me in the car and

drove like the clappers to get us here,' Jenny said.

'The new Galway to Dublin Road is so much quicker,' Dylan explained, as Jenny briefly introduced him to Conor, Lisa and Joy.

'Can I see Sean?' she pleaded.

'Come on and we'll ask the nurse,' said Conor.

Jenny was only allowed to stay a few minutes with her brother, and came out in tears.

'He looks so bad. So banged up! What the hell were himself and Dara up to?'

'They were in the new car Dara got for his twenty-first,' explained Conor. 'But look, they didn't do anything wrong. Apparently a truck ahead of them just jackknifed in the rain and went out of control, and came right across their lane. The ambulance men said it was a miracle any of them are alive.'

'Where is the truck driver?' asked Joy.

'The doctor said they were operating on him earlier, but he wouldn't give us any more information.'

Jenny sat curled up on the bench beside Dylan, while Lisa dozed against Conor. Joy sat loyally beside Alice as the staff came in and out and Alice was let in once or twice to check on Sean. The hospital was quiet except for the odd siren as an ambulance arrived into the busy casualty department.

Then the sounds changed as the Friday night shift began to end and the new Saturday daytime staff came on. The tea trolley trundled along with the patients' breakfasts, the cleaning staff came up and down on the lift, and the teams of new junior doctors and trainees waited to start their rounds.

'You go and have some breakfast,' urged Alice. 'I'll stay here.'

Conor took Lisa down to the cafeteria for breakfast, and they brought Alice back a piping hot bacon roll. Joy went down then, to have some breakfast with Jenny and Dylan.

Alice stretched and went off to the nearby bathroom to freshen up a bit. She looked awful. There were grey circles under her eyes, and her mouth and lips were dry. She had aged ten years overnight, and she just prayed that soon there would be good news.

She threw water up in her face, and reapplied her lipstick, and dragged her tiny hairbrush through her hair. She had just emerged from the bathroom when she spotted Liam. He looked equally exhausted, and she knew he hadn't slept a wink either. The two of them automatically put their arms around each other.

'He might die,' she gulped. 'Sean could be brain-damaged, Liam, they just don't know how bad it is or if he'll come out of this!'

'Ssshhhhh,' he murmured, holding her close. 'It's all right, I'm here, Alice. I'm here.'

The new day-shift nurse took them both into intensive care and asked for the registrar to come up to talk to Sean Kinsella's parents.

'The fact that there is no change might seem bad to you,' explained the serious young woman doctor with the glasses. 'But to us it shows that at least Sean is stable. He's had a good night and all his vital signs are fairly normal. Head injuries are slow to heal. They are never quick, as the brain needs time to repair and recover, which is what we all want.'

'Can he hear us?' asked Liam, holding Sean's hand.

'You should assume he can. Talk to him when you are visiting him. It's reassuring for Sean to hear familiar voices around him.'

'Buddy, Dad's here,' said Liam, putting his arm around their youngest son. 'Mum and I are together and Jenny and Conor are here, too. We're all here, all wanting you to get better and wake up and talk to us.'

'I'm around all day, Mr and Mrs Kinsella, if you need me. My boss Professor Murray will be around to see Sean later.'

'Thank you, Doctor Collins,' said Alice, reading the young doctor's name badge.

297

They sat with Sean for a while and then went back to the waiting room, Jenny flinging herself into Liam's arms.

'Oh, Dad, thank God you're here!' she said, breaking down. 'Sean would want you to be here.'

'It's OK, Jenny. I'm not going anywhere,' Liam promised.

She introduced him to Dylan, and Alice had to suppress a smile, as even in the circumstances they were in she could see Liam trying to make an assessment of the tall gangly young student that his daughter was dating.

'Nice to meet you, Mr Kinsella,' said Dylan politely. 'I've heard a lot about you.'

At least Jenny had the good grace to blush, thought Alice. God knows what she had told Dylan about her father's love affair.

Lisa hugged Liam, too, and Alice could see she was relieved that Conor's dad hadn't let them down.

'Thanks for coming,' said Conor quietly.

'As if I wouldn't come immediately to see my own boy!' Liam protested. 'I came as fast as I bloody well could, Conor, you know that . . . don't you?'

'Yeah, Dad, I know you did,' said Conor, standing up and putting his arms around his father.

'It's OK, Conor,' said Liam huskily, patting his shoulders.

Joy disappeared off to get coffee for everyone.

'Alice, I think I'll head home now. Unless you need me to stay?' she said as she passed around the plastic cups of coffee.

'Joy, thanks for being so good – for bringing me here and staying all night. You must be wrecked.'

'Nothing a few hours in my own bed won't cure!' Joy insisted. 'If there is any news about Sean will you let me know? I'll come back in if you need me.'

'Go home and get some sleep,' ordered Alice. 'And I promise if there is any change I'll be in touch.'

It was mid-morning before the consultant came to see Sean. He talked to Liam and Alice afterwards.

'I'm sorry, but there is no change . . . so we are just going to have to play a waiting game for the moment, and see what happens with your son.'

'Will he get better?' asked Liam.

'I cannot guarantee that,' Professor Murray said cautiously. 'But I would be hopeful. In these kinds of cases young men will often take days to regain proper consciousness. We all just have to be patient and to take care of his other obvious injuries. He's had a major shock, and his body and brain need time to adjust.'

'What about the ventilator? When will he be able to come off that?' asked Alice.

'That's a tricky one. We could try taking him off it now, and hopefully he might do OK, but what I don't want is for your son to get distressed and us to have to put him back on it. I know it looks awful and uncomfortable, but Sean is not aware of it. We have him sedated so that he is not in pain. Doctor Collins and the team are here to look after Sean, and I know it is an awful time for the family, but everyone is doing their very best for your son.'

'Thank you, Professor Murray,' said Liam, shaking his hand. 'We know that, and we really appreciate it.'

Back in the waiting room, Alice felt like a wet rag. No one could tell them what was going to happen.

'Mum, why don't you go home for a bit?' suggested Conor. 'You look exhausted.'

'We all do!' she admitted. 'But, Conor, I'd prefer you and Lisa and Jenny and Dylan to go home now and your dad and I will keep watch here. Then when you've had a rest you can come back in later.'

'Anyway, your mum and I would like a bit of time together here,' insisted Liam, taking Alice's hand.

Chapter Thirty-four

The next few days were a blur to Alice as they all took turns staying in the Mater Hospital to be near Sean, watching and hoping for some sign of recovery.

Liam, to give him credit, rarely left their son's bedside. None of them could face the prospect of something happening to Sean. When they were beside him they talked about all his favourite things: music, pizza, rugby, his friends, Lizzy Nolan, his first girlfriend, himself getting expelled from Irish college for speaking in English, himself going to Paris for two months to learn French, his computer and all his games ... anything that might bring him back to them. As the hours and days passed Alice tried to stay positive, and believe that Sean would come back. The neurology team were regularly checking Sean and ensuring that he was getting adequate fluids and nutrition intravenously and maintaining a good circulation.

Having Jenny and Dylan staying for a few days was great, and she could see the strong bond that had developed between her daughter and her boyfriend. Conor and Lisa had been wonderful, too, and were bending over backwards to help and support her. Her dad and her brother Tim and his wife Patsy, Liam's family and Sean's close friend Becky had all visited the hospital and stayed constantly in touch; even Elaine had come discreetly with Liam to visit Sean at a time when Alice was not around. All her friends were praying for him and sending messages and texts. Jack and Molly Cassidy next door had even volunteered to take over minding the dog.

She had called over to Catherine O'Loughlin to ask about Dara. 'We're waiting, too . . . waiting to see about his liver. They say he may need a liver transplant,' Catherine said, breaking down in the kitchen. 'He keeps asking about Sean, wanting to see him. We told him Sean can't walk, and is too sick to come and see him. Dara looks awful: he has a collapsed lung and they had to remove his spleen, and he's in a lot of pain. His liver was badly lacerated and torn. I just can't believe the two of them . . . they always did things together . . . even being in a bloody accident!'

'Will you let me know, Catherine, if there is any news?'

'Of course,' said Catherine. 'Please God, the two of them will recover and get up to their old antics.'

It was early on Sunday morning and Alice was at home asleep in bed when Conor phoned her with the good news that the doctors felt that Sean's coma was easing, and that he was beginning to show some reactions.

Alice got dressed immediately, and she and Jenny went to the hospital.

'On the Glasgow Coma Scale he is showing more responses,' explained the doctor on duty. 'He opened his eyes when the nurse called him loudly. She had noticed he seemed to be reacting when she was changing the dressings on the cuts on his knee, so she tested him. It is a small sign but it is a good one.'

Alice and Liam tried not to get too excited about it, but felt like they had been given a present. Within twenty-four hours Sean was opening his eyes for a few minutes at a time, and seemed to be trying to pull at his IV drip.

On Monday Professor Murray told them Sean's coma was definitely lifting.

'We will be monitoring him very carefully,' he

explained, 'but my hope is that by the end of the week Sean may be out of intensive care. A lot will depend on his respiration, though.'

Alice cancelled the Tuesday night class, and got get-well messages for Sean from everyone in the class.

'We're all still going to meet up, so we're going to the pub in Monkstown,' Lucy texted her, 'and we'll all be thinking of Sean.'

They really were such a great group of people!

On Wednesday night Sean tried to talk. He was agitated and moving, trying to ask about Dara.

'It's all right,' Liam assured him. 'Dara is all right.'

Professor Murray and Doctor Collins both came to the unit to examine Sean, and the next time Alice saw him he had been taken off the respirator.

'What will happen if he stops breathing?' she said, concerned, frightened now if he wasn't on the machine.

'Well, we'll know all about it because the alarm will sound,' explained Doctor Collins, 'and then we will have to reconnect him to it. But let's hope that won't happen!'

Twenty-four hours later Sean had been moved out of the intensive care unit and into a small four-bedded room beside the nurses' station.

'We want to be able to keep a good eye on him,' the staff nurse explained.

He sounded hoarse, and sometimes a bit like he was drunk, but Sean was finally out of his coma and able to see his family around him and – with difficulty – talk a little.

'I can't believe it,' cried Alice. 'We got him back!'

'Take things easy and slow with him,' advised Doctor Collins, 'but you should see a difference every day.'

Alice was content to sit by Sean's bed and simply hold his hand. He was getting better. They had been given a second chance.

Chapter Thirty-five

Kitty changed quickly, pulling on her good camel-coloured trousers, a white top, and her new red cardigan. Checking her hair, she put on a little make-up. She was knackered tired after minding her little grandson Danny all day, but going out to meet Rob, Tessa, Lucy and the rest of 'the class' was probably just what she needed.

Clodagh had been delayed at work so Kitty had given two-year-old Danny some of the egg, sausage and chips they were having for his tea before he was collected.

'Bye, Nana,' he called, getting into the car.

'Bye, pet!'

'Are you not going out to your cookery class tonight?' Larry had asked, disappointed, when he surveyed the fried egg, sausage and chips on his plate. He was getting used to the fancy fare she cooked on a Tuesday night, and the past few weeks had waited to eat until she came home from her cookery class. They had enjoyed some delicious meals: lamb, beef, fish, tarts, pies and cakes. The last few weeks Larry had even opened a bottle of wine as they sat in the kitchen, and complimented her on the food and chatted just like the old days when they had first got married.

When they were younger she remembered she used to cook all kinds of things! Larry's stomach would be rumbling with hunger for all the lovely dishes she'd serve up. Back then, she had tested out recipes from the big cookbook she got for a wedding present, and from magazines. Then, of course, the kids had come along, and it was all about what they wanted: burgers and chips, spaghetti, lasagne, stew, roast chicken, fish fingers and bloody mince. Plain food. She had just gone along with it, the only treat being the big Sunday roast with all the trimmings that she still cooked.

'There's no class on today,' she had explained. 'Alice's youngest boy was in a car accident and is in a coma. We've all been praying for him. It's awful for poor Alice and her family. Sean's a nice boy, I met him a few times, so tonight we're all still meeting up and going to the pub in Monkstown for a drink instead of having our class.'

'Oh, I'm sorry to hear that! I hope the young lad gets better.'

'So do we all! Anyway, I'd better get going. We're just going to have a drink or two.'

'Listen, Kitty, do you want me to drive you? That way you can have all the vodka you want and not worry about drink-driving.'

'Are you sure?' she had asked, gobsmacked. Despite all her pleading, Larry had point-blank refused to come to the party a few weeks ago, and yet now here he was offering to bring her!

'Yes, and I'll come back and get you when you're finished. Just give me about fifteen minutes' warning.'

The others were all sitting near the back of the pub and Lucy, whose mum, Nina, was a friend of Alice's, was able to update them on Sean's progress.

'At least he's stable and the doctors are pleased with him,' said Kitty, who didn't know what Larry and herself would have done if any of their brood had been badly injured like that.

Rob had gone up to the bar and got the order in for everyone.

Gemma and Paul were still delighted at the success

of their party, and couldn't believe how many people had turned up.

'Maybe we'll have a barbecue later in the summer!'

'Count us in,' called Leah and Rachel.

Lucy had got a 'Get Well' card for Sean, and a 'Thinking of You' one for Alice, and they all signed them, also putting in some money to buy some flowers for Alice.

'I'll buy some really nice ones and drop them around when she's home,' promised Lucy.

'Everything OK, Kerrie?' Kitty asked. She couldn't put her finger on it, but there was something up with that young one. She could always tell with her own girls, and something about Kerrie's strained face and tense, thin body told her that all was not well with the young bride-to-be. 'How are the wedding plans coming?' she asked gently.

'We're still on track for September in France,' Kerrie said. 'There's just a few of us flying over, but it will be lovely. Who wants a big wedding these days? The restaurant we are using has a Michelin star, and the food there is just wonderful. They're doing a very special menu for us.'

Kitty thought of her own girls' weddings, the big family parties they'd been, and felt sorry for the poor little thing. Food and menus were the last things people remembered about weddings, but she couldn't very well tell Kerrie that.

Sometimes at home she got out the DVD of Clodagh's wedding, or Niamh's and Shane's, and put them on in the machine, and just sat down and cried and laughed for the hour or so at the special days that were there. There was her dad on film, Lord be good to him, waving as he went into the church the day of Clodagh's wedding, chatting to everyone, messing and playing to the camera. He'd died about six months later of bowel cancer. There was Auntie Rose and her cousin Gerald, all gone now, but still there for them all to see in their finery on film. Clodagh was all-out pregnant with Danny at Niamh's wedding, squashed into her bridesmaid dress. Danny always laughed when Kitty told him that he'd been in Mammy's tummy at Auntie Niamh's wedding. She even noticed how well Sheila had looked then, in that gorgeous fuchsia-pink outfit. Sheila and herself doing a little dance and drinking champagne . . . Sheila well and healthy and happy then, only months before they found the lump that was killing her now.

'We want our wedding to be perfect, simple and a bit sophisticated and low-key, the kind of event that Matt and I prefer,' confided Kerrie. 'We're not into crowds or fuss or any of that kind of thing! So that's why we've chosen to have it in France, with just a few people there.'

'Every bride must have the kind of wedding they want! It's yours and Matt's day after all,' encouraged Kitty. 'Anyway, I'm sure that you and your mum and sisters must be having a lovely time organizing it all, just as I had with my girls.'

'Yes, of course.'

'And we'll all be dying to see the photographs!' joked Kitty as she ordered another glass of vodka and orange and joined in the chat with Rachel and the rest of them.

'It was so embarrassing!' laughed Rachel. 'There's me going to a cookery school and asking all Pete's family over for dinner to celebrate his mam and dad's anniversary, and going to show off and do that lovely stuffed fillet of pork Alice taught us, and the gratin potatoes. I followed everything step by step exactly. There I was, the table set, candles and everything ready, and Pete topping everyone up with champagne, when I realized that there was something missing. You know in Alice's you always get that lovely smell when we're all cooking? I suddenly realized that there was not a whiff of a cooking smell! Nothing! I was mortified. Everyone starving and waiting to eat, and I had forgotten to put on the stupid oven!'

'What did you do?' Lucy laughed.

'What could I do? Put the oven on pronto . . . but it took ages. Pete's mam and dad and everyone got so tipsy! The food turned out great, but Pete's dad was absolutely bunched, and fell asleep at the table and snored his head off!'

Everyone began to swap stories of dishes they had tried, and what a success they had been!

Kitty hadn't realized the time, and was about to text Larry to come and collect her when she spotted him coming through the bar. She couldn't believe it!

Larry had put on his new wine jumper, the one that Shane had given him for Christmas.

'Over here!' Kitty called to her husband.

She introduced him to everyone, and Emmet made space for him to sit down.

'Will you have one for the road?' Larry asked her, going up to buy her a vodka and getting himself a red lemonade and ice. Kitty couldn't believe that Larry was making such an effort! Had Sky TV broken? Had every sports event in the world been cancelled? She watched in disbelief as Larry chatted away, real friendly, and told everyone just how much he missed his regular Tuesday-night dish!

'I have to give it to my Kitty, she's a fine cook!'

Chapter Thirty-six

Kerrie O'Neill glanced quickly at her screen, seeing how well Fintan Sweeney's portfolio was doing. Today shares in Eire Air were up, as they were about to announce a merger with the major supplier of wind-energy platforms in Kerry. Fintan Sweeney, one of her major clients, was already in, but a further investment if there was a closing dip would be worth it as it was a company he'd expressed an interest in.

She checked the latest share prices and decided to hold steady for the next few hours. Running over the numbers on Global ITI she saw it had lost another 0.5 per cent market share to rivals, and she knew her boss Sven Johnnson would not be happy. She needed to find out what the hell was going on over there. She grabbed her latte . . . it was cold. She needed another one! She looked around to see if any of the interns were around, and spotted Eva Macken busy checking the screen.

'Eva,' she mouthed and held up her cup. The twenty-two- year-old finance student copped on immediately, and disappeared to the canteen to get her a fresh one. She smiled. Eva reminded her a bit of herself when she had joined Barrington Holdings, bright and intelligent and too eager for her own good. Kerrie had started at the company six years ago, one of an elite group of ten finance graduates hand-picked by Sven for a demanding career as an investment manager in one of Ireland's top asset-management companies. Kerrie O'Neill mightn't have had the same pedigree and background as some of her more wealthy colleagues, but she was the one who had graduated top of her Master's class in UCD.

'It is a dog-eat-dog world out there,' Sven had told her when he'd hired her. 'And I suspect that you are, like me, a mongrel who will rise to the top.'

'Here's your latte,' announced Eva, putting the paper cup carefully on her desk.

'Thanks!' Kerrie said, making a mental note to try to give Eva something more interesting to do over the next few days.

Today, Kerrie had back-to-back meetings with Sven and the senior managers about services they should be offering to their loyal customers, who trusted them with their investment portfolios and ways to promote them.

She was sipping her coffee when Matt phoned.

'Kerrie, are you coming straight home from work tonight?' he asked.

'Yeah. Why?'

'Mum and Dad phoned, and they are in Dublin! They want to meet me and are coming over to the apartment to have dinner with us. They were meant to stay at Georgina's tonight, but the kids are sick with a vomiting bug, so I said that they could stay with us, if that's OK?'

'Have dinner and stay with us tonight?' Kerrie repeated, appalled. She couldn't imagine anything worse than having Maureen and Dermot landed on them. It certainly wasn't OK. His parents were hard-going at the best of times, but to have them staying in the apartment!

'Why do they have to stay with us, Matt?' she quizzed. 'Can't they book into a hotel?'

'I'm not having my folks go to a hotel when we have loads of room,' he said stubbornly.

'Then why don't we all just go to some nice restaurant, eat out?' she suggested, trying to keep her voice level. 'I'll book a table.'

'No, don't,' said Matt. 'Apparently, Dad really needs to talk to me about something, so he asked if we could just stay in. I thought maybe you could cook for the four of us.'

'OK,' said Kerrie, trying to hide her dismay, and wondering what the hell was going on with his parents.

'Listen, I'm going to be stuck here for a while, so maybe you could stop off in Superquinn and get some food, and I'll see you at home later . . . thanks,' Matt said, putting down the phone.

Kerrie's first thought was that she could stop at Polly's Pantry on the way home and pick up something to heat up, but then she realized that it was far too risky: Maureen Hennessy would be snooping around her kitchen, and might discover what she had done. No, she'd just have to cook something. Taking out her iPhone she searched for her Cookery School recipe folder and opened it. There must be something there that she had made with Alice that she could manage to cook again.

She stopped off in the supermarket on the way home, piling her groceries into the back of her car. Hopefully she hadn't forgotten anything.

The apartment was spotless, so at least she didn't have to worry about that, she thought, as she began to prepare the meal.

Think what Alice would make, she had told herself, and had opted to begin with Maryland crab cakes. The combination of breadcrumbs with crabmeat, spices and egg was simple enough to do, and the cakes looked perfect as she popped them in the fridge to chill. Medallions of pork with a cider sauce was something she should be able to manage, and when she had made it in class a few weeks ago it had turned out way better than she had expected it to. She was serving mash with it: unlike her previous disaster, this time it had a perfect creamy consistency. For dessert she was really keeping it simple, and had opted for the easy apricot crumble they'd made a few weeks back, mixing the flour, brown sugar and oats together before adding the butter to make the crumble topping, and sprinkling it over the halved apricots in the ovenproof dish.

With everything in the kitchen fairly well organized, she changed quickly and freshened up, hoping that Matt would at least get home before his parents arrived.

Maureen and Dermot were looking around the apartment when Matt appeared. They had put their overnight bags in the spare double bedroom, which was decorated in teal, white and red, with a series of Japanese prints on the wall behind the bed. Kerrie gave them extra pillows and left the grey wool throw along the bottom of the bed in case they felt cold during the night.

'I see you two have gone for that modern minimalist look everywhere,' remarked Maureen, as she wandered around the apartment.

'I don't like clutter,' admitted Kerrie, 'and I prefer clean lines.'

'Kerrie's a bit of a perfectionist,' teased Matt, arriving in and greeting his mother.

'Well, that's quite obvious,' Maureen said, inspecting their bedroom and hot press and bathroom.

'Well, I like it, and I think you've got yourselves a fine-sized property in a really good location,' remarked Dermot, standing out on their large balcony and surveying their surroundings.

'Matt, get your mum and dad a drink, I'm going to start cooking dinner.'

Kerrie was glad to escape to the kitchen and let Matt deal with them. It was a Thursday night, they both had to work in the morning, and what the hell were the Hennessys up to, landing themselves on them like this?

She tried to remain composed as she cooked. Nothing was burning! Nothing was falling apart! Nothing was exploding or disintegrating before her eyes! She couldn't believe it as she placed

318

the perfect golden crab cakes on a small bed of mixed leaves with a little dill and mayonnaise dressing and called the others to the table.

The table, with its expensive tableware and beautiful Louise Kennedy designed glasses looked great, and they had an amazing view from the ceiling-to-floor glass windows out over the redeveloped docks area, which now housed the Grand Canal Theatre and the impressive Grand Canal Square, with its long red rods of light illuminating the place.

'Well, that's some scene!' said Dermot. 'You could be in the likes of New York or London, instead of here, in the heart of the old abandoned docklands. It's such a transformation!'

Matt helped Kerrie serve the pork medallions, and as she passed Maureen some of the spring-onion mash Kerrie could see she was impressed.

'I hadn't realized that you were such a good cook!' Maureen said.

'I'm getting there.' Kerrie laughed. She was so relieved that it was going OK.

The crumble went down a treat, and Kerrie was finally able to relax as Matt made coffee for everyone. The talk at the table had been a bit strained, and

Kerrie wondered what was going on to bring the Hennessys to their apartment for the first time.

'Mum, Dad, is everything OK?' asked Matt, who was naturally worried.

Kerrie could see the anxious expression that flashed between Maureen and Dermot.

Dermot looked awkward as he played with the remnants of his crumble.

'Your dad is in a bit of trouble,' said Maureen slowly.

'Dad?' Matt asked, alarmed. 'Are you sick or something?'

'He's not sick,' interjected his mother. 'But he's in a bit of financial bother . . . we thought you might be able to help him, give him some advice about what we should do.'

Kerrie couldn't believe it: Dermot Hennessy in financial difficulty! The Hennessys were wealthy, they had money and property and investments. How could they be in trouble?

'What's happened, Dad?' asked Matt firmly, staring straight at his father. 'What the hell has been going on?'

Kerrie looked at the defeated expression on Matt's father's face, and felt sorry for him.

'Have Gerard and Alan Mullen got anything to do with this?' Matt asked.

'Your father and Gerard have a partnership,' added Maureen. 'You know that, Matt!'

'Dad, I know that you and Gerard have been involved in a few deals over the last few years, but Gerard surely has had no involvement in the rest of your business or in grandfather's company?'

'Dermot, for God's sake will you stop trying to protect Gerard, and worry about yourself, and tell Matt all that has happened and about the bank,' snapped Maureen angrily.

'What's happened with the bank? Dad, what's happened?'

'They've closed us down, refused any credit and are seeking immediate repayment of loans.' Dermot sighed heavily. 'But there is no way of repaying them at the moment.'

'So what are they looking for?'

'To raise capital to buy some of our investment sites I used my own property as collateral. We were building a big portfolio and investing, and we expected in the long term to see healthy growth and profit.'

'Like half the country,' said Matt flatly. 'I presume most of the stuff is worth nothing now.'

'I took a punt! And I lost . . . lost big time,' said Dermot despondently. 'So now they are going after my assets.'

'Can you believe your father, gambling like that?' interjected Maureen. 'People like us have a position to keep . . . an expectation . . . a standard. If your father has jeopardized our standard of living . . . our way of life, put that at risk, I will never forgive him. What if he's ruined us?'

'We are not ruined, Maureen . . . well, not yet. Don't talk like that. This will get sorted out . . . I promise.'

Kerrie felt awful for Dermot, but could understand Maureen's worries.

'Matt, I've brought everything along: all my paperwork, contracts, documents. I have a meeting with the bank tomorrow afternoon in the head office, and I wondered was there any chance you could come along to the meeting with me? You know the jargon, how to deal with these people!'

Poor Matt, thought Kerrie, being dragged into this.

'Dad, why didn't you say something about this earlier? Warn me what was going on?' Matt said sharply. 'I'll have to try and cancel a load of meetings I had tomorrow. I need to see and to read everything. And try to understand what the hell you've done to get yourself into such trouble.'

Kerrie could see Matt was angry with his father. He disappeared for a second, and came back with his calculator and a pad of paper and some pens. 'Come on, let's clear the table! Then we can spread out all the documents and paperwork you've brought along and see what you've got. I need to try and put this thing together. Have you spoken to a lawyer?'

'Just Barney Kerrigan . . . he drew up some of the documents, and looked over most of the agreements for me and for Gerard.'

Matt put his head in his hands . . . Barney was one of those cute hoor local solicitors who had a hand in every deal going in the locality.

Kerrie filled the dishwasher and packed away the place mats.

'Maureen, why don't the two of us go in the living room and give them a chance to look over things?' she suggested. 'I'll make a fresh pot of coffee.'

Maureen looked tired, and spent the next hour complaining to Kerrie about Dermot.

'We have a social standing, Kerrie, dear. You've seen where we live, you understand how much we have to lose if Dermot doesn't sort this out properly. We owe some money, but surely the bank can be reasonable with people like ourselves. I mean, if this bank thing gets any worse, how would I show my head in the golf club?'

Kerrie tried to mask her own annoyance and irritation.

'I knew you'd understand, dear ... you can imagine how your own parents would feel if they were faced with the indignity of this ultimatum by the bank.'

Kerrie thought of her mam and dad, who had scrimped and scraped all their lives and only had a tiny savings account. They had never borrowed money, and if they couldn't afford something had simply done without it. Holidays, clothes, treats, cars, house repairs and redecoration had all been put off until they had saved enough. Her father was terrified of running into debt.

'How's Georgina?' she asked, hoping to change the subject.

'Georgina is fine, but far too wrapped up in those children. She will have them spoilt. I've warned her, but of course she won't listen.'

Kerrie tried not to get angry, and to stay calm as Maureen then began to give out about Ed, Matt's older brother, and his lack of ambition or drive. Ed Hennessy had struck Kerrie as a bit of a waster who assumed that family money would keep him going as he dabbled in property and ran some kind of management agency which tried to fundraise for various business schemes. He wasn't a patch on Matt and everyone knew it.

'He just wants to be out drinking and having fun

with these so-called friends of his,' Maureen complained. 'Heaven knows where it will end. And as for some of the girls he's dated! They are certainly not what Dermot and I would expect.'

'I'm sure that Ed will settle down when he is good and ready,' Kerrie said.

Maureen was tired, her face pale and strained. Kerrie was relieved when a while later she said goodnight to them all and disappeared to bed.

Matt and his dad were still engrossed in paperwork and documents.

'You OK?' Kerrie asked, making them some more coffee and giving them some cheese and crackers. She was ready to hit the bed herself.

'Sit down and look at these,' Matt said grimly, indicating some of the documents and his notes spread all over the table.

Dermot looked surprised.

'Dad, it's OK. Kerrie probably has a better financial brain than I have, and it's good to get another eye on the problem.'

An hour later Kerrie couldn't believe how foolhardy her father-in-law-to-be had been! It was like he had been putting bets on horses running in the Curragh Races, but instead he had gambled heavily on property and invested far too much in some high-risk retail and hotel schemes. His accumulated debts now were massive, and she doubted he had anything like the necessary funds to service them. Grabbing Matt's calculator she began to do her own rough calculation of his debts.

The Hennessys' villa in Marbella would definitely have to go, their summer place in Connemara and, she suspected, Moyle House would also need to be sold off if Dermot was to have any chance of showing the banks he was making an effort at least to service his debts.

Leaving Matt to be the one to explain this to his dad, Kerrie crawled into bed. She had an early-morning meeting in the office, and wouldn't get to see Dermot and Maureen before she left.

Chapter Thirty-seven

Alice looked over at her class. All were in their striped aprons tonight, eager and ready to learn to cook. They had been so supportive to her since Sean's accident, and it was such a huge relief to her that if all went well then Sean was on track to return home next week. She couldn't wait to have him back here with her.

'Before we begin, I would like to thank you all for your amazing support over the past few weeks. It has been a difficult time for all of my family, but your messages and texts and lovely flowers and cards were all very much appreciated. Thank you for bearing with me.' They all gave her a clap, and Alice had to restrain herself from going and hugging each and every one of them.

'I hope that you have all been doing a bit of practising in the meantime!'

'I made a brilliant dinner for my boyfriend.' Lucy grinned.

'I had a dinner party for six, and the sea bass turned out amazingly well,' added Emmet. 'I impressed them all with it.'

'I managed to cook dinner for my mother-in-law, who is cordon bleu trained, and nothing disastrous happened.' Kerrie beamed. 'In fact, Alice, everything turned out perfectly. I still can't believe it!'

'I'm glad to hear it!' Alice laughed, delighted. 'And hopefully tonight's dishes will also turn out equally perfect. We are starting with monkfish with a salsa and stuffed red peppers, followed by a French favourite of mine, a delicious cherry tart, for dessert.

'Now, let's get started,' she said as she showed them how to prepare the sweet pastry tart and bake it blind before filling it with the frangipane and topping with the pitted and halved cherries, then baking again before serving. The monkfish was easy and she showed them how simple it was to poach it and then serve it with the salsa and the stuffed peppers.

As they all got on with their preparation and cooking she had to admit to a feeling of achievement at the level of calm and confidence that now permeated her cookery class. Most nerves had disappeared by now, and each member of the group was doing their very best to achieve perfection in serving food that was both enticing and tasty. How would her next group fare? she wondered. She had another ten people beginning next week!

After class Rob, Paul and Gemma sat around eating, and she joined them. She opened a bottle of red wine and they chatted easily as they finished off the evening's meal. All were in raptures about the cherry tart. Usually she would have had Sean and Dara here, so it was good to have some company.

'Alice, are you free next week to come to the cinema or for a drink with me?' Rob asked as he got ready to leave. 'You know I've missed our outings.'

She had been so tied up with hospital visits she'd had no time to see anyone for weeks, but with Sean home in a few days, and her new class starting, she really wouldn't have time for cinema trips. Sean would need her at home, and that's where she planned to be.

'I'm sorry, Rob,' she said, explaining about Sean. 'He's going to need to have his mum around for a while, and to tell the truth I'd be too nervous to leave him.'

She could see the disappointment on Rob's face, but it was only fair to let him know where her priorities lay for the moment, and not to lead him to expect any more from her.

Chapter Thirty-eight

Bringing Sean home from hospital was overwhelming, and when her son gave a whoop of excitement as he crossed over the threshold of their home, Alice almost collapsed in tears herself.

A few weeks ago his life had hung by a thread, and now he was back in Martello Avenue, safe and sound with her; back to his bedroom and the routine at home. He would miss the rest of this year's college term and doing his second-year exams, but the college had already agreed he could repeat the year next year. For the moment he had to concentrate on getting well and getting back to normal gradually. He would join a programme out in the National Rehabilitation Hospital, which was fortunately near them, and had been told to take things slowly until he began to feel better.

Jenny had come from Galway, and Conor and Lisa and even Liam were all there for his homecoming, and she had to act like a sentry on duty as so many of his friends wanted to see him and talk to him. She had to limit his visitors – even Becky, who clearly was very close to her son and cared about him – but she had to make sure that Sean didn't tire himself out trying to do too much. The doctor had advised him to avoid using the computer for a while and not to go on Facebook or email, as his brain still needed to rest. Even reading a page of a newspaper or book exhausted him!

Seeing him lying on the couch playing with Lexy she gave a silent prayer of thanks for his recovery.

Liam called frequently, and she tried to let him and Sean have time on their own together. Sean needed his dad, and that was obvious.

One evening when Sean had gone to bed early after having too many old school friends call to him, Liam came down to the kitchen and she made coffee and reheated some of the chicken casserole she'd made for dinner earlier for him. It felt strange having him back in the house . . . a weird sense of déjà vu.

'Alice, I'm glad we're on our own, as I need to talk to you,' he said seriously.

She immediately felt her hackles rise, on guard for whatever he was about to throw at her.

'I wanted to apologize for being such a shit over the past two years,' he said slowly, 'apologize for being such a bastard to you. I guess going through all this with Sean has made me realize how much my kids and you mean to me, and how I just took it all – my family – for granted. I can't turn the clock back, but I promise to try to do better by you and the kids.'

She didn't trust herself to look at him. He had hurt her so badly, but now she was beginning to live without him. He was no longer a pivotal part of her life. He was the father of her children, her ex-husband, ex-lover, but she had learned the very hard way to survive and manage without him.

'It's been so tough without you, Liam, but I have learned how to live my own life now,' she said firmly.

'I know that.' Liam looked somewhat ashamed. 'I see you now, and you've changed. You have your cookery school, and your friends and a busy life. You've got on with your life!'

'What did you want me to do?' she said bitterly. 'Cry over you for ever?'

'No!'

'I've had to stand on my own two feet. I needed money and am doing my best to be financially independent of you or anyone else.'

'I admire you for what you have done, Alice, believe me!' he said. 'I just wanted to let you know that I've talked to my solicitor and have organized that the house will be totally transferred into your name.'

'Why?' she asked, immediately suspicious of his so-called generosity.

'We both paid for the house,' he explained. 'But you and I know that it was really your inheritance from Betty that paid off most of the mortgage and transformed it. It was all your money that you put into this place. So I guess for the sake of fairness it should be yours. The kids might be grown-up, but they still need a home to come to. It's also become your place to earn some income. I may be a right shit, but after all we've gone through in the past few weeks I can't take that away from you.'

Alice held her breath. She couldn't believe it. She had been expecting a battle with him over the house, and now he was prepared to cede it to her.

'Liam, thank you,' she said, taking a deep calming breath.

'The office and the apartment in Ballsbridge are, however, still in both our names,' he said, 'and I need you to agree to them being transferred into mine alone.'

'Oh,' she said, surprised. 'Why?'

'I want to offload at least one of them, even if the market is poor. A lot of my work is now on contracts with Johnny Leonard in the UK, and I am back and forward there a lot. I don't need a big office with all the overheads here in Dublin any more. Something smaller will do.'

She had never had any interest in the apartment he'd bought as an investment about ten years ago, and as for the office, it had always been his as far as she was concerned. He could have it!

'Whatever you want, Liam. If we need to sign papers and go to solicitors to set it up, just go ahead and organize it.'

'Thanks.'

She could see the gratitude on his face.

'Well, it looks like we are both getting on with our lives.'

She smiled half-heartedly.

'I'll be in the UK more and more, Alice, but you know I'll be here if you or the kids need me. I'm just a phone call away.'

'I know,' she said, actually believing him. 'What does Elaine think of you being away so much?'

'She understands I have to go where the work is. She's even talking about moving over herself, as her brother Tony has a wine bar in Putney and is thinking about expanding.'

She looked at Liam. Was he going to give the money to Elaine? But actually, she thought, it was none of her business what they did or didn't do any more.

'Well, I hope whatever happens, Liam, it all works out for you,' she said, realizing that she genuinely meant it. Liam was no longer hers. As her husband he was so much a part of her past but she accepted the fact that he would have very little to do with her future.

'Look, I'd better go,' he said, standing up. 'I said I'd collect Elaine after work.'

They hugged each other awkwardly at the front door.

'I'll be in touch about the legal stuff, Alice,' he said, walking out to the car.

It occurred to Alice, as she watched her husband sit into his car and drive away that, for the first time in over two years, she was no longer angry with him, and that another part of her life with him was finally over.

Chapter Thirty-nine

Tessa checked the dining room. It was strange to see her mother's old dining room in use again. She'd polished the table and set it with her mother's good Waterford crystal glasses and Wedgwood dinner service. She'd picked pink and mauve peonies from the back garden, and they made a pretty display in vases on the table and sideboard. She'd polished the silver and cleaned the big mirror over the sideboard, and with the light from the large bay window the room seemed brighter and airier, especially with all her mother's old boxes, that used to be stored under the sideboard, banished to the garage. The room was ready, she thought, as she placed some candles on the table.

Florence Sullivan had gone to the hairdresser's for a wash and a blow-dry and had tried on about three outfits before settling on a pretty turquoise two-piece to wear for tonight's dinner party. Tessa's mother was almost as excited about Tessa having a few friends to dinner as she was.

'Mum, they are just some of the group from my cookery class!' Tessa had reminded her. 'It's no big deal.'

In London she had regularly entertained her friends and had people in. It was one of the things she had missed most since moving home. She'd mentioned it to Emmet one night and been surprised when he suggested that if so, it was high time she invited some of her new friends over to her home. She'd agonized over it, but had eventually asked Emmet and his friend Steven, Paul and Gemma, and Kitty and Rob. She'd also been surprised when Kitty had asked if she could bring her husband along.

'Larry's not a great one for going out, but I think that he might come along if he knew it was just the class crowd.'

Tessa opted to cook something a little fancy, and she hoped that she could pull it off, given that she was using a pretty antiquated gas oven. She had cooked a large leg of spring Wicklow lamb with garlic potatoes and spring greens. For starters there was a creamy salmon mousse, and she had made a sticky pecan toffee tart for dessert.

She had changed into a simple pale-blue shift dress that she hadn't worn since returning home, with a pair of nude slingbacks.

It was no surprise that Rob was first, as he had promised to bring along some good wines for the night. He had also brought a gorgeous bouquet of flowers, which she put in the big glass vase in the hall.

'They're lovely, Rob,' she said, hugging him, as she brought him into the sitting room where Florence was in her favourite chair.

Rob had already met her mother, as they had got into the habit of going for weekly walks, and once or twice when he'd collected Tessa he'd come in and had a bit of a chat with Florence.

'You're looking very stylish tonight, Florence,' he complimented, as Tessa sliced some lemon and fixed three glasses of gin and tonic.

It was a lovely bright evening, and Tessa opened the French doors out to the garden. She'd mowed the grass the previous day and strimmed all around the edges of the flower beds. The big lilac tree was in full bloom, and some of the roses were already out. She'd always loved this room, with its sunny aspect, comfortable chintz-covered couches and polished wood bookshelves.

A few minutes later everyone seemed to arrive at the

same time, and she got caught up introducing them to her mother while trying to fix drinks and top-up glasses.

'What a lovely house!' said Emmet, hugging her and presenting her with a box of handmade chocolates. 'You look gorgeous, Tessa, darling!'

'And you look great, too!' she said, noticing he was wearing a beautiful linen jacket and crisp Ralph Lauren shirt. Steven was great fun, and was charming Florence by telling her how he and Emmet first met.

'And you've been friends ever since?' She twinkled, holding his hand.

'You could say that!' He laughed.

Kitty looked amazing: she had a beautiful soft mauve wrap-around dress on her, and had done something new with her hair.

'I've stopped getting it permed, and am letting it grow a bit longer,' she confided. 'It was making me too old-looking.'

Larry, her husband, was deep in conversation with Paul about growing vegetables in a garden and the use of nets to prevent birds attacking strawberries, something he seemed to know a lot about.

Tessa asked Kitty into the kitchen to give a quick check with her that everything looked OK, and then called her guests into the dining room as Rob attended to the wine.

Tessa held her breath as they tasted the mousse. Everyone complimented her on the delicate flavour of the fish on the cucumber and lettuce bed as she passed around the warm baby brown scones she'd made to go with it.

The lamb was melt-in-the-mouth tender, the rosemary sprigs she'd picked from the garden giving it a lovely flavour. As she looked around the table she could see everyone was really enjoying it. She carved some extra slices and saw them disappear in a trice, Rob saying that it was one of the best legs of lamb he had eaten in a long time. Gemma was chatting away to Florence, telling her all about her garden flat.

'Did I tell you that I am thinking of opening a little café-cum-coffee shop?' said Emmet, who was sitting beside Tessa.

'What?' said Tessa, surprised. 'Where are you thinking of opening?'

'I've been scouting around for suitable premises, and there's a place on the seafront near Monkstown Village that has just come up. It's literally only a two-minute walk from the beach and the DART station,' he explained. 'It's a great little premises, used to sell toys and trinkets, and I think it's in a good location. I've been talking to the landlord, and we are trying to come to a deal on the rent.'

'But it's so different from what you normally do!'

'Did,' he corrected. 'There's very little work for architects at the moment, unless you are prepared to go overseas. Half of my office are travelling the globe, and I can't just hang around hoping something will happen. So I guess opening a little place of my own has always been a bit of a pipe dream, and Steven has encouraged me to just go for it.'

'What kind of place will it be?'

'Well, nothing too fancy, and it will only open during the day. I have no intention of competing with the local restaurants! But you know something, Tessa? If you walk all along the seafront there is hardly anywhere to just chill and meet friends for coffee or lunch and grab a bowl of soup or have a nice slice of cake. So a simple café might work!'

'Sounds great,' said Tessa. 'Just the kind of place most of us would drop in to!'

'That's what I hope.' He sounded pleased with himself. 'Well, that's if I can get the premises.'

'Fingers crossed!' wished Tessa.

They all stayed chatting for ages, Tessa making pots of coffee and opening the bottle of Baileys that Kitty and Larry had brought along, as Florence loved a glass of the creamy liqueur.

Eventually Florence admitted she was tired and

went off upstairs to bed, saying goodnight to everybody before she left.

'She's such a sweetheart,' said Emmet. 'No wonder you are so mad about her.'

As they all drifted off home in taxis, Rob was left behind. He and Tessa cleared the table and moved into the sitting room to enjoy the remnants of the fire.

'That was a lovely night, Tessa.'

'I'm so glad that I made the effort now,' she admitted. 'I was a bit nervous about everyone coming here with Mum and all, but she has had nearly as good a night as I have!'

'It was perfect.'

'Thanks for helping with the wines.'

'My pleasure.'

She smiled to herself. He really was so old-fashioned and kind.

'You've cooked me a lovely dinner, Tessa, so I hope that you will let me in return bring you to dinner next weekend?' he said. 'That's, of course, if it suits you!'

'The two of us go out on our own to dinner?' she asked, taking in his serious face and greying hair.

'Yes.'

'No Bingo?' she teased. 'That dog is always with us.'

'No Bingo, I promise.'

She noticed the way he laughed, those funny creases around his eyes making him seem younger.

'Just the two of us,' he promised, as he kissed her cheek. Then he got his jacket and said goodnight.

As Tessa blew out the candles in the sitting room and locked up it hit her that Rob was the kind of man she liked. They were comfortable together, relaxed. He made her feel attractive, and she certainly found him not only interesting but handsome in a well-preserved way. The age difference between them was nothing, really. They were already friends but maybe ... maybe there could be more ...

Chapter Forty

Lucy snuggled up to Finn on the couch. She had just made the most gorgeous coq au vin, as Alice called it, and Finn had practically licked his plate clean. They polished off the rest of the bottle of wine and as she curled up in his arms Lucy realized this was the place she wanted to be. She could hear his heart beat, his breath, feel his ribs move. Finn was so much part of her.

'Lucy,' he said slowly, 'I've been thinking a lot about it lately, and I was going to ask if you'd be interested in moving in with me?'

'Move in here with Duggy and Karl?' she said. She spent a huge amount of time here, but Lucy couldn't imagine anything worse than being officially just another flatmate, and paying rent to stay in this kip of a place.

'No.' He laughed, sitting up a bit and looking at her. 'I meant you and me on our own moving in together and finding a place. I love you. I just want to be with you all the time, and now that I have a bit of money maybe it's time we kind of made it official and the two of us started living together.'

Lucy couldn't believe it. It was exactly what she had been hoping for, practically from the minute she'd started dating Finn: to be with him all the time. She loved him so much, and living together was something she felt they were both ready for.

'Where will we live?' she asked.

'I dunno.' He shrugged. 'But it's got to be somewhere nice. I've had enough of dumps like this!'

'We can get in touch with some letting agents, check online,' suggested Lucy, excited. 'We are bound to be able to find somewhere nice. Somewhere that's pretty central.'

'And we are not having T-shirts all over the place,' he warned. 'This place we move to is going to be our home, not a bloody warehouse!'

Lucy laughed. At the moment they could barely fit into his bedroom or the hall, as they had boxes of printed 'Busy' T-shirts everywhere. Sales were going great, and the business was really beginning to take off, and their online website was just about to launch.

'Wait until Mum and Dad hear!' she joked. 'I'm sure they'll be glad to get rid of me.'

'No one would ever want to be rid of you, Lucy,' said Finn, touching her lips with his. 'Unless they were some kind of madman!'

Lucy wrapped her arms around him, kissing his eyes and face and neck. 'Finn, you are the best thing that has ever happened to me,' she said as she began to kiss him everywhere else.

They were curled up on the couch still when Duggy arrived home.

'Hey, what did you guys eat?' he asked. 'It smells great.'

'There's some left in the fridge if you want it,' offered Lucy. 'It will only take a few minutes in the microwave.'

She laughed as she watched Duggy dig into the chicken.

'What's up with you two?' he asked. 'You look like two Cheshire cats!'

'We're moving in together,' explained Finn.

'In here?'

'No, I wouldn't inflict that on Lucy,' he joked. 'Nah, we are going to find a place of our own.'

'When are you moving out?'

'Well, as soon as possible,' teased Finn. 'I'll do anything to get away from you lot!'

'Great!' said Duggy. 'Maybe now I'll get a bit of a chance to use the couch if you two lovebirds are not around!'

'Duggy, you spend half your life on this couch,' jeered Finn. 'It's practically your office!'

'A lot of good ideas have been generated on that old couch.' Duggy laughed. 'But it's not going to be the same without you.'

'Well, I won't go far,' promised Finn.

'And I'll have you over for some great dinners,' added Lucy. 'We're not going to let you starve.'

'Then we're all cool,' said Duggy, squashing in beside them.

Lucy had dragged Finn around half of Ranelagh. The price of accommodation for two people was outrageous, and the landlords had you over a barrel because they knew that you were a couple. Some of the flats and apartments they viewed wouldn't fit a dwarf, they were so small and cramped. Most suffered from some form of damp or mould, and anything half-decent was way out of their budget. Finn was getting more and more disappointed with what they were being offered, but Lucy refused to give in. She was determined that their first home together would be something special.

They viewed the top floor of a house on Grosvenor Square in Rathmines. It was a hell of a hike up a rickety staircase, but there was quite a view from the small attic rooms. It wasn't perfect, but they were about to agree to take it when Finn decided to push back the massive wardrobe in the main bedroom, and discovered a wall of damp coming from a leak in the ceiling! They practically ran out of the place. There was a modern one-bedroomed flat to let in a block in Terenure, but having to live, eat and cook all in one room – and sleep on a pull-out sofa bed – was just too much, no matter how cheap the rent was.

'We are never going to find anywhere!' complained Finn. 'We'll be stuck with Duggy for ever!'

'We'll find somewhere,' she insisted, refusing to give up searching. They were going to look at a house on the Ranelagh Road at 8 p.m. which contained eight flats. The road was a bit noisy, and the flats were pretty grim, but at least the landlord had ensured the place was dry and warm. The ceilings in the room were very high and she imagined it would be hard to heat them during cold spells, and the only form of heating was storage, which she knew cost a fortune. The furniture was ancient, and looking at the bed she knew they would definitely need a new one.

'Can we come back to you tomorrow?' she asked. 'We need to talk about it.'

'I don't like it,' insisted Finn. 'I know it's the right location, but the house is so wrong.'

They were trudging back down towards Donnybrook when Lucy spotted the 'Flat to Let' sign up on a large three-storey house on Belmont Avenue.

'This isn't on our list!' she said, rooting through her printout.

'Well, let's just knock and see if anyone is there,' said Finn.

A middle-aged man opened the door to them.

'We are enquiring about the apartment you have to let.'

'That's quick. I literally just put that sign up,' said the owner. 'And the advert is meant to be going on to the websites on Friday!'

'We were walking by, and we are looking for somewhere in this area to live,' Finn explained. 'What size is it?'

'It's a one-bed apartment with a living room, small kitchen and bathroom in the basement. My daughter and her boyfriend used to live in it until a few weeks ago, but now they've bought a town house in Clonskeagh as they are expecting a baby and this place would be far too small for them.'

'Can we look at it, please?' begged Lucy. The man would hardly have his daughter living in a basement hovel, would he?

'I wasn't going to show it till the weekend, as I'm still decorating it, but if you don't mind wet paint you're welcome to have a look.'

Grabbing a key he led them down the steps to the outside door to the self-contained flat. The hall was narrow, with only a small space for hanging coats and storage, but once they stepped in they both couldn't believe the small but perfect cream kitchen with its window overlooking the front.

'I put in a new hob only two years ago for them,' explained the man.

The living room was big with a fireplace, a window, and a door opening on to a small paved terrace which held a barbecue and a wooden table and chairs. The bedroom was great, and had a fitted wardrobe. Everywhere was clean and bright, gleaming with magnolia-coloured paint.

Lucy looked at Finn and knew they were both thinking the exact same thing. It was perfect. Just what they wanted, but the awful thing was it was probably going to be way over their budget.

'How much is the rent a month?' ventured Finn.

Lucy held her breath, barely daring to inhale.

She couldn't believe it when the owner came back

with a figure that was only thirty euros above their budget, and this lovely little flat was well worth it!

'We'll take it,' said Finn. 'We'll need to move in almost straight away.'

'Well, once I have your deposit and we get the rental agreement drawn up I can give you the keys by Monday, if that suits you,' offered the owner. 'The wife and I live upstairs, so, to be honest, I suppose having had Niamh and Brian living here I'm happy to have another young couple like yourselves take it.'

Lucy couldn't believe it! They had found a flat. They were actually going to move into this place. It was exactly what they both wanted, and was near to town and everywhere!

'I love it,' she said, squeezing Finn's hand.

Outside, back up on the street, they looked at each other. They had found a place of their own. This was the first step, the first move in their life together.

'Can we really afford it?' she asked Finn hesitantly.

'We are just going to have to sell a lot more T-shirts every month,' he said, sweeping her up into his arms.

Chapter Forty-one

Kerrie O'Neill watched as Matt got ready to go home to Moyle House for the weekend.

'Please, Kerrie, come with me?' he pleaded. 'I can't face it on my own.'

'No! I'm not going, Matt,' she insisted stubbornly. 'I've had enough of it! I've had enough of your parents and their problems. You are not going to be able to solve it, Matt, you know you're not. Your dad is in far too deep. The bank told you that. His losses are enormous.'

'He's under huge pressure from them. I've got to try and help him. For God's sake, he's my dad.'

'Matt, he's no bloody saint. He got himself into this mess. He owes the bank a fortune. It's a wonder they didn't call his loans in sooner.'

'Gerard Mullen is responsible for most of this,' he

shouted at her. 'Dad would never have got involved in all this mad buying if Gerard and that bloody solicitor of his hadn't encouraged him.'

'Face it, Matt, your dad gambled and now he has lost! I feel sorry for him and your mum, but you know as well as I do that the banks just want to get some sort of settlement and repayment schedule set up.'

'Come down, then, and help me explain it to them.'

'No,' said Kerrie firmly.

The past few weeks had been an utter nightmare, with Matt having to deal with the bank and the revenue and do everything in his power to try and sort out his dad's finances. There were constant phone calls and messages, and Dermot Hennessy regularly visiting their apartment, trying to sort out some sort of viable rescue plan. Matt was up till all hours on his laptop going round and round in circles doing calculations and trying to find some way out of the quagmire his father had managed to get himself into. He looked exhausted, and was barely sleeping. She loved Matt for his kindness, and she knew he was just being a good son, but he was so wrapped up in his family's affairs that she felt totally pushed aside. All he cared about was the Hennessy name and reputation, and trying to save it.

She was exhausted with it. Dermot Hennessy's business with Gerard Mullen – 'Goldsmith County Investments' – had been put into receivership, and on paper it looked like Matt's dad owed five to six million to the banks. What the hell had the Hennessys been up to? She knew if Matt had had the money himself he would have used every red cent of it to bail his father out, which irked her even more.

She saw it every day in work: clients who refused advice and just literally wanted to take a gamble on some company or other, or shares, or invest in an off-the-wall scheme. Sometimes their gambles paid off, but more often than not the money was gone and they had to accept that they had lost.

'Just come down for a day, Kerrie,' Matt persisted. 'We're having a big family meeting. Mum and Dad would want you there.'

'Matt, they wouldn't!' she shouted back. 'I'm hardly your parents' favourite person. Your mother barely tolerates me!'

'Don't say that about her!' he said defensively. 'She's been having an awful time of it, you know that.'

Kerrie bit her lip. She was not going to tell Matt exactly what she thought of his mother. 'Listen, Matt, it's far better you go down and try to persuade them about selling the house quickly before the bank does.

You need to sit Ed and Georgina down and explain exactly what is going on to them. Get your dad to agree to appoint an auctioneer. Anyway, you are far better able to handle your parents without me around.'

'But I want you there, Kerrie,' he kept on angrily. 'Why won't you come?'

'Every weekend it's been the same,' she retorted. 'All we talk and think about is your parents and the house and what is going to happen to them. I'm not doing it this weekend.'

'You are so selfish, Kerrie . . . so self-centred,' he said, zipping his bag and grabbing his car keys. 'This is just too messy for you. It's like this apartment, and our wedding. You want everything perfect and clear-cut! Nothing out of place for perfect Miss Kerrie O'Neill, or you will tidy it up and put it away.'

'I am being selfish,' she shouted as he walked out the door and banged it after him. 'I'm going looking for my wedding dress. I'm going to try and sort out the accommodation for our wedding. I'm going to phone that little French priest that we want to marry us . . .'

Chapter Forty-two

'Are you sure you two will be OK?' Alice asked, unable to disguise her anxiety at leaving her youngest son for the night.

'Mum, stop fussing!' Sean replied stubbornly. She knew he'd endured more motherly fussing than most twenty-year-olds over the past few weeks, but she couldn't help it!

'You know I have my phone with me, and I will leave it on silent just in case you need to contact me.'

'Mum, for heaven's sake.' Conor laughed. 'We are only going down the road to the pub for a curry and a few pints! I think the two of us will be safe!'

'I know.' She sighed. 'I know!'

Alice grabbed her black jacket and glanced quickly at the mirror in the hall. Sally and Hugh would be here to collect her in a few minutes. Sally had insisted she come along and join them on their table at 'The Innovation Ireland Dinner' in the Four Seasons Hotel. 'It will be fun!' Sally had promised, refusing to accept Alice's various attempts at declining the invitation. 'I don't care what you say, Alice, you are coming and having a night out!'

Conor was staying for two nights at home as Lisa was away at a hen weekend in Kilkenny with some of her hospital friends. Conor had decided it was high time he and Sean went for a few pints, and that his kid brother began to take steps back to a normal life.

The Four Seasons Hotel was packed, the crystal chandeliers sparkling, a pianist welcoming them as the waiters passed around glasses of champagne. Alice was glad that she had worn the simple fitted black satin dress, with the scoop neck. She felt elegant and classic, and that she was not competing with some of the younger women, who were wearing a stunning array of halter-neck multicoloured chiffons and thigh-high cocktail dresses.

'Wow!' said Hugh, as he surveyed the crowds. 'The women get prettier and the dresses get shorter every year.'

Alice helped herself to the champagne, and began to feel the tension ease. She relaxed. She was with Sally and Hugh, and Trish and Brendan were also on their table, so it was definitely going to be a fun night. The noise level grew and grew as everyone chatted and mingled, and she couldn't believe it when she met Rachel, who was wearing a stunning purple sheath dress, her dark hair up in an almost beehive style.

'You look gorgeous, Rachel!'

'I think we all look a bit better without our aprons.' Rachel giggled, introducing Alice to her husband, Pete.

'Pete, this is Alice Kinsella, the lady who changed our lives and got me cooking!'

'You certainly have,' he joked. 'Rachel and Leah are gone mad at it now; instead of spaghetti and pasta we are trying out all kinds of things. Rachel's even getting me into it.'

'Rachel is an amazing cook.' Alice smiled. 'And I'm sure she'd love to have you try out some of the recipes, too.'

'I'm working on it!' Pete admitted sheepishly.

'What a lovely couple,' remarked Sally. 'You must have some fun in your class!'

'We do.' Alice laughed. 'And now I have a new crowd that has just started, and one of them speaks hardly any English, which is causing even more chaos!'

After a few more drinks they left the reception area and began to file into the large ornate ballroom. The tables were all beautifully adorned with candles and stunning pink and purple lily arrangements.

'This way, Alice,' called Sally, showing her where their table was. Alice, spotting her name card, was relieved to see that she was sitting beside Hugh, who was always brilliant company, with Brendan and Trish down the other end from her.

They were just settling themselves at the table when Alex Ronan appeared and slid into the seat on the other side of her.

'Sorry, I got delayed a bit, Hugh, but I had to drop Aisling somewhere,' he apologized.

Alice blushed. She hadn't seen Alex since she'd left Ronan, Ryan & Lewis last year, and she was sure the senior partner was hardly expecting himself to be landed sitting beside her. She glanced over at Sally to see if she understood the situation, but Sally was deliberately ignoring her and chatting away to a small balding man and his wife.

'Nice to meet you again, Alice,' said Alex, as he began to study the menu. 'We still miss you at the office.'

Alice blazed. Was he being sarcastic or polite? She couldn't really figure it out. She would kill Sally for putting him beside her . . . kill her!

She watched the wine waiter top up her glass with white wine. It was going to be a long night, she thought, sitting here beside Alex.

'What have you been doing since you left us?' he asked politely. 'Hugh mentioned you were setting up some type of business from home.'

Alice found herself telling him about The Martello Cookery School and her group of students, and how much she enjoyed passing on her culinary knowledge and skills to others.

'I love food and am pretty passionate about it.'

'Passion is a pretty rare commodity these days,' he mused, 'so I'd imagine you are a very good teacher!'

'Thank you,' she said, surprised by the compliment.

'I always suspected from the minute I met you that your talents were wasted in our office,' he added.

Alice could see the twinkle in his blue-grey eyes, and was unsure if he was teasing her or being sincere. She found herself laughing, remembering the disasters she had inflicted on the accountancy office, and the consternation she had caused.

'I don't know how I would have survived without Kelly to keep an eye on me,' she admitted.

'Kelly keeps an eye on us all!' he agreed.

The food was delicious, the service impeccable, and Alice found she was really enjoying the meal as Alex encouraged her to try the red wine with her beef.

'Hugh really knows his stuff,' he whispered. 'I wouldn't dare order wine if he's around.'

Alice told him about all the bottles of Hugh's wine she had enjoyed at dinners together over the years.

Hugh entertained them with a story about a trip to a vineyard in France with Sally. 'It was meant to be the most exclusive wine, a rare vintage they produced there from a blend of local grapes. Sally and I had to make a special arrangement to visit the château and to be able to have a tour around. At the end we were treated to a sample of the wine, and it was all we had expected, it was heavenly . . . probably one of the best wines I have ever had the good fortune to have encountered in my life. I wouldn't dare tell how much it cost, but we decided to order a case and have it shipped back home here. It was the perfect end to a perfect trip to Bordeaux touring around the vineyards.' Hugh continued, 'Anyway, a few weeks later the case arrived, and we were patting ourselves on the back, as the next night we were having Sally's brother and his wife and our next-door neighbours for dinner. I decided to open two bottles of our special vintage to let it breathe.

'The dinner was great, and when we sat at the table I was telling everyone about this new wine we'd discovered and poured a glass for them all. I could see by their faces that they were tasting it and not liking it! The stupid thing was that I hadn't tried it myself, and when I did it was vile . . . pure plonk. We opened the second bottle, the third bottle . . . each one was viler than the last!'

'What did you do?' asked Alex.

'Fortunately I usually have a few good bottles on hand, and we opened them. Sally and I checked out the rest of the crate afterwards and every single bottle was awful. What an expensive lesson to learn!'

'I think they saw you coming, Hugh!' joked Alex.

Alice was surprised to find Alex such good company. She knew that like herself he was separated. In the office the gossip had always been that he was a bit of a player, and everyone assumed that he'd been unfaithful to his wife and left her, but as they both had an Irish coffee he told her about raising his son Niall and daughter Aisling, mostly on his own.

'We got married in Washington. Sarah's from there, but decided to come back here to live and have a family. I was busy building up the accountancy practice with Hugh and Emer, and I guess Sarah found it really difficult to settle in Dublin. She was constantly back and forth to the States to see her family. Eventually the trips got longer and longer, and then I discovered she had met someone else. Talk about a kick in the teeth! She got herself involved with some guy there and moved back, and that's where she is now. They got married eventually ten years ago, and have another son. The kids still see her and visit her. However, Dublin is home for them. It isn't an ideal situation, but it's the best we can all do.'

'I'm sorry,' Alice said.

'Don't be! I have two great kids, and I wouldn't change that for the world,' he confided. 'You know marriage. It's a lot like Hugh and his wine: there are no guarantees . . . no guarantees that it's all going to work out.'

As the meal finished the music started, and Alice soon found herself dancing around the floor with Hugh as the band got everyone up. Trish was in great form, and dragged Alice off to the loo for a chat about men.

'Give that lovely man beside you a chance,' she urged. 'Just give him a chance!'

'Shut up, Trish!' Alice protested. 'He's my old boss!'

Brendan then had her up dancing and swinging around the floor to some Abba classics. Exhausted, she retreated to the table to sit for a few minutes, watching the other dancers as she sipped a long cool glass of iced water.

Alex returned to the seat beside her.

She felt embarrassed. He'd clearly disappeared to the bar to escape her. They sat in silence watching the others dancing, Sally out on the floor hanging on to

Hugh as they did some weird version of the twist.

She'd slip away to the loo again in a few minutes, she decided. Let him go back to the bar.

As the music ended she reached for her bag, and was about to stand up when the band began to change tempo and play Sinatra. Alex touched her hand, asking her if she would like to dance.

'Alice, this is one of my all-time favourite songs,' he explained as he led her on to the dance floor.

For the rest of the night they danced and laughed and chatted, and she felt so at ease with him. Maybe he did this with every woman he came across, but Alice felt pretty and attractive and interesting when she was with him, and had to admit she found him attractive, too. For a big man he was unexpectedly light on his feet, and was a bit of a music buff, which surprised her.

When the music ended and everyone began to file out to collect their coats and jackets she felt strangely reluctant to go.

Sally and Hugh offered her a ride home in their taxi, but as she felt the pressure of Alex's hand in hers she turned them down.

'Hugh, I'm taking this young lady to the Residence for a last nightcap,' Alex explained. 'But I promise I'll look after her.'

'You'd better!' warned Sally drunkenly from their taxi.

Alice found herself ten minutes later in the Residence, the exclusive private members' club on St Stephen's Green, with Alex ordering some more drinks for them. They found a quiet corner to relax and talk. They danced a little more to some soul and jazz, and Alice felt like she was young again as they talked and laughed. It was well after 4 a.m. when they finally left and got a taxi home, Alex's arms around her as they stopped at Martello Avenue.

'Thanks for a wonderful night,' she said, giving him a quick hug as she got out of the car.

'I'll be in touch, Alice,' he promised, and somehow Alice knew that he meant it.

Chapter Forty-three

Alice enjoyed a blissful Sunday morning lie-in, the house quiet until Conor and Sean came into her bedroom.

'What time did you get home last night, Mum?' asked Sean.

'Late, very late,' she said, rolling on to her side. She had absolutely no intention of telling either of her sons what time she had actually got home.

'We're having lunch with Dad,' reminded Conor. 'Do you want us to get you a cup of coffee or something before we go?'

'No thanks,' she said, wrapping the duvet around her. 'I'm fine.'

'It's lovely out!' Conor said. 'Really sunny.'

An hour later the doorbell went, and she remembered

that she had invited Joy for brunch. She managed to find her flip-flops and raced down the stairs in her pyjamas to let Joy in.

'Look what the cat dragged in!' teased Joy, as Alice poured them each a large glass of orange juice. 'Where's Sean?'

'Conor's taken him over to meet Liam for lunch.'

'Bit of fatherly bonding,' quipped Joy.

'I suppose if there is one good thing that has come out of the accident it's that Liam is making an effort with the boys.'

As Alice hopped in the shower upstairs and dressed, Joy made bacon and scrambled eggs and a mound of French toast for them.

'Don't burn it!' warned Alice.

After they had eaten, Joy persuaded Alice to put on her sunglasses and come for a walk. It was a glorious day and they wandered down to the little beach in Seapoint, which was only a few minutes from the house. They watched the gangs of kids and toddlers in shorts and togs splash and play around.

'Summer's here!' They laughed, seeing all the exposed white skin being revealed for the first time.

Alice watched as the sunlight bounced off the water, and a load of small yachts flew by, their sails catching the light breeze. Such a beautiful day! A perfect summer Sunday! The marina in Dun Laoghaire was busy as boats sailed in and out of the harbour.

Alice's phone had a message, and when she checked it she saw that Alex had sent her a text.

Lovely night, Alice. Let's do it again. What about dinner in the Unicorn on Friday?

Alex Ronan

She smiled. Sally or Hugh must have given him her number.

She texted him back.

Yes please . . . Looking forward to it.

She put her sunglasses back on, and as she walked in the sunshine she began to tell Joy all about meeting Alex.

Chapter Forty-four

It had been an awful week. Matt had barely spoken to Kerrie since coming home late on Sunday night. They had avoided each other at breakfast, and on Monday he had texted her to say he was working late and not to wait up for him. She had her cookery class on Tuesday, and afterwards sat in her car crying for an hour eating the melt-in-your-mouth shortbread slices that Alice had showed them how to make. Matt was, by the way, asleep in bed when she eventually went into the apartment. She lay on her side of the bed wide awake for hours, listening to his breathing and wondering what was happening to them.

He was out on Wednesday, and on Thursday she met Ruth and they went around the shops looking at possible bridesmaid dresses.

'You OK, Kerrie?' asked her friend, concerned.

'Fine,' Kerrie lied as she despatched Ruth into the changing room to try on some more dresses.

On Friday when she came home she found Matt had left a note for her to say he was heading down to Moyle for the weekend. This time he hadn't even bothered asking her to accompany him.

She couldn't sleep all night and knew somewhere deep inside that their relationship was starting to unravel, spinning out of control. She was losing him . . . losing Matt.

On Saturday she couldn't settle to anything. She felt sick and scared, and, after trying to waken herself with an invigorating shower, found herself pulling on a clean pair of jeans, a white knitted ribbed sweater and a jacket, and getting into her car and driving home.

She passed the massive new high-rise developments of apartments and hotels in Tallaght, many empty, some now at least let to students at the local college. She gazed at The Square shopping centre and the hospital. They'd all been built since she was a kid. When they'd moved there, their estate had been surrounded by green fields. The green fields were long gone, replaced with more and more housing.

She had loved the freedom of it, the wildness of the place where they could run and roam with gangs of kids, all playing together. Slowing down at the traffic light she turned into Forest Road and took a right into Riverfield Grove. A group of five small boys were kicking a football, and her little nephew Jamie was among them. He gave her a shy wave. This road had been home for so long, a place of security and comfort, with the Murphys and the Kennedys next door, along with the Griffiths and the Conroys and a whole host of families that had all grown up together. Their mothers had kept an eye on them all, and their fathers had worked hard to put food on the table and pay off the mortgages they'd taken on to buy the three-bedroomed semi-detached houses.

She stopped outside Number 248. Nothing ever changed. The red painted gate hanging from the pillar, the big palm tree in the front garden, and her mam's sparkling clean net curtains in the window.

'You should have told me you were calling today, Kerrie, pet, and I'd have got something in.'

'I just felt like coming home,' Kerrie said, trying not to cry as her mother hugged her. Her dad was out the back, pottering like he always did, fixing a bicycle.

'Mike's young one nearly came off it the other day going to school. It needs a new chain,' he said, greeting her. She watched as he checked the tyres on the bike.

'Is everything OK?' he asked.

'Dad, can I not just call home like everyone else?' she said, wishing he wasn't so perceptive.

'Sure you can, pet,' interjected her mam. 'This place is like a railway station at times with all the comings and goings. Martina's gone off into town shopping for a few hours, and little Max is upstairs having a nap, and Jamie is somewhere outside.'

'He's fine, he's playing football.'

'Come on then, and we'll have a cup of tea while things are quiet.'

'The place looks great.' Kerrie admired the kitchen which had been painted a fresh creamy white, and there was a new silver fridge standing in the corner.

'Your dad and Mike painted it two weeks ago and it looks so much better now. The poor old fridge gave up the ghost last week so we went down to Power Electrics and got a new one!'

'Well, it all looks great!' Kerrie said, noticing the tumbling mass of petunias and geraniums in her mother's window boxes and planters and tubs.

She sat at the big pine table, where she had spent so much of her life, as her mother made a pot of tea and produced some of Kerrie's favourite Club Milk biscuits.

'How's everyone?' she asked.

Claire O'Neill began to give her the weekly

rundown on the family. Mike's wife Nicola was expecting again; Andy's little girl Emma might need to get her tonsils out; Tara was getting on well in England, and loved the London hospital where she was working; Martina's husband Darren had just been taken on by an electrical contractor in Walkinstown, which was great news; and Kerrie's little sister Shannon was studying so hard for her Leaving Cert exams that her ma was worried she'd make herself ill.

'Where is she?' Kerrie asked.

'At the library. She says it's quieter there for her to study at the weekends.'

Kerrie felt guilty. Shannon was eighteen, and a lot like her. The teachers said she was very bright, and she was aiming to get into college and study science. Why hadn't she tried to help her little sister more, encourage her?

'She'll be home at teatime . . . you can talk to her then,' said her mam, as if reading her mind. 'How's Matthew?' asked her mother. 'Everything OK?'

'Matt's fine, Mam, he's gone down to stay with his parents for the weekend.'

'Down to that lovely big house of theirs? Why didn't you go, too?'

Kerrie didn't know what to say, and could see the concern in her mother's eyes, and found herself blurting out all about Matt's family's troubles and Matt's involvement in trying to fix things.

'Matt's a good boy,' her mother said, pouring more tea. 'Maureen and Dermot seemed fine types of people. A bit different from us, I'll give you, but they must be finding this all very hard. Imagine losing your home or business at our age! The poor things, Kerrie. Is it any wonder your Matt is trying to help them?'

Kerrie stared at the photos on the kitchen wall. They were family photos of herself and her brothers and sisters when they were younger, and now there were also the new grandchildren. Her mam had a heart of gold and, instead of being angry at the Hennessys, pitied them.

'Thank God, your dad and I own every stick and stone and tile in this house. No one can touch it, as our mortgage was paid off four years ago!' she said proudly. 'We paid off the car last summer, and we've a bit of money put by for our pension and holidays and emergencies like the fridge. You know your dad! He wouldn't have it any other way. That man is as straight as they come!'

'I know that, Mam, you and Dad are the best,' Kerrie said, jumping up and hugging her.

'Kerrie, what about your wedding plans?' her mother said softly. 'How are they coming?'

'Everything is a bit up in the air at the moment,' Kerrie said. 'I've the church booked for the ninth of September, and Father Louis, the priest who's going to marry us, speaks English, so the mass will be in English. I'm trying to find someone to sing in the church. And the restaurant is all organized, but I'm trying to sort out the menu. You and Dad need to book your flights, and there is a lovely hotel over-looking the water. I've provisionally booked twelve rooms there. The church is only a few minutes away . . .'

'Kerrie, is everything all right?' pressed her mum.

Kerrie had been rabbiting on about the wedding arrangements, unaware that tears were running slowly down her face.

Her mother passed her some tissues from the box she kept in the kitchen.

'Matt and I have had a fight . . . we're barely speaking. He hates me . . . He's gone down to his parents again this weekend, and he barely even told me that he was going.'

'Did he ask you to go with him?' quizzed her mother.

'Yes, he did last week. I just didn't want to go down. His mother is such a snob, she hates me . . . hates that Matt and I are getting married. She thinks that I'm not good enough for her precious son.'

'I see,' said Claire O'Neill quietly, her hands resting on her patterned apron, her brown hair flecked with grey, her eyes sad. 'Is that why your father and I and your brothers and sisters, well, those who can manage it, are being dragged off to France, Kerrie, for this wedding of yours?'

Kerrie stopped.

'No, Matt and I love France. We want to get married there. We—'

'Are you ashamed of us, Kerrie? Ashamed of your family, where you come from?'

'No, I'm not. It's just that his family are so different from ours,' Kerrie trailed off lamely.

'Matt is a nice boy,' her mother said firmly. 'What his family are like makes no odds to your father and me, once he is a good kind husband to you and a good father to your children. That's what makes a man. Not the money in his bank account, though that can ease things a bit, or where he did or did not go to school, or whether he grew up in a big house or one of the council flats like where Darren came from.'

'I know that, Mam. It's just that the Hennessys are used to different things from us. I love Matt, but sometimes I feel I don't really fit in with them.'

'Lord rest your Granny O'Neill, but she was a right rip. When I married your father she thought I wasn't good enough for him. Told me to my face! She made my life a misery with her sour face and ways. My father worked in Guinness's brewery and she was always going on about it. I only found out after she died that her husband John had been turned down by the brewery. She held a right old grudge about it, as John got a job in the Swastika laundry then, but sure, that had none of the benefits Guinness's had! There was no widow's pension when he died and he left her with a young family.'

'That's different!'

'Don't you think your daddy and I think it strange that Matt has never been to this house? All the other boyfriends and girlfriends practically lived in the place. Your dad used to have to throw Darren out at midnight when he and Martina were going steady.'

'It's just that Matt's busy . . . with his job and . . .'

'When you went to college, we were all so proud of you, Kerrie. You are the first person on both sides of the family to not just get a university degree but to do a Master's. Why do you think young Shannon is working so hard? She wants to be just like her big sister! I see her looking at the photo of you in your cap and gown on your graduation day, and I know it spurs her on. Why would you be ashamed of what you are, what you have achieved? We are all so proud of you. But I'm proud of all our children and their achievements.'

'I know that.'

'Do you love Matt?'

'Yes.'

'Then be honest with him. You can't hide things in a marriage, it never works.'

'I know,' Kerrie said, feeling a huge pang of regret for what she had done. All the deception! Things couldn't go on between Matt and herself the way they were. They had to be honest and open with each other. If he didn't want to marry her, he had to tell her!

Little Jamie came in from playing football. He'd cut his knee, and Kerrie wiped his tears, found a big plaster in the medicine box and stuck it on. Later she gave baby Max his bottle and changed him. His chubby fingers grabbed on to her blonde hair as she played with him.

Her sister Martina came back laden with shopping bags from town, and did a fashion parade for them, showing off her new outfits and shoes.

'These are the first new things I've bought since Max was born,' she said, giving a twirl around the kitchen in her new red dress. 'Now that Darren's got work again things are looking up!'

'You'll all stay for tea,' insisted Claire O'Neill. 'I'll make my meatballs in tomato sauce for everyone. Jamie loves them.'

Kerrie jumped up and offered to help, cutting up the onions and helping to shape the seasoned balls of minced beef.

'I don't believe it!' teased her mother as Kerrie told her all about her cookery classes, and the kind of things she had learned to make.

After dinner, when Martina and the kids had gone, Kerrie stayed in the kitchen talking to Shannon while her mam and dad sat on the couch together and watched a DVD.

'Mam says you are working really hard!' Kerrie smiled. 'Good girl, that's exactly what you need to do for the next few weeks . . . get through the exams and get what you want.'

'If I want to go to Trinity College or UCD I'll need to get at least four hundred points,' her younger sister, with her long dark hair and skinny face, explained. 'I'm hoping to pick up an A or two in maybe physics or maths or even chemistry. My teacher, Miss Hanratty, says that I'm on track, but I just need to keep going. I want to be like you, Kerrie, and do well!'

Kerrie looked at the big brown eyes and long dark lashes; her sister was so beautiful and so focused.

'If you need any help with anything, Shannon, I'm here for you. Any help I can give you with revising or going back over things, let me know. I'm still pretty hot at maths, you know.'

'I just hope I make it into bio-medical science,' Shannon confided. 'I'd love to be doing research and finding out things the whole time . . . it would be a cool kind of job to have.'

'What about the rest of your subjects, how are they?'

'OK, I guess. My French is a bit ropy, but I should pass it, and I like Irish, believe it or not!'

'Do you need any help with the French?' Kerrie pressed.

'Maybe.'

'Well, how about for the next few weeks we get together and go over your French until the exams? It's one of my favourite languages,' offered Kerrie.

'That would be great.' Her sister grinned.

'I'm staying here tonight, so maybe we can go through some work after breakfast.'

Wearing a pair of Shannon's pyjamas, Kerrie slept in her old bedroom, which now contained a baby's cot and changing gear, and a cardboard cut-out of Dora the Explorer stuck on the wardrobe door.

'Night, pet,' said her mam, creeping in to give her a kiss. 'It's nice to have you here. Sleep well.'

* * *

She had slept well for the first time in weeks, and woken clear-headed and refreshed. Going home after a massive family Sunday lunch, she had taken some of the family photos, promising to make copies and return them to her mam the following week. There was a photo taken on holiday in a caravan park in Wexford, with them all running into the waves grinning in the sunshine in their swimming togs; a photo taken in the back garden when Shannon made her first Holy Communion, and one of Kerrie's mam and dad on their wedding day. She had also discovered Fred, the old black and white teddy bear she'd had since she was about two, on the top of the wardrobe, and had shaken the dust off him and taken him home, sitting proudly in the front of the car with her.

Matt would be home later tonight. She needed to talk to him. They had to sit down and be honest with each other. She had been so stupid, so scared of losing him! Hiding things! Pretending. It was pathetic. But now there could be no more pretending, no more lies. She'd had enough of it!

Chapter Forty-five

Kerrie sat on the couch, waiting for Matt to come home, watching the lights of the city below come on. A breeze drifted in from the balcony as she listened to Kings of Leon, one of Matt's favourite bands. She had Coronas chilling in the fridge, and some food in, as he might be hungry.

She heard his footsteps outside the door, and his key turning in the lock. He looked beat, exhausted, and she hugged him tight, savouring the smell of his skin and sweat and the remnants of his aftershave.

'Matt, can we talk?'

'Kerrie, I'm absolutely shattered,' he said, flinging himself on the couch. 'Can it wait till tomorrow, or another time?'

'No,' she said seriously. 'It can't. I need to talk to you tonight.'

He looked wrecked, but she had to talk to him now, before her courage deserted her and the pretence all started again.

'Have you eaten?'

'I had a massive meal before I left. You know what Mum's like.'

'What about a drink?'

He nodded, throwing his head back on the head-rest of the couch. He looked so good: his long handsome face, and scruffy dark hair, and lean legs in their pale chinos, and his pale blue Massimo Dutti shirt. She loved him so much that it hurt.

She fetched two chilled beers from the fridge, and curled up on the chair opposite him.

'What's this all about?' he asked warily.

'It's about us . . . well, it's about me,' she said. She could tell that she had Matt's attention.

'Matt, you know all the meals and dinners we've had since we moved in here?' she said softly. 'All the lovely lasagnes and chicken and beef dishes and the banoffi pies and fudge brownies you adore . . . well, the truth is that I didn't make any of them. I couldn't cook, so I bought them and pretended to you that I could.'

'What?' he said, perplexed, sitting forward. 'You didn't make them, any of them? But I saw you in the kitchen . . .'

'You saw what I wanted you to see, for you to get the impression that I was a good cook,' she admitted. 'I know it was crazy, but I just couldn't admit to not being perfect. So I lied to you! And on Tuesday nights I haven't been doing a course in work since January. I've been doing a cookery course in Monkstown. I'm actually trying to learn to cook.'

'Why couldn't you tell me?' he said, hurt. 'Kerrie, I never expected you to be able to cook, to be perfect! Why would you think that it would matter?'

'You are right about me . . . what you said the other day . . . I wanted our lives to be perfect. I thought that's what you would expect of me,' she said, trying not to cry.

'Cookery lessons on a Tuesday,' he said, putting his hand to his forehead. 'There was I, worried that you were seeing some guy from work, as you always seemed so happy when you came home.'

'What?'

'We've both been pretty stupid. I should have asked you.'

'There would never ever be anyone else,' she said, her eyes welling with tears. 'How could you even think that, Matt?'

'Is the big confession over?' Matt said wearily.

'No,' she said. 'This is only the start of it.'

Matt sat up on the couch, his beer in his hand.

'Matt, I didn't grow up in safe middle-class Terenure, in a big house with a garden and my daddy working for one of the banks. I didn't go to one of those fancy fee-paying girls' schools ... I didn't just swan into college with the rest of my social set.' She took a deep breath, trying to control the shake in her voice.

'My life is the complete opposite. I grew up in Tallaght, on a big estate, and went to Riverfield Community School, one of the biggest schools in the country, with some of the most disadvantaged students. And I busted my guts to get a place in college and drag myself up. I went to America one summer on my J1 – that's where I got to know Ruth and Christine and Laura and Caroline – and I just hung out with them, and when we got back to college people began to assume that I was part of their gang. We went everywhere together – holidays in Greece, backpacking in Europe – and later, when we all started working, shopping trips to New York and skiing in Austria and France and ...'

'Meribel,' he said slowly.

'Matt, I studied so hard and worked so hard ... maybe I even began to believe that I was like them. I learnt about art and literature and architecture and style ... All the things to help me fit into the world I wanted to belong to ... your world.'

She looked at the expensive wooden floor, noticing

the rich colour of the natural wood that had been imported from Canada, the width of each board, the perfect symmetry of it.

'I'm a fraud, a liar!' she said despairingly. 'I haven't been honest with you. I could understand you hating me. It's just that I can't pretend any more . . . I've had enough of it.'

'I knew about your school,' said Matt gently. 'Well, the fact that you didn't go to Castlemount or St Mary's or Annefield. Georgina's best friend and her four sisters all went to Castlemount, and when Georgina mentioned your name none of them had heard of you. Lindsey went to St Mary's, and Georgina went to Annefield.'

'You never said anything.'

'I thought that you would tell me yourself when the time was right. What school you did or didn't go to makes no difference to me! You are the brightest, most intelligent, girl I know, and that's what matters.'

'Oh,' she said, surprised.

'And the night we brought your parents to see Paul McCartney your dad let slip that you lived nowhere near Terenure, and that he had as little dealings with the banks as possible and preferred to use the post office, as he used to work as a postman.'

'My dad works in the sorting office,' she said, not trusting herself to speak. 'He's due to retire next year.'

'Is there any more?' pressed Matt. 'A secret husband, kids, another life I know nothing about?'

'No.' She sniffed, tears running down her face. 'But I've let you down. I should have been there for you . . . gone to help with your parents if you wanted me to.'

'Kerrie, I can't blame you for not wanting to come down to Moyle. Georgina and Mum had a massive fight, and Ed says they've blown his inheritance . . . the lazy shit.'

'I'm sorry.'

'Listen, I love you, not where you came from, not what school you did or did not go to, not your family, and whatever is going on there. You are the person I fell in love with and respect, and want to marry. You don't need to lie to me . . . to pretend.'

She couldn't believe it. Matt still loved her, wanted her, wanted to marry her!

'Are you sure?'

'Yes,' he said firmly. 'And are you sure you won't object to taking on the son of a disgraced bankrupt, my snob of a mother, and God knows what other family scandals are coming down the track?'

'I'm not marrying them . . . I'm marrying you,' she said, running over and jumping on to his lap. Matt held her as she cried and cried and cried. Matt stroked her hair and told her that it didn't matter, everything was going to be all right.

Chapter Forty-six

Tessa had made breakfast, and was downstairs listening to the radio, when she realized that it was almost ten o'clock and Florence hadn't appeared. It was unlike her mother to be such a late riser, but she had seemed a bit tired the past few days. Putting on the kettle, Tessa made a fresh pot of tea and toasted a few slices of McCambridge's brown bread, putting them on a tray to bring up to her. There'd been a slight shower overnight, but the weather forecast for the day was good, and maybe they could go for a bit of a drive or a walk if her mum felt up to it.

'Morning, Mum,' she called. The curtains were drawn, and her mother stayed asleep as she put down the tray and opened them, letting the sun flood into the bedroom with its rose-patterned wallpaper.

'Here's some tea and toast for you.'

Florence Sullivan looked so peaceful, her eyes shut, her white hair spread out against the pillow.

'Mum,' Tessa called again, trying to rouse her.

It was only when she sat on the bed and went to touch Florence's hand that she realized that her mother had died. She wasn't breathing but wasn't completely stone cold either.

'Mum, Mum!' Tessa called, trying to wake her, rouse her, bring her back to life, knowing in her heart that it was far too late, and that Florence Sullivan was gone . . . had passed away some time in the last few hours.

She sat holding her mother's hand for an hour, just wanting to sit there quietly and peacefully with her as she said her own personal goodbye.

Then, gathering herself, she phoned their local GP. Doctor O'Connell agreed to come straight away.

She tidied the bedroom a bit, waiting for the doctor's arrival.

'She looks so peaceful,' said the doctor when she saw Florence. Tessa waited downstairs while the doctor made her examination.

'As we suspected, it was heart failure,' Dr O'Connell said gently, coming into the kitchen. 'Very peaceful, and just the way Florence would have wanted to go. No hospitals, no drama, asleep in her own bed. She's a lucky lady.'

'Yes,' said Tessa, finally giving in to her tears.

'What should I do now?' she sobbed.

'Well, you need to contact the rest of your family, and the funeral directors – they will help you with the arrangements – and then maybe there's a friend or someone you could phone who would come over to give you a bit of support,' she said kindly. 'Someone who would stay here with you for a bit.'

'Yes,' Tessa nodded.

'Will you be all right?' asked the doctor.

'Yes, of course. I'll make a few phone calls.' Tessa found herself gabbling. 'I'll start to organize things. My brother is in California, and my sister is in Hong Kong. They'll need to book flights home at once. They'd want to be here. Be here with Mum.'

'And don't forget to phone someone to come over,' reminded the doctor, as she got ready to leave. 'You have my number if you need me, Tessa.'

Tessa phoned Marianne first, and her sister cried hysterically when she told her the news.

'I should have been there,' she sobbed. 'She's my mother. Why wasn't I there?'

Donal was almost silent when she told him, and she could tell he was crying.

'I'll be home as soon as I can, Tessa,' he promised. 'I'll book flights straightaway and we should be home in Dublin by tomorrow or the next day.'

Afterwards Tessa sat there feeling totally alone, unsure what she was meant to do next. She could run across to her mother's elderly neighbour, Rose, but she too was old, and frail. She didn't really know any of the newer younger neighbours who had moved in over the last few years. She picked up her phone and she didn't know why, but she phoned Rob's number, certain that he would be the one person who would know what to do.

Rob Flanagan came round immediately, and she sat in the kitchen while he made her tea and arranged for Andrew Furlong from Furlong's Funeral Directors to come to the house to make the arrangements for her mother's funeral. They would look after the coffin, the hearse, opening the grave.

The mass would be in St Teresa's, their local parish church. Florence had always loved the church, and had attended it ever since moving into the district, always geting involved in parish activities. She would be buried with their dad in the graveyard in Wicklow.

'Where do you think you want to go back to after the funeral?' Rob asked gently.

'I don't know,' Tessa wailed.

'We had it at home when Kate died,' he said simply. 'It's what she would have wanted: to have it at home, not in a hotel or bar. What do you think Florence would have wanted?'

'We never talked about it, but I suppose Mum loved this house . . . so she'd have liked everyone to come back here.'

'Then maybe we should start to organize it: see about a caterer and get some drink in,' he said calmly. 'I'll phone two or three of them, and ask them for quotes, and get them to send you some menu options, and then you can talk to your brother and sister about it.'

She didn't know what she would have done without Rob. He always seemed to be there, at her side, advising her and supporting her. Even when Donal and Marianne and their families arrived home he stayed on in the house and explained what arrangements he'd helped her to set up.

She could see her brother and sister were curious about this older man who was involved with helping to organize such a big family event.

'I'm a friend of Tessa's,' he explained, 'and I had a great regard for Florence.'

It was strange to think of the house now filled with her children and grandchildren and Florence not there to welcome them, and see them and talk to them.

'I miss Granny!' sobbed Chloe, Marianne's eldest girl who had been especially close to her.

'Where did you meet such a lovely man?' whispered Marianne, when Rob was fetching a box of glasses from the off-licence and a crate or two of wine.

'At a cookery school.' Tessa laughed.

Father Molloy, the parish priest and great friend of her mother's, said the funeral mass, with all the grandchildren saying a bidding prayer each, and Marianne and Tessa doing the readings, while Donal gave a lovely eulogy about Florence to the packed church.

Many of Florence's generation were gone, but all the relatives and friends of Donal, Marianne and Tessa turned up, and Tessa couldn't believe it when she saw that Alice and so many of the cookery school group had come along, too.

The sun shone as they journeyed to the graveyard, and back home they sat outside enjoying the sunshine and the garden in full bloom as the day became a celebration of Florence's long life and friendships and interests. It was a way of remembering Florence's enduring love for her family, and the great spirit that she had possessed right till the end.

Tessa fell into bed exhausted and slept till lunchtime the next day. Marianne had taken over the cleaning-up duties, and after eating something Tessa gave in to the waves of exhaustion that suddenly overwhelmed her, and crept back to bed. The next few days were filled with reminiscing as Tessa and her brother and sister relived their childhoods growing up in the house, and began to sort out some of Florence's personal effects.

'What are you going to do now, Tessa?' asked Marianne, concerned. 'The house is here for you as long as you need it, but are you going to stay here or go back to London?'

Tessa couldn't think straight. The reason she had moved back to Dublin was to be with her mother and help care for her. She had absolutely no idea what she should do now that Florence was dead. The house and its contents, and all her mother's possessions, had been left equally between the three of them, with a small bequest for each of her grandchildren. Florence Sullivan had always been both generous and very fair.

A week later Donal and his two kids had returned to San Francisco and Marianne and her husband Kevin and their three children had flown back to Hong Kong. The house felt strangely lonely without them all. Did she really want to stay here living in the old neighbourhood? To rattle around this house on her own with no proper job or reason for staying here?

But now, with Florence Sullivan gone, what was she supposed to do?

Going on the internet, Tessa looked at flights to London and also at the London job agency sites for opportunities in human resources management. She couldn't return to Bridgetown & Murrow. Instead she would make a fresh start if she returned to London, and find a new job. With her mother's death there was nothing to hold her here in Ireland. Once probate on their mother's will had come through, Donal and Marianne and she were all in agreement about putting the house up for sale.

Chapter Forty-seven

Alice studied herself in the figure-hugging black trousers and loose knitted beige jumper. Her hair had got longer, and she was lightly tanned. She looked younger, felt younger. She had been seeing Alex for the past few weeks. They had enjoyed a wonderful dinner in the Unicorn, and since then there had been lunches and walks and a big dinner party in one of Alex's friend's houses and a few drinks in Gleeson's with Joy and Fergus. Next week Hugh and Sally had invited them to their place, which she felt was a sign that her friends, despite their surprise that Alex and herself were seeing each other, actually approved of the relationship.

Tonight they were going to a concert at the RDS. Horslips, a favourite Irish rock band of Alice's, had re-formed to put on a few concerts and Alex had somehow managed to get two of the much sought-after tickets.

'Back in the day I was a huge fan,' he confessed.

'So was I,' she said excitedly, as they joined the huge crowd of fans streaming into the Royal Dublin Society's grounds in Ballsbridge for the open-air concert. 'I went to all their gigs.'

The first twang of the electric fiddle as the band broke into their particular edgy Celtic rock sound sent shivers down Alice's spine, and she found herself joining in every song and up on her feet. Alex was having an equally good time.

'Trouble ... trouble,' they shouted along with everyone, as the band went into one of their favourites.

Alice felt like a teenager again, with Alex beside her relaxed and totally at ease. The band played, and fireworks lit up the night sky almost two hours later as Horslips launched into their final song.

'Oh, Alex, thanks for bringing me,' Alice said, hugging him. 'It's been such a good night.'

'You know something? I wish we'd met when we were younger ... bumped into each other at one of the concerts,' he said softly, as he took her hand and they manoeuvred their way out through the crowds.

Alice looked at him, his dark eyes serious. She

thought of Conor, Jenny and Sean. She wouldn't change the past. Liam and herself might not be together any more, but theirs had been a good marriage for the most part, and their kids were great.

'I'm glad we've met now!' she said. 'At this stage of our lives. Alex, you've got your kids, and I've got mine. You know you wouldn't change them for all the money in the world!'

'Yeah.' He grinned as he put his arm around her. 'I know that.'

They walked to his car and en route to Alice's home stopped off for a nightcap; Alex had a pint of Carlsberg while she had two glasses of chilled white wine. Driving her back, he stopped the car and pulled her into his arms, their kisses in only a few minutes turning more passionate. Like two teenagers making out, they both wanted more. Alice found herself giggling as Alex bashed his rather large knee off the handbrake.

'We're too old for this!' he complained.

'Speak for yourself,' she teased, as she pulled him over towards her side of the car.

'Alex . . . I can't invite you into my place as Sean is there and Jenny is home for the weekend.'

'Aisling has three girlfriends staying the night in my place,' he groaned. 'They were having a pasta and Prosecco night, whatever that is!'

'A more grown-up version of a sleepover.' She laughed.

'It's not funny!' he complained.

'There's nothing we can do,' she said softly.

Alex stopped and straightened up.

'We're not broke sixteen-year-olds! I'm taking you to the Four Seasons,' he said, reaching for her hand. 'No kids or complications there.'

They stood in the foyer as Alex checked them into a room in the hotel. He was using his golf shoe bag as his luggage, and Alice tried to remain composed as the receptionist swiped his credit card.

'The porter will show you to your room, Mr and Mrs Ronan. You are on the third floor.'

Alice had to fight to control her giggles as they went up in the lift, and the minute the porter left the room the two of them collapsed into a heap on the king-size bed, laughing.

When Alex disappeared to the bathroom she sent Joy a text.

If kids are looking for me please say I am staying with you. Alice

Joy texted:

Where r u?

In the 4 seasons with alex.

Hussy . . . have fun. Joy

Then she sent Sean a text to say not to worry, but she would not be home as she was staying with Joy.

They raided the minibar, and Alice found herself curious to touch Alex and explore the rest of his body as they kissed and kissed and he pulled her on to the bed.

She lay in Alex's arms aware that she felt totally happy. There was no embarrassment or shyness as they held each other close, and eventually both drifted off to sleep.

The next morning they slept in and ordered room service: rich roast coffee and pancakes with blueberries and maple syrup and crispy bacon. They were both tempted to stay on for another day, and not bother even leaving the hotel room.

'I'd better get home. Jenny is going back tonight,' she explained. 'She'll think it very strange if I don't turn up.'

Reluctantly, they checked out. Alice really didn't want to leave Alex, and missed him the minute they said goodbye to each other at the end of her road.

She laughed when she was getting lunch, because Alex texted her:

Can we do it all again next weekend? Miss you already.

Chapter Forty-eight

Kitty sat at the kitchen table. It had been an awful, awful day. Sheila's daughter Melissa had phoned her at lunchtime, telling her to come to the hospital, as her mum was very weak. She wasn't surprised as Sheila O'Leary had gone downhill rapidly over the past ten days. The weight seemed to have fallen from her frame, and her eyes had looked scared. The doctors had her on a morphine pump to help with the pain, but at times Sheila hadn't been able to bear it. The cancer was everywhere, and you could hear it in her breathing. Even a few words and she would be coughing and fighting for breath.

'Don't talk, Sheila, love . . . let me do the talking,' Kitty had pleaded, as she had sat by the bed and held Sheila's hand, and told her about her cookery class, and the recipes, and people in it, and the family, and the places the two of them would go when Sheila got back on her feet and was well again.

Sheila had looked like she was asleep. Her skin had gone a strange yellow colour, as her kidneys weren't working any more, or her liver.

Kitty had sat with her for hours. Then Sheila had opened her eyes. She had been smiling. Kitty had leaned forward and kissed her.

'You go girl . . . go away from here and all this pain,' she had said slowly. 'We'll meet up again. Best friends for ever.'

Sheila had drifted back to sleep again, and Kitty had returned home, leaving poor Martin O'Leary holding his wife's hand as all their family gathered together to say goodbye to Sheila in the hospital. There was nothing more to be said or done . . . just waiting now . . .

Melissa texted Kitty at 3 a.m. to say it was over.

Mammy's gone. RIP.

Kitty got up and grabbed her dressing gown. She couldn't sleep, and made her way downstairs to the kitchen. Larry was still fast asleep on his side of the bed. She put on the kettle. The tears came hot and hard as she thought about Sheila. She looked out at the garden, and a small vixen looked back at her, startled. It was burrowing in among the tall grass

402

under the holly tree. A lovely fox with beautiful eyes and glossy red coat . . . its colour reminded her of Sheila's hair. It stayed staring at her for what seemed like ages. She'd seen the odd fox out in the road late at night, or up in the park when it started to get dark, but they'd never had one in the garden! The vixen sat down, looking at her through the kitchen window. It was so strange. Next thing, she heard the kitchen door open and the fox was gone. Larry stood there in his striped dressing-gown.

'Are you all right, Kitty, love?' he asked sleepily.

'No . . . I'm not,' she said, crying again. 'Sheila died a while ago. I've lost my best friend in the whole world . . . I'm going to miss her so much.'

'I'm sorry,' he said, sitting down beside her. 'I know how close the two of you were.'

'What will I do without her, Larry?' she moaned. 'We had so many plans, things we were going to do. We were going to go to Paris: get the lift up to the top of the Eiffel Tower, go on one of those riverboat cruises on the River Seine, say a prayer in Notre Dame and see the big paintings of water lilies Monet did.'

'Monet?'

'The French artist. She loved his paintings. She had a calendar of them in her kitchen,' Kitty said softly. 'And poor Sheila is not going to be there for when

Paddy's new baby is born in September. She was there for all the other grandchildren being born. It isn't fair, Larry, she's too young to be taken.'

Larry leaned over and hugged her, before switching on the kettle and making more tea and some hot buttered toast for the two of them.

Chapter Forty-nine

Tessa wrote a few more labels, and using the wide brown tape secured more cardboard boxes. There were old books, old records, old clothes, old scarves and handbags of her mother's all ready to be brought to the charity shop. Someone else would have the benefit of reading Florence's large collection of Agatha Christie and Barbara Cartland novels.

The scarves and bags were probably vintage at this stage and worth something, and she had cleaned and carefully folded the clothes that were worth selling: the Pringle cashmere twinsets, Cleo tweed skirts and jackets, and a collection of evening wear in pristine condition.

She was booked to go to London the following week, and she had to try and clear some of the stuff from the house, as there was far too much in every room, and the auctioneers had advised a serious de-clutter before putting the house on the market.

At least she had made a good start on it.

It was sad getting rid of things, but her mother had been a great age and was of the generation that believed things should be recycled and shared.

Tomorrow she would have a go at the kitchen presses and the dining room cabinet, as her mother had a huge collection of ornaments and bric-a-brac that could be got rid of, too.

She was scrawling 'Gardening Books' on a box when Rob Flanagan surprised her by ringing the doorbell.

'What are you doing?' he asked, surveying all her work, and the boxes scattered over the floor of the hall and the sitting room.

'Packing up, Rob.' She sighed. 'I'm just trying to get rid of some of Mum's stuff. Donal and Marianne picked out what they wanted, and, well, most of the rest is just going to have to go to charity. I'll go over to St Vincent de Paul with it tomorrow, as I won't have room for any of it myself.'

'Oh,' he said.

'I told you I'm going back to London next week. I've booked my flight.'

He said nothing.

'Listen, I'm going to take a break. I've done

enough today. Do you want a coffee?' she offered.

'Why don't I take you out instead?' he offered.

'I'm not exactly dressed up.' She smiled.

'Come on, Tessa, let's go for a drive,' he suggested.

She didn't know if she was in the mood for one of their walks or talks. She felt a bit low and sad after clearing away her mother's things – talk about being emotionally drained! – but Rob was insistent. He'd been so kind to her since Florence's death, and so helpful, that she felt she couldn't refuse him.

Grabbing her bag, keys and jacket, and putting on a pair of shoes instead of her flip-flops, she sat in beside him in his Volvo. It was warm but dull, and she hoped that it wouldn't rain.

'Where are we going?' she asked.

'What about the beach? Brittas?'

Tessa smiled. She hadn't been there for years, the beach with the miles of golden sand, tall dunes and rolling waves. As a kid, it was one of her favourite places. Her mum and dad used to rent a mobile home there for a month every summer in the big caravan park overlooking the beach. Alice's parents used to own the nearby hotel. She still remembered it: playing pitch and putt there; her parents going for dinner to the hotel, which was very fashionable then; Florence all dressed up in a summer print dress, linking her father by the arm.

*　*　*

The traffic was light, and an hour later Tessa and Rob were climbing the path up through the sand dunes to get to the beach.

Clouds scudded across the sky, and only a handful of people were on the strand: a few swimmers, dog walkers and mothers with small children and toddlers.

'I love this place.' She sighed. 'I have such good memories of here.'

'I know,' he said, taking her hand as they began to walk. 'You told me.'

She found herself confiding in him about the family situation, with the house left equally between Donal, Marianne and herself.

'They say that I can stay on as long as I want in the house, that there is no big rush to sell it, but I feel that's not fair. Anyway, Mum's dead, and the reason I came back home is gone, too. I need to refocus and get back to work. Go back to London, find a new job, and get on with my life.'

'Do you want to go back to London, Tessa?' Rob asked quietly, staring at the foaming white waves tumbling in across the sand ridges. 'Is that what you really want to do?'

'I suppose so. What else is there?' She suddenly felt so torn, so lonely.

'Maybe there is no need to rush into making a decision. Not yet . . .'

'Rob. It's all organized. I'm going next week. I have four job interviews set up. There is nothing to keep me here!'

'Are you sure about that?' he said forcefully. 'You have friends, people who care about you here.'

'That's great, but I have friends in London, too,' she said gently.

'Then I don't want you to go,' he said angrily. 'I don't want you to leave.'

She stopped, spinning around to look at him.

'What are you saying, Rob? It's too late.'

'No, it's not, Tessa. I don't want you to go. I want you to stay here in Dublin. Give us a chance.'

'Us?'

'Yes, the two of us and what we feel for each other. We both feel it, you know we do. We work well together. I never thought after Kate that I would meet a woman again that I could have feelings for, but you've changed all that, Tessa.'

'The two of us!' she said, her eyes welling with tears.

'Yes, the two of us. Why wouldn't it work? Maybe I'm too old . . . I'm sixty-two, for God's sake, and you are only in your thirties, I have no right to—'

'I'm thirty-nine, Rob. I'll be forty in December,'

she said, gripping his arm. 'Age does not matter!'

'Are you sure about that?' he teased. 'I'm old enough to be your father.'

'You are nothing like my father.' She laughed. 'Anyway that's not an issue,' she said, touching his face and tracing his jawline with her fingers. 'So don't even think it!'

'I don't think it!' he admitted honestly. 'When I am with you I feel different. Young again, as if I'm starting over. I have another chance. I loved Kate with all my heart and will always miss her, but this is something new, something different. A chance to begin again.'

'I'd like that,' she said.

'I want to be with you . . . not just for a few hours, or a day or two here or there, but to become a proper part of your life, Tessa.'

'I want that, too,' she said. 'I thought that first night when we were at Gemma and Paul's and we were dancing that I was imagining it, but when Mum died, the only person I wanted to call, to really be there, was you! I can't explain it . . . I don't know why, but I just knew that I needed you, and that I could rely on you to be there for me.'

'Cancel your flights and those appointments, Tessa. Don't go to London! We both know loss and loneliness,' he said, his eyes staring into hers. 'Maybe we both need a new beginning.'

'But it's all booked and organized,' she said, trying not to cry as she saw the expression on his handsome face.

'Unbook it! I don't want you to go. I'm here for you, Tessa, here for whenever you need me,' he promised, pulling her into his arms.

They sat on the sand until the sun had almost gone down, talking about the future, what would happen if she stayed, making plans together. Both decided to give their relationship the chance to grow and develop; they wanted to discover if they could love each other.

Chapter Fifty

Alice checked to see how Sean was doing. His face was pale and strained, and she knew that he was nervous about seeing Dara, who had finally come home from hospital. They had talked on the phone and texted each other over the past weeks, but she hoped that seeing each other again wouldn't bring back bad memories of the car crash.

Catherine O'Loughlin rushed to open the door, flinging her arms around Sean and bursting into tears.

'Sean Kinsella, I never thought that I'd see you walk back through that door again!'

Sean didn't know what to say, and just hugged her back.

She led Sean and Alice into the sitting room, where Dara was on a leather armchair. Wearing jeans and a hoodie, he looked pale and very thin and fragile. Sean gave a whoop of joy and flung himself into his best friend's arms.

Alice and Catherine discreetly retired to the kitchen where they could talk at their ease and leave their sons together.

Alice had made a dozen and half chocolate brownies, the type she knew Dara liked, and had brought them over.

'Thanks Alice, they're Dara's favourites. I'll make some coffee and give them into them.'

'How is he?' Alice asked.

'Great . . . it's so great to have Dara back home with us . . . but he's changed. Sometimes I find him crying . . . thinking about it, going back over it! If only we hadn't given him that bloody car for his birthday!'

'That had nothing to do with it,' reminded Alice. 'It wasn't Dara's fault, you know that, Catherine.'

'I know, but if he hadn't been driving he would have been nowhere near where the accident happened that night.'

'The truck driver, God rest him, had a massive heart attack. It was a freak accident, a one in a million. Dara and Sean had nothing to do with it!'

'But our boys were there!' Catherine insisted. 'They were in the wrong place at the wrong time!

413

Dara's been so sick. We thought we'd lose him.'

'I know,' said Alice, reaching for her hand. 'It's been awful.'

'He has liver problems, no spleen and has had most of his lower body crushed.'

'He's alive, they both are! Listen, they are laughing and joking. We got our sons back,' Alice said encouragingly. 'OK, so they are damaged, but they're young, they'll recover. Every day Sean is getting a bit better, and I'm sure that Dara is the same.'

An hour later Alice got ready to go. Sean was sitting in beside Dara, the two of them listening to one of their favourite bands on Dara's iPod, and chatting away like old times.

'I'll drive him home in another two hours,' promised Catherine. 'We don't want them to get overtired.'

'It's going to be Sean's twenty-first in ten days,' reminded Alice. 'He's not up to a big party yet, so we are just going to have a bit of a family dinner, but we would love it if you and Ciaran and Dara could come along, too.'

'That sounds great,' agreed Catherine. 'We wouldn't miss it for the world.'

At home Alice did a few things, including checking up on the menus for tonight's class. Rob had put in a special request to learn how to make a proper shepherd's pie, and she was also going to show them all how to make choux pastry and chocolate éclairs. Emmet had phoned her to ask if he could come over ahead of the others as he wanted to discuss his new business venture with her. He'd brought her along to see the empty shop, and Alice had had to agree it was an ideal spot for a café. Being an architect, he had all kinds of décor ideas, and he was such a perfectionist he was sure to get it right. She was happy to advise him on food and menus and equipment, and, from her own experience, what she thought he could do to make the café work.

Throwing off her shoes, she lazed back on the couch. As Lexy settled beside her Alex rang.

She liked the sound of his voice, and hoped that no one in his office was listening to their conversation as they arranged to join Joy and Fergus for a bite to eat in Gleesons tomorrow night – it was high time they all met up. They also made plans for a romantic night away on Saturday in Ardmore, in a beautiful hotel with a Michelin-starred restaurant and views to die for.

'And don't forget the following Saturday we are having Sean's twenty-first birthday dinner here. I'm dying to introduce you to everyone!'

Sean had already met Alex and had insisted she bring him along, as Liam would be bringing Elaine.

Chapter Fifty-one

Lucy stood at hatch 5, waiting her turn. Brian was behind it as usual.

He passed her the regulation unemployment benefit form that she had to sign and she passed it back to him.

'You need to sign it,' he reminded her, 'otherwise you cannot go and collect your money.'

'I'm signing off today.' She grinned. 'I'm coming off the dole. I've got a job.'

'Oh! Where?' he asked.

'Selling T-shirts!' she opened her denim jacket and let him see her 'Busy Stargazing' T-shirt.

'My boyfriend and I make and sell these,' she explained. 'We've set up a T-shirt business!'

She could see straightaway that Brian the dole official was interested.

'That's great, Lucy, really great. It's fantastic to hear some good news in this office!'

'I brought you a present.' She reached into her bag and got out a large-size 'Busy Queuing' T-shirt with 'hatch 5' on it and gave it to him.

'Hey.' He laughed, looking at it and recognizing his hatch number. 'That's cool!'

'We've sold quite a few already.' She laughed. 'They're very popular, but I'm kind of glad that I won't be queuing here any more!'

She met Finn afterwards, outside on the step. Both of them had signed off.

'Coffee?' He grinned as they made their way to the usual spot.

It was late, and Lucy looked at the screen of her laptop. She had butterflies in her stomach with nerves as she clicked on the link to their new website. Duggy and his friend Killian had done a great job, and she laughed as she looked at the photos of Finn and herself outside the dole office in their 'Busy' T-shirts. Then there were photos of them in the Temple Bar market selling them with Duggy in his 'Busy' T-shirt. There was also a funny section with the story of how 'Busy' T-shirts came into existence, and the inspiration behind the 'Busy' brand.

She checked out the page of designs with sizes and prices and the payment options. It looked really cool and edgy, and was easy to negotiate, which was important. There was a 'follow us' link to Twitter and a link to their Facebook page, and she couldn't believe how many people had already uploaded photos of themselves wearing a 'Busy' T-shirt.

She recognized two or three of the bands she had sent T-shirts to, and couldn't believe it, but they had actually worn them at gigs and when they were doing publicity shots. Maybe Duggy could do a link to the bands' Myspace so fans could check out the music and the T-shirts!

Finn was busy on the other side of the room at the big kitchen table they had bought in IKEA. He'd had another idea and was sketching out a rough concept: 'Busy Boarding' with a guy jumping the waves on his surfboard!

She loved it.

'Hey!' he said, pulling her onto his lap and kissing her. 'None of this would have happened if it wasn't for you, Lucy.' He touched her face with his finger. 'You are the best thing that has ever happened to me . . . you are my lucky charm. My other half. My better half.'

'And you're mine.' She felt exactly the same way about him, too. The minute they had moved in to the flat together it had felt like they were always meant to be together.

Suddenly he got up and disappeared into the bedroom. He came back a few seconds later, knelt down on the floor near her, and took her hand.

'Lucy, I hope it's not too soon, but I really love you, and I want to ask you something really important: will you marry me?'

Lucy flung her arms around him, the two of them falling in a heap on the rug on the wooden floor.

'Of course I'll marry you, Finn,' she said, burying her face in his chest, trying not to let tears of sheer happiness engulf her. 'I love you so much.' She gulped and sniffed as Finn gave her the ring.

It was small and perfect – a simple diamond on a slim platinum band – and it fitted her finger perfectly.

'Finn McEvoy, we're broke! You know we don't have the money to buy a ring,' she protested, shushed by his lips kissing her, his hands on her waist and hips.

It was only as she began to unbutton his shirt she noticed Finn's new T-shirt. It was black and white, and showed a guy and a girl kissing, and the words: 'Busy Loving You!'

Chapter Fifty-two

Over the busy June bank holiday weekend Matt and Kerrie decided that they would visit both families. On Saturday they would go to Kerrie's parents' house to meet some of her family, and on the Sunday she would go down to Moyle House with him.

From the corner of her eye Kerrie watched Matt's expression as they drove to Tallaght and turned off the main road and into Riverfield Estate. Passing row after row of white and grey houses almost identical to each other, it was very different from his world, she knew, but this was her place, where she grew up, and he needed to understand that.

It was really hot, and they were both in cut-off jeans and T-shirts, Matt bringing along wine, beer and sweets for her family, while Kerrie had made a strawberry tart for dessert and bought a large tub of Ben & Jerry's ice cream.

Everyone was in the back garden, and her dad had the barbecue lit. Her mum and Mike and Niamh, Martina and Darren were all sitting under the green parasol at the big wooden garden table and chairs. Johnny was helping her dad, and a smaller table was set up for the kids, who were all racing around and playing, the toddlers down at the old sand pit with buckets and spades.

'Welcome,' said her mam, hugging them and getting up to get everyone drinks.

Matt was polite, getting to know everyone and shaking their hands, and playing football with little Jamie, Emma and Rory.

Her dad was busy cooking hamburgers and sausages, his face red from the heat of the charcoal as he flipped and turned them, and there were buns and salad and a big bowl of her mother's potato salad. Kerrie and Johnny's wife Fidelma passed around the plates of hot food to everyone.

'This is great,' said Matt, slathering tomato ketchup and raw onions on to his burger as little Jamie sat on his lap munching a massive ketchup-covered sausage, and destroyed his clean T-shirt.

'He's gorgeous,' whispered Martina, when Matt went off upstairs to try to wash some of it off. 'No wonder you kept him so well hidden,' she teased. 'When is the wedding? France in September, isn't it? With Darren only just back working you know we won't be able to go. You'll just have to count us out.'

'And I'll be the size of a house by then!' added the pregnant Nicola.

Embarrassed, Kerrie suddenly felt less certain about going away to get married. Why shouldn't her brothers and sisters and little nieces and nephews be there? They were her flesh and blood. But the chances of rearranging things and finding a venue for a wedding in Ireland would probably be pretty impossible at this late stage.

'Hey,' said Matt, reappearing in a tight-fitting clean grey Harvard T-shirt.

'Shannon gave me this to change into.' He laughed as Kerrie's younger sister appeared behind him.

'Sit here,' insisted Kerrie, making sure Shannon had a big burger and all the trimmings. 'It's brain food.'

'I'll take a little break for an hour and then I'll go back to study,' Shannon promised.

'What a girl!' said her dad. 'Shannon is up in that attic room of hers studying so hard. She's just like Kerrie was, stuck to the books!'

'My exams are in a few days, Da,' protested Shannon. 'I'd want to be stuck to the books!'

Afterwards Kerrie's brother Mike got down her dad's guitar and began a sing-song with everyone joining in. Mike sang some Radiohead and Thin Lizzy songs. Then Martina sang some Mary Black before her dad took over and did some Dylan and Elvis.

'I told you my dad was great,' said Kerrie proudly. Matt sang along, too, Jamie back up on his lap again. She looked round at the garden, filled with her mother's plants and flowers and the big old mountain ash tree. Everyone had a drink and was relaxing in the deckchairs as the light began to fade and the sun went down. It was getting time to pack up and head home. The kids were getting tired, little Emma sucking her thumb as she curled up in her mammy's lap.

'Sit down, Ma, and I'll make you and Dad some coffee,' Kerrie offered, disappearing into the kitchen.

'This is always the time of evening I like best during the summer,' said her dad. 'The older ones are out playing in the road, and the smaller ones are ready for bed, and your mother and I can just sit out here in the garden and take our ease. Watch the sun go down!'

Matt reached for Kerrie's hand as she brought in the coffee and they sat in the garden chatting for a long while before saying their goodbyes.

* * *

'I like them,' said Matt as they drove home. 'The more I get to know your mum and dad, the more I appreciate them. Your family are great, and Shannon seems a lot like you. Jamie is a bit of a handful, but just the kind of kid I hope we have some day.'

'Hey, we have to get married first!' she said, suddenly turning serious. 'That's what I wanted to talk to you about, Matt, getting married. I'm not sure about having the wedding in France any more . . . it's just so far away.'

'I thought that's what you wanted: to have this small exclusive wedding with only our parents and a few family members and close friends present.'

'I did . . . but now I've changed my mind.'

He laughed aloud. 'I hoped that maybe you might.'

'I want all my family there,' she admitted. 'I've been so absolutely stupid, Matt. So caught up in this fabrication of mine . . . My brothers and sisters can't afford to pay for expensive flights to the South of France and hotels in high season! Who'd mind their kids?'

'Finances are a bit tight on my side of the family too, at present,' Matt teased.

'I've been such a fecking wagon!'

'Mmm,' he said, agreeing with her.

'If it's not too late, Matt, do you think we could have the wedding in Ireland? There must be somewhere that could take the crowd!'

Chapter Fifty-three

The next day they drove to Moyle House. Kerrie was shocked to see the auctioneers' huge 'For Sale' sign attached to the railings beside the gateway as they drove up to the house.

'How are they both taking it?' she asked.

'Badly!'

The dogs ran up to greet them, and Kerrie patted Lady on the head as Maureen Hennessy came out to welcome them.

Maureen looked tired, as if the stuffing had been knocked out of her; she had lost some of her strength and vitality.

'Where's Dad?' asked Matt.

'He's in the sitting room reading the paper.'

Dermot Hennessy seemed to be dozing in the

armchair, his chin on his chest. The abandoned newspaper was spread loosely across his lap.

'Dad,' said Matt gently. 'Dad.'

Dermot Hennessy began to stir and, stretching his arms and shoulders, he woke up.

'Good to see you, Matt, boy, and Kerrie.'

Kerrie was shocked at the change in him too. He seemed to have shrunk, and his colour wasn't good. He looked so pale.

'Just having a read of the Sunday papers . . . lot of rubbish, most of it!'

Feeling awkward, Kerrie slipped away upstairs with her bag. Matt and his dad needed time on their own together.

Maureen was busy in the kitchen when she came downstairs.

'I'm sorry about all that has happened,' said Kerrie hesitantly. 'It must be so hard for you and Dermot and everyone.'

'Well, the one thing I will say for all this trouble is that you soon find out who your true friends are. We've had a few let-downs, like the Gallaghers not inviting us to their big summer garden party over in Killeen Abbey two weeks ago – we've always gone to it! How could people forget all the good things that Dermot and Gerard Mullen did for this town and area? The shopping centre they built, those lovely family houses up on the Forge Road, the medical centre and the new nursing home!' she said angrily. 'Dermot is no saint but he's not a bad man, Kerrie! At least some of our old friends have been loyal, and thank heaven I have the golf club.'

'You still go up there?'

'Most of the ladies there have enough sense not to give a toss about people's husbands' reputations!'

It was lovely outside and when Maureen suggested a walk with the dogs Kerrie was pleased to go along. The dogs scampered backwards and forwards as they wondered all around the grounds of Moyle House.

'It's at its best now,' said Maureen, as they walked through the garden with its herbaceous borders filled with tall delphiniums, lupins and foxgloves. Masses of climbing roses covered the stone wall. 'I can't believe that this will be my last summer here in the garden,' she said, trying to control her emotions. 'And that next year someone else will have taken over the place. The whole thing is too bloody sad to bear!'

'Do you know where you and Dermot will move to?'

'No, but we both want to stay fairly local.'

'Maybe you'll find somewhere smaller close by or in the village,' Kerrie suggested.

'Can you imagine Dermot living in a cottage in the village?' Maureen snapped bitterly.

Kerrie couldn't imagine them living anywhere but here. No wonder it had been so hard for Matt trying to get them to agree to sell.

'Lots of people in Dublin downsize as they get older and their families grow up,' she said gently.

Maureen pretended that she didn't hear her.

They walked down to the old tennis court.

'I'd always hoped that Georgina and Matt and Ed's children would play tennis on this court, just like in the good old days.'

Kerrie looked at the uneven grass surface and almost threadbare net, knowing that she was looking at remnants of a world that had vanished long ago. It was just that the Hennessys couldn't see it.

As they reached the old paddock the dogs chased after a rabbit, barking furiously. They passed by the old stables and quarters, now empty and abandoned.

'It was a busy yard before our time,' reminisced Maureen. 'We kept a few ponies and mares, but the Butlers had a full yard. There's the old water pump and the saddle stone, and the mounting block they used to help the ladies on to their horses.'

Kerrie wandered around, exploring. Amazingly,

although the old stables looked a bit decrepit from the outside, inside they were still in pretty good condition, with dry walls. There were fifteen stalls, a kitchen, a large tack room and steps up to a big loft area.

'Some of the stable boys used to sleep up there to keep an eye on the horses,' explained Maureen. 'They were valuable animals.'

Outside, around the small courtyard, there were a number of ramshackle outhouses. The sun shone brightly; wildflowers had colonized the cracks in the broken paving and the gaps in the stone walls.

'It's lovely here, Maureen. What a beautiful place!' Kerrie said.

'It's just a stables,' said Maureen. 'It's never been used for anything else, except maybe some storage.'

'Half the mews houses in Dublin in Leeson Street and Ballsbridge and Donnybrook and Dun Laoghaire were old stables and coach houses that people converted. They can look amazing,' Kerrie said quietly. 'I'd imagine if you already own one it is a lot less hassle to convert them than to build something from scratch . . . but I'm no expert.'

'What are you saying?'

'You own these stables already, Maureen, and the courtyard. You could probably retain them when you sell the rest of the property, if the auctioneer agrees.

Also it would slightly reduce the cost for a buyer. They could make a lovely mews-type house. Easy to manage.'

'Matt told me that you were a clever girl,' Maureen said, patting Kerrie's arm. 'But I'd want to find out the feasibility of doing something like that, without too many people knowing about it! I wouldn't want to get Dermot's hopes up if it was not possible or cost too much. With the business gone, and all that has happened, he's like a lost soul about the place.'

'I have a friend who is an architect, his name is Emmet Ryan – maybe I could ask him to contact you and come down here and see what he thinks,' Kerrie offered. The first time she had met him Emmet had told her about a mews conversion he had done down near Herbert Park for some musician. She remembered seeing photos of it in one of her house design magazines.

'Yes, that is something definitely worth looking into. Downsizing! Is that what you called it?'

Kerrie tried to control her smile. Maureen had been listening to her after all.

'As you say, lots of people in big houses like ours have to downsize and move to a smaller property on their own land. We'd still be in Moyle House, whether it is a mews or a lodge or whatever you call it!' Maureen called the dogs and they continued their walk.

* * *

Dermot was quiet at dinner, the four of them sitting in the dining room. Maureen had gone to a lot of trouble and done salmon en croute, something that Kerrie wouldn't even dare to attempt. The pastry was cooked to perfection, concealing its delicious filling of fish and dill, and served with lovely new baby potatoes.

'How are the wedding plans coming?' asked Maureen.

'They're not,' admitted Kerrie truthfully. 'We're thinking of changing everything and having it in Ireland if we can find somewhere to hold it. But at this stage it might be impossible.'

'We're both taking a few days off next week to have a look at places,' explained Matt. 'We're seeing what we can find that's free in September. A lot of the big venues will be gone, but maybe we can find an old country house or hotel that we both like.'

'Much better to have it in Ireland instead of dragging everybody away,' added Dermot. 'To be honest, I don't know if I'd be up to flying myself at the moment.'

'That's what's made us change our minds,' admitted Kerrie. 'Too many people we love wouldn't have been able to come to France, and, Dermot, we really want you and everyone we care about to be there.'

* * *

That night, as she lay curled up in Matt's arms, Kerrie wondered what would have happened to this house by next year. Dermot looked very unwell, and Matt said the doctor had put him on some kind of medication for stress and suspected he was developing an ulcer.

'I'm going to miss this house,' Matt sighed.

She told Matt about her conversation with his mother about the old stables.

'I dread the thought of the two of them moving away and having to start all over again,' he said.

'Matt, it's only an idea, but if you want I'll ask Emmet about it.'

'If he's coming down I'll come with him. Maybe there is a way they could salvage something from this disaster, Kerrie,' he said, getting excited. 'If we could manage without too much cost to convert the old stables and yard they'd still be able to stay living here at Moyle.'

Chapter Fifty-four

Alice couldn't believe their luck. The weather had held. What a perfect June evening to celebrate Sean's twenty-first birthday. She'd made him a special breakfast that morning and given him her present of a surfboard and some Quiksilver shorts.

'Mum, it's just what I wanted. Dara and I can't wait to give it a try in August.'

She was nervous about him learning to surf, but Conor and Jenny had made her realize that she couldn't wrap him in cotton wool for ever!

All day long his friends had been calling and texting, and Sean was so excited. A big group of them had gone to Chicago for the summer, but they had still remembered him and phoned. In September, when they all got back, there would be a night for his college and school friends but tonight's celebration was a family one. Indeed, it was a very special one as Conor and Lisa had surprised them all by getting engaged while away in Croatia, and were planning to get married the following summer.

Tanned and happy, Conor had helped his mum to string fairy lights all around the garden, and take out the barbecue and set it up for cooking. Alice had marinated lots of chicken in a rich hickory sauce, and made prawn and vegetarian kebabs and her usual homemade beefburgers. There were chunky sweet potato fries, and small baby new potatoes, and big bowls of tossed green salad. She put the finishing touches to a big chocolate cake with twenty-one candles on it, and, looking around the kitchen and garden, thought everything looked ready to go.

Jenny, in a pretty pink gingham dress, was setting up the glasses, while Dylan tried to fit as much drink as he could into the fridge to chill, as it was so hot and balmy outside. Sean had uploaded music on his iPhone, and set up speakers to play it in the garden.

Alice's dad, Barry O'Connor, had arrived early and was sitting with a Guinness outside, chatting to Sean, Hugh and Sally.

She had a few minutes to change out of her work clothes and into the simple beige linen shift dress and her slingback shoes. A slick of peach lipgloss and she was good to go. Everyone was in great form, and when Dara and his parents arrived Alice couldn't stop herself crying as the two boys posed for photos. This day was so special to all of them. Next year, hopefully, Sean and Dara would be up to going off on the traditional student visa working for the summer in America. Three of the girls from Sean's course at college had turned up wearing the shortest skirts she had ever seen, and were making a huge fuss of her son, along with Nick, Brian and Eoin, some of his old school friends.

Liam and Elaine arrived as she began to light the barbecue and cook. Elaine, in a revealing wrap-around dress, was nervous as Liam introduced her to the family. Alice did her best to be polite, even though she had no interest in having a conversation with Elaine and was only letting her attend for Sean's sake.

Joy arrived with Fergus and Beth both in tow. She gave her godson the Xbox 360 Kinect he was dying for.

'Thanks, Auntie Joy,' he said, delighted.

'Fergus is a sweetheart,' said Alice, hugging the tall man with the glasses and great sense of humour who was such easy company and was crazy about blonde-haired Joy. 'You know he's mad about you!'

'I know.' Joy blushed. 'Can you believe it?'

* * *

Patsy, Tim, Jenny and Lisa all helped Alice with the cooking, and everyone came up with their plates to help themselves to burgers and chicken and kebabs. Hugh and Conor poured out the drinks. 'What a spread!' said Dylan, filling his plate with a bit of everything.

Alex arrived with flowers for her and a present for Sean. He'd had his hair cut, was wearing a red and white striped shirt, and was unaware of the stir he caused by kissing her full-on in front of everyone. She laughed, seeing Liam's reaction to the new man in her life. He looked seriously put out!

'I didn't know that you were seeing someone,' he said peevishly as he followed her into the kitchen to get more drinks.

'Alex is a lovely man,' she said, grabbing a bottle of tonic water from the fridge and some ice. 'You hardly expected me to live my life on my own, Liam, did you?'

She could see he was uncomfortable. 'Alex works with Hugh; he's the senior partner there. That's how we first met.' She smiled, getting another gin and tonic for Joy before slipping back outside. 'And as I said, he's a lovely man.'

It was getting dark when they lit the candles and

carried the cake out to the garden on a tray. Sean was just like he used to be as a kid: all excited as he blew the twenty-one candles out, with everyone chanting and singing and cheering, toasting Sean and then toasting Conor and Lisa.

Later they sat and chatted, Alice delighted to see that Sean's girlfriend Becky was sitting on his lap. She'd flown back from France for the weekend to surprise him.

When everyone was fed and well-served with drinks, Alice finally sat down herself, Alex coming over to take the seat beside her.

'Great party!' he said. 'Great kids.'

She appreciated the compliment.

'Sean's having a wonderful time. That's what matters.' She laughed, holding his hand, relieved to see how well Alex fitted in with everyone. Funny how it had all worked out . . . if she hadn't gone to work in Hugh's office would she ever have met Alex? Fate was a strange thing. She still couldn't believe how they'd found each other.

They stayed outside till midnight, Alice slipping away to bed not long after Alex went home, leaving the young crowd and cousins to party on into the night.

Chapter Fifty-five

Alice looked around the kitchen. She couldn't believe that tonight was her final night with the class. Ten strangers had joined her cookery school in January, and now she would really miss each and every one of them. They were more than her students . . . they were her friends!

They had been such a diverse group at the beginning. She had tried to disguise her dismay at the different levels, wondering how she could possibly teach such a group. Some of them had been hopeless, and terrified of cooking, but it amazed her how week after week their confidence in the kitchen had grown and grown.

They had all given her such support, and trusted her, from that very first night when they had watched her demonstrate and taken down her recipes. She suspected that she had learned almost as much from them over the past few months as they had learned from her. Even little Lucy, who had been despondent and now was madly in love and engaged to that gorgeous boyfriend of hers, and running a very successful business with him by all accounts. Nina and David still couldn't get over it.

Then there was Kitty, who had been such a stalwart. She had only signed on for something to do, and yet seemed to have rediscovered her love of cooking. She was a natural. And Emmet, who Alice had always suspected of having a more important reason to develop his proficiency in the kitchen, and was now bravely set to open a place of his own. They were a wonderful bunch. She would miss each and every one of them!

Tonight was a very special night, this last night together, and they were making a three-course dinner: pan-fried scallops, rack of lamb with rosemary potatoes and a lovely light meringue roulade filled with raspberries and cream. She had set the big table and afterwards they would all dine together and have a glass of wine.

Fixing on her apron, she showed them how to prepare and pan-fry the scallops.

'Delicious,' said Paul. 'My all-time favourite fish.'

She watched as they all very competently took their turn, giving advice or a hand when necessary. The meringue roulade was tricky, too, and there was a knack to getting it right as you gently rolled it up with the filling.

The time flew and she couldn't believe it when the last rack of lamb was ready to serve and the class was almost over. Finally, the ovens were off, and everything was finished.

Tonight no one was rushing home and they all sat down to eat. What lovely food, she thought, and what lovely people. She would miss them all.

'What a fantastic meal you have all prepared,' she said, smiling, 'and what a time we've had together learning all about food! I'd like to congratulate you all on completing the course, and also to congratulate Lucy on her recent engagement. Let's have some wine to celebrate!'

Lucy blushed and showed everyone her ring.

'Wine, definitely!' said Rob, hugging Lucy before slipping into his usual place as Alice passed him the bottle and the opener.

'Lucy, congratulations on your engagement,' everyone said, as Alice took some more glasses from the press and passed around knives, forks, spoons and napkins, and they all sat down to eat.

'We're broke, so we won't be getting married for ages!' Lucy laughed. 'If we do get any money it's going straight back into our business. This summer we're at all the big festivals. We've a stand at Oxegen and Slane and Electric Picnic, and are even going over to Glastonbury to sell our T-shirts. Lots of the bands are starting to wear them, and then people just want them. Finn and I can't believe it!' she said happily. 'But maybe if things go OK we might be able to get married the summer after next.'

'We've some good news, too,' announced Paul. 'Gemma and I are going to have a baby in December.'

'You will be wonderful parents,' said Kitty, hugging Gemma, who everyone couldn't help but notice had refused the wine and was drinking fizzy water.

'And don't forget my new business! Café na Mara will be opening in about ten days' time,' reminded Emmet. 'I hope you are all going to come along to the opening on Friday week.'

'Of course,' they all chorused.

'It's wonderful to see a new venture opening,' said Rob seriously. 'Emmet, I wish you so much luck with it. Living so nearby, I plan to be a regular customer.'

Alice opened another bottle of wine, topping up Tessa's glass.

'When are you heading back to London?' she asked.

Tessa had mentioned her plans to return to London once she had organized and settled some of her mother's affairs.

'Alice, I'm not going anywhere.' Tessa laughed, her serious face animated. 'I've decided to stay on here in Dublin.'

'I managed to persuade her to stay,' said Rob, taking Tessa's hand and making it quite clear to everyone that he and Tessa were very definitely together.

Alice smiled to herself. Why hadn't she seen that Tessa was perfect for him? They were made for each other: two lonely people who had somehow found each other here at her cookery school! There had been something different about Rob the past few months. How had she not guessed about their romance?

Around the table, everyone began to talk of their plans for the summer.

Rachel and Leah were off to holiday houses beside each other in Lahinch, and in the autumn would do a child swap so they each got a romantic break away for a few days with their husbands. Kitty was joining her daughter's family in Waterford for a few weeks, and had been flabbergasted to discover that Larry had, out of the blue, gone and booked tickets for the two of them to go to Paris in late September.

'And of course, Kerrie, you'll be off to France for your wedding. You must be so excited!' said Alice.

To be honest she'd worried so much about Kerrie when she had first joined the class. She had seemed so tense and unhappy all the time; but now as her wedding got nearer she seemed to have finally relaxed.

'Alice, everything's changed.' Kerrie laughed, her eyes sparkling.

'You're not getting married?' blurted out Kitty without thinking.

'No,' protested Kerrie, 'Matt and I are getting married, but not in the South of France! We've decided to have our wedding at home now. We're having a big family wedding down in Meath at his family place, Moyle House. It's going to be a bit tight trying to squeeze everyone in, but we have hired caterers and barmen and are praying for a dry sunny day. My three sisters and Matt's sister are being my bridesmaids, so it's mad because this is June and we're still trying to find bridesmaid's dresses that suit everyone, and I have two little flower girls and two little pages, too. And those kids are all a bit wild! There'll be a band, and a bouncy castle for all the kids, and one of my brothers is going to let fireworks off on the lawn, and we've hired a bus to bring people back to Dublin afterwards.'

'Lucky you,' said Lucy enviously.

'Moyle House is a wonderful house,' enthused Emmet, 'perfect for a wedding.'

'It's kind of a last hurrah for the house,' Kerrie admitted. 'My parents-in-law-to-be have to sell it, and it looks like a family from Germany are the buyers. Emmet was down giving Matt and his dad some advice about converting some of their stables into a mews with a courtyard garden, so that's how he came to see it!'

'A proper wedding! So much better than a handful of guests in France,' said Kitty, making everyone laugh.

'Kitty, we're still going to France for our honeymoon,' insisted Kerrie.

'Here's to Alice!' toasted the class, as everyone stood up. 'And to her cookery school!'

Alice blinked away the tears in her eyes. Funny, but she would really miss them. This year might have begun with some doom and gloom and trepidation, but it had brought so much change for all of them gathered here around the table. There had been so many new beginnings!

So much had happened in her own life over these past few months, too. She had learnt to let go of Liam and the hurt of it, and to stand on her own two feet, which had been much harder than she had ever imagined. She took the risk of opening a cookery school, worrying about getting it off the ground! Then there had been Sean's accident and the awful reality of almost losing her youngest son. The wonderful support of her friends and family – even these people, her students – had helped her get through those dark days. And then there was the milestone of Sean's twenty-first party last week. It was so good to see Sean well again. And to have the opportunity to introduce Alex, the new man in her life, to the people she loved.

She still sometimes couldn't believe it!

The Martello Cookery School's reputation was growing, and next year she hoped to run classes three nights a week and was even considering holding a class one morning a week, too. Her business was taking off in a way she had never imagined, and even Patsy, her sister-in-law, and Nina had signed up for the autumn.

Then there was Alex! Lovely Alex!

The two of them were off to Lake Como for ten days in three weeks' time. He had booked them into a magnificent-looking five-star hotel overlooking the lake. Alex Ronan was such a lovely man – generous and big-hearted and romantic – and when they were together he made her feel special, young and happy again!

She was so lucky to have been given this second chance – to have somehow found the courage to open her heart to happiness and to finding love again with Alex when she least expected it.

Acknowledgements

Thank you to my lovely editor, Linda Evans, for her wonderful support, encouragement and work on my books.

To all the team at Transworld UK for their dedication and work on this and all my books, and for making it seem so easy, especially Joanne Williamson, Vivien Garrett and Kate Tolley, and my copy-editor, Lucy Pinney. And to Eoin McHugh and Brian Langan in the Transworld Ireland office.

To my agent, Caroline Sheldon, for her constant support and belief.

To Rosemary Buckman for helping to bring my books to far-flung shores.

Thanks to the ever-supportive crew at Gill Hess, Dublin, for all their work and efforts, especially Gill and Simon Hess, Declan Heaney and Helen Gleed

O'Connor, Sophie Hess, Fergus Gannon, Eamonn Phelan, Nigel Carre and Ian Davidson.

To all the Irish booksellers for giving such wonderful support to both me and my books over many years.

To my ever-patient husband, James. You are my 'rock'.

To my wonderful family who make sitting round a table telling stories fun: Mandy, Laura, Fiona and James and Michael Hearty and Michael Fahy.

To my gorgeous grandchildren, Holly and Sam Hearty.

To Ann Frances Doorly, who was so much more than a friend. I'm going to miss you so much.

To my lovely friends. I know I drive you crazy talking about ideas and characters, but I'd be lost without you all.

Thanks to all my writer friends, especially Sarah Webb, Martina Devlin and Larry O'Loughlin.

To Maeve Binchy for all her wonderful stories and her constant encouragement of her fellow writers.

To Sharon Slowey, a bookworm after my own heart! Thanks for sharing so many good books with me.

To my friends in Irish PEN – a great club to be in!

And finally, to all my wonderful readers – a sincere 'thank you' from this very grateful author.